SOMETHING ABOUT
DARLING ISLAND

POLLY BABBINGTON

OH SO POLLY

Words, quilts, tea and old houses…

My words began many moons ago in a corner of England, in a tiny bedroom in an even tinier little house. There was a very distinct lack of scribbling, but rather beautifully formed writing and many, many lists recorded in pretty fabric-covered notebooks stacked up under a bed.

A few years went by, babies were born, university joined, white dresses worn, a lovely fluffy little dog, tears rolled down cheeks, house moves were made, big fat smiles up to ears, a trillion cups of tea, a decanter or six full of pink gin, many a long walk. All those little things called life neatly logged in those beautiful little books tucked up neatly under the bed.

And then, as the babies toddled off to school, as if by magic, along came an opportunity and the little stories flew out of the books, found themselves a home online, where they've been growing sweetly ever since.

I write all my books from start to finish tucked up in our lovely old Edwardian house by the sea. Surrounded by pretty bits and bobs, whimsical fabrics, umpteen stacks of books, a plethora of lovely old things, gingham linen, great big fat white sofas, and a big old helping of nostalgia. There I spend my days spinning stories and drinking rather a lot of tea.

From the days of the floral notebooks, and an old cottage locked away from my small children in a minuscule study logging onto the world wide web, I've now moved house and those stories have evolved and also found a new home.

There is now an itty-bitty team of gorgeous gals who help me with my graphics and editing. They scheme and plan from their laptops, in far-flung corners of the land, to get those words from those notebooks onto the page creating the magic of a Polly Bee book.

I really hope you enjoy getting lost in my world.

Love

Polly x

1

J ane Le Romancer sat glumly at her desk with her chin on her hand, staring at her laptop. Another cup of tea, another day in the office, another ten hours of quite possibly not seeing anyone at all. Another round of cheese, onion, and salad cream sandwiches. Another day in a small life. A very small life. Wasn't there a TV show about small lives? Smalltown or something? Jane sighed. She'd be able to top any TV show ever broadcast with her smallness. Jane Le Romancer's life was the epitome of small. Not that anyone knew how small it really was on the inside because from the outside Jane's life didn't look half bad, not bad at all. A nice house, a very nice house, in fact, a high achieving son, good health, a great career, a pretty good body for her age; her mind wasn't too shabby either. She was well educated, independent, and had excellent shoes. But smallness? Yes, Jane Le Romancer's life was most definitely small.

Jane wiggled the mouse, flicked her computer back to life, and looked at the pile of manila archive boxes stacked up beside her. It wasn't as if she didn't have anything to do in her small life. She was at the beginning of a case at work, meaning she had enough to keep her occupied for a long time. Billable lots of time laid out in front of her for the foreseeable future. For the rest of her small life, it seemed.

Her phone pinged with a message from the parcel tracking company; she'd got to know its ping, different from the pings she'd allocated to her four friends. She knew the tracking company alerts because they arrived far too often, sometimes more than once a day and because her parcels were, more often than not, the only thing that kept her company. She pushed her chair out and sighed. At least when she got a tracking ping, she had an excuse to leave her office and possibly exchange a few words with Laura, the receptionist, downstairs. She'd go down and collect the parcel from reception and then save it for the evening; it would give her something to look forward to on a Friday night. Her Friday nights regularly consisted of unboxing new wares. They were about the only thing she had going on.

Standing alone in the high-tech lift, she waited as it whisked to a halt and delivered her into the marble-floored reception area. On the far side, a gleaming mirrored desk, a bank of Macs, harsh lines of dazzling downlights, and shiny glass. Three white orchids in a row stood on top of the desk, as if guarding the space behind them. Jane's neutral sky-high shoes clipped across the floor; she could see Laura, the receptionist, standing at the desk looking at the spot where she usually sat, speaking to a man in a black shirt who was fiddling with Laura's phone headset. The phone engineer's huge black backpack overpowered the floor beside the desk, his head bent forward. Jane stood in front and waited, looking on as Laura, her hands deep in her pockets, frowned at the engineer. The little pearl drop earrings at Laura's ears dangled as she nodded her head when the engineer asked her a question. 'Yes, yes, it's always a headset issue.'

'So that shouldn't happen again,' the engineer said, seemingly oblivious that Jane was standing in front of him. It seemed 'oblivious' was a regular part of Jane's non-happening life.

Laura chuckled. 'I've heard that before. I'll be wearing the headset all day, so we'll soon find out.'

Jane listened and observed patiently, used to feeling as if she merged into the wall, when Laura suddenly realised someone was standing there and looked up. 'Oh sorry, Jane, I didn't see you there.' The engineer also peered up from what he was immersed in with a look of mild interest. His eyes ran Jane up and down and when they got to the top, they looked away again; eyes not interested in a life that was small.

Laura continued, 'Did you want me for something?'

Jane nodded. 'All good, nothing serious. I've just had a message that a parcel has arrived, so I thought I'd pop down and collect it. Save you the bother.'

Laura frowned and walked around the desk, stepping over the engineer's gigantic black backpack. 'Oh, I don't remember one coming for you. Hold on a minute, I'll go and have a look in the pigeonholes.'

A few minutes later, Laura was back with a small padded packet in her hands. She passed it over the shiny desk with a smile and a question on her face. 'More little earrings?'

Jane nodded as she took the small packet. 'Yes.'

'Lovely. No doubt I'll see you showing off your purchases next week, will I?'

Jane nodded. Inside, the nod was a wry one; she certainly wasn't going to be going anywhere else to show off her new things.

Laura continued to chatter on, flapping her hands around enthusiastically in front of her. 'I loved that necklace you bought last week. The one with the little gold bee on the chain. So sweet. So fragile and pretty. It looked lovely on you.'

'Yes.' Jane smiled. 'Thank you.'

'Have you worn it anywhere nice?' Laura asked.

'Oh, no, no, not really.' Jane sighed inside. Chance would be a fine thing.

Laura smiled brightly, her elbow leaning on the side of the desk. 'What are you up to this weekend? Lots on?'

Jane felt embarrassed to say that yet again, as she did every single Friday, she had nothing on *at all*. The next time she had to be anywhere or do anything would be 9 a.m. on Monday morning when she was taking a flight to Edinburgh to work in a dreary business hotel with other faceless forensic accountants on a case. She was well-practised though at not appearing too boring and forced herself to inject a faux cheery tone into her voice. She flicked her eyes up as she spoke.

'Oh, you know, this and that. I've got a friend coming over for dinner and a few things on,' Jane outright lied. She had nothing in place of the sort. The only time she ever had anything on was when she occasionally got together with one of the group of four friends she'd had since school or an event for her son.

This weekend, same as the last, the one before that, and stretching away into the future, there was nothing on for Jane at all. The last time she'd been out, more or less, was when her friend Lucie had celebrated a huge engagement party. Jane flicked her attention back to Laura and finished her sentence with a big fake smile, as if to say that she too was looking forward to the weekend. She wasn't looking forward to it in the slightest. It was the same as any other weekend as far as she was concerned; lonely, small, long and beige.

'That sounds lovely.' Laura beamed, the little pearl earrings wiggling again in her earlobes. 'I just *adore* having people over for dinner, but it gets tiring when you're entertaining all weekend. I've had a run of it. People here, people there! Know what I mean?'

Jane nodded as if she agreed, when in actual fact, she couldn't remember the last time she'd had anyone over at all, let alone for the weekend. She asked the obligatory question in return without needing to listen to the answer; Laura's social life was the opposite of small. 'What about you? Are you doing anything fun this weekend?'

Laura launched straight into it. 'You know me! I haven't got a minute to sit down all weekend and when I say *all*, I mean it. I've got so much to do it's ridiculous!' Laura tapped the side of her head and whooshed out a dramatic little sigh. 'What I wouldn't do for a night in on my own with a pizza and Netflix. First world problems, who'd have 'em, eh?'

'Ahh, nice, sounds like you're going to be busy,' Jane replied, dreading her regular Friday and Saturday night trawling through Netflix and iPlayer looking for something to keep her company. She tried to sound interested in Laura's bursting-to-the-brim social life and nodded enthusiastically.

'Yes, I love my weekends!' Laura exclaimed, her eyes dancing with happiness.

Jane plastered her 'I'm interested' smile on her face as she listened to more of Laura's plans. Her mind drifted off a bit as Laura waved her hands around and rattled on. 'So many things to do, so little time! I've got breakfast with an old school friend tomorrow morning, then straight to the pub for lunch with Eliza, more or less. Then remember those work friends I told you about from my old office?' Jane nodded as Laura paused and her earrings jiggled again. 'One of them is having a huge birthday party. To be honest, I could do without it, but, oh, you know what it's like. You have to do what you have to do.'

Jane nodded, smiled, and did a little shrug of her shoulders as if she totally got what it was like. As if she also was on the receiving end of so many invites at the weekend that she could do without them. It couldn't have been further from the truth. 'Oh, I know,' she replied, batting her hand in front of her face and raising her eyebrows. 'Go, go, go, isn't it?' She went to turn. 'Have a lovely time then, and I'll see you at the end of the week. I'm off to Edinburgh for that case meeting on Monday.'

'Yeah, yeah, will do. I'll be exhausted by the time Monday

arrives,' Laura replied with a little laugh. 'It'll be nice to get away from this place, though. Thank heavens for the weekend.'

Jane's heels tapped on the floor as she made her way to the lifts. *Thank heavens for the weekend?* She didn't think that *at all.* Not even a little bit. What even was the weekend? Her weekends were no different from her weeks. Her days merged into one bland bank of beige time punctuated by cases at work. Her weekends were just a nondescript blend of being on her own, cleaning the house, trying to keep on top of the mountain of work, and doing the garden. At least the garden wasn't beige, there was that. She'd always loved a potter in the garden; now it was about the only thing she had in her life. That and the incessant lonely tightness in her chest.

As she got back to her desk, she picked up her phone and scrolled through her Facebook feed. A post from the container gardening group she pottered along with, one from her online reading club, and another from the group she loved all about the ins and outs of living in a chateau in France. She kept scrolling through the funny little groups she perused between long hours of forensic accounting. The online posts that kept her sane and gave her something to think about in her small little life.

How to grow potatoes in a bin bag. Ten books to read when you are down. Easy ways to cut your hair at home. Really?

She clicked on her groups, idly scrolling down and down. It went through her mind that she really needed to skinny down her online content consumption. Too many groups for a person with a tiny life. Did she really need to belong to a group on Korean farming methods when her gardening consisted of pottering in her small garden in her (very nice) London suburb? Was it actually necessary to be part of a group on producing less waste in an urban environment when the most waste she had in a week was one very small bin full? She smiled as she came to the group for a little community on an island where her friend

Lucie lived. Jane was the main planner in Lucie's upcoming wedding and had joined the community group to aid in planning the event. She'd found all sorts on there and had all kinds of ideas for the wedding preparations. She scrolled down and read through absentmindedly; a friend of Lucie's, Mr Cooke, was giving away a lawnmower, someone called Sara had a bunch of cuttings to share, and there was a post about a local event, Dinner on Darlings, and its organisation. Jane smiled at the posts as she read through; the little island going by the name of Darling was so very quaint and friendly. As she swiped up, she stopped and sat up as a post caught her eye.

House Swapper Wanted.

Come and stay in my gorgeous old mews house on Darling Island and enjoy all the coastal delights on the best little island just off the coast. With its floating bridge, vintage trams, bustling Darling Street, delightful pubs, old fishing boats and secret cafés, while away your days with long walks by the sea. Not far from the blue waters of Darling Island's bay, get to experience the Darling flora and fauna and spend warm evenings tucked up in the house just like a resident.

The house includes a sitting room, a gorgeous bespoke handcrafted kitchen with an original refurbished Aga, three bedrooms, a bathroom with a roll top bath, and from the loft room divine distant views out to sea. The mews house is a beautifully renovated period property with a small courtyard garden, freshly painted in muted antique whites and comes complete with scrubbed floorboards, potbelly stoves, oversized iron bedsteads, cloud mattresses, and top quality Portuguese linens.

The brick walled courtyard is spilling with pots, plants, and herbs with a seating area to enjoy the Darling Island hazy blue sky. Enjoy a lazy glass of wine in the afternoon, swing in the hammock from the apple tree, or snuggle up under a quilt on the Adirondack chairs in the evening next to the chiminea.

I am looking for someone to swap houses with for at least three months. I need to be within commutable distance to the city in a comfy house where I can sometimes work from home. This swap is for you if

*you are looking for some time to get away from it all in a peaceful
environment and want a quiet oasis to get your life together... or start
a new one on our little island so very far from care.*

*Five or so minutes walk to Darling Bay in a quiet, safe area near
the historic town of Darling with its many beaches, heritage listed
library, post office, and a short ferry ride to the mainland.*

*I am looking to swap with a tidy, non-smoking, single professional.
This is for you if you are after a peaceful environment. Leave your car
at home and enjoy zipping around the island on my beautiful cruiser
bike. DM me for more info and a chat.*

Jane smiled at the description. She had stayed in a holiday
home in the mews area for Lucie's engagement party, so if it
was the same row of houses, she roughly knew its location and
that it was a gorgeous spot. She nodded at the sound of the
house and allowed her mind to wander; how lovely it sounded.
Some lucky person would be spending three months in
someone else's home, living someone else's life and a very nice
life at that. A life on a little island surrounded by hazy blue and
accessed by a delightful floating bridge. She clicked her phone
off and wiggled the mouse for her computer. How wonderful
would a house swap be? How funny to live in someone else's
house, someone else's life. She shook her head to rid it of the
words from the post. She had no time for pipe dreams and
lusting after houses on little islands online. She had numbers
coming out of her ears and work piled up to see her through the
next few months, if not years. Jane Le Romancer's life was way
too small for pipe dreams and house swaps. But as she sat at her
computer in a sea of work, her mind kept flitting back to the
post; the house, the swap, and the island did, actually, sound
rather nice.

2

The following week, Jane sat on mustard yellow chairs in the foyer of an international hotel in Edinburgh. Hotel lounge music piped through the speakers and a thoroughly grotesque amount of downlights glowed onto shiny marble floor tiles. Huge sculpted pillars topped with brass stood to attention all around and the whir of a continuously revolving door sounded beside her. A hotel worker dressed head to toe in black banged trolleys together and slammed china cups and glasses onto a shelf. The slamming of a fridge door, the clip of heels, a whooshing of a coffee machine behind the bar.

Jane rolled her neck around, the muscles and tendons cracking under the surface of her skin. She'd been stuck in a mahogany panelled, airless meeting room all day, its insipid walls and faux wood desks adding to the bland feel of her life. There had been a lot of numbers, many words exchanged, air conditioning humming, insipid tea, and plates of dull sandwiches. Two forensic accountants with greying hair, generic striped business suits, off-white shirts, and laptops. Comparing, syncing, tap tap tapping on the keys. Jane sighed as she looked around the hotel lobby. All of it was as nondescript and beige as her life. A faceless template of a hotel lobby with nothing much to say. Just like her.

She pulled out her phone and waited for face recognition to open the screen. Not much excitement there either. She replied to a message from her friend Tally, flicked up on her screen to open Instagram, navigated away, and then tapped on her groups. More posts in the little gardening group she liked to peruse, a notice that her online book club choice for the month would be going up the next day, and a notification that Mr Cooke on Darling Island was taking a group out to the other side of the island to look for rare shells. Jane scrolled up. The little Darling Island community posts always brought a smile to her face. There was always someone giving something away, an event going on at the sailing club, or a little get together at a coffee shop. Her friend Lucie had moved to Darling Island after a break-up with a partner, and when Jane had been to visit, she'd loved the community feel. It was a place where people seemed to know each other and care. A place where perhaps life wasn't quite as small.

Mindlessly scrolling, she came again to the house swap post she'd read the week before while sitting in her office. She scanned through the details again, more slowly than before. It did sound nice. It sounded very, very nice. She tapped on the comments underneath and read through. A few people had commented on the post offering their suggestions; an idea to try putting the house on Airbnb, someone saying they had a friend with a flat in Kingston which offered a good commute, and another person suggesting a great boutique hotel.

Jane let her eyes wander to a couple of women sitting in the hotel reception chatting over huge glasses of wine and mused the house swap idea. What would it be like to swap a house, a life, with someone else? In terms of what the Darling Island swapper wanted, Jane's house couldn't be better; it was a lovely old place, on a tree-lined little road in a South London suburb some called the village of the city. Lots of nearby cafés, a short stroll to the tube, a leisurely walk to the Common, not far to get anywhere in the city. In fact, it was one of the most highly sought after areas to live in London.

She thought more about swapping houses with someone. What would it actually be like in reality? What would she do? If she did it, would she be lonely? She contemplated the scenario for a moment and realised that, actually, it wouldn't alter her life much wherever she lived. She couldn't really get any lonelier or her life less small. She shook her head as she came to the conclusion that her house made no difference. Unless she was talking to someone about work or messaging one of the four friends she'd had since school, who now lived in different parts of the country, she didn't do anything much at all. Her life wouldn't be any different wherever she lived in the country, in the world, in fact.

She mused her little London place further. Sure there were a handful of friendly neighbours in her road, a few people she nodded her head to here and there in the village. There were lovely people in the coffee shop where she bought the same cup of coffee on her way to the tube station every morning and had done for years. The same Italian family who owned the restaurant on the corner of her road, who delivered her little parcels of food every now and then because she looked after their cat. But overall, she had not a lot in her life. Swapping her house for someone else's wouldn't really make much difference to her at all.

Jane swiped down and clicked on the photos accompanying the house swap post. A smile crossed her lips as she enlarged them one by one; this was not your average house by any stretch of the imagination. Whoever this Catherine person was, she knew what she was doing in the styling department. The pictures looked like something that had just stepped out of a fairytale; a dreamy, higgledy-piggledy, unfitted kitchen with an

Aga, a ginormous old retro Italian fridge, pots and pans hanging from a vintage ladder suspended from the ceiling, flowerpots full of herbs, a roll top bath, a gorgeous courtyard, little white gates, a brass bed, dolly planters. On and on it went in photo after photo of deliciousness.

Jane sighed. She was no stranger to having a nice house and garden; her house was about all she had going on in her life. She spent her evenings and weekends pottering around with nothing else to do, but this house on Darling Island was on a whole other level. She slammed the case on her phone shut and sat staring into the distance and the goings-on in the hotel bar. She couldn't do a house swap. What an utterly preposterous idea.

Jane's thoughts were snatched away from the swapper post by a notification and a ping with a text from the airline. She closed her eyes, tutted, and shook her head as she read the message. Fog and a severe weather morning meant the flight would be unable to land in London, or indeed, take off from Edinburgh. All flights in and out had been cancelled. She sighed, contemplating for a quick second whether or not to start looking at finding an alternative way to get home: hiring a car, booking a train, or possibly a coach. Quickly dismissing the idea, she sighed; she'd been stuck in Edinburgh more than once before and each time, after a lot of faffing, had ended up getting a hotel room for the night anyway. As she glanced out the window to the wind howling around the pavement, fog, and drizzly rain on the windows, she decided to cut her losses. Acting quickly, she walked over to the hotel reception desk, smiled, and rolled her eyes towards the weather outside as one of the other accountants came out of the lift dragging his bag behind him. She watched as he scurried towards the revolving doors as she stood in a queue at the reception desk.

She listened as the man in front of her let out a long, dramatic sigh, explaining to the bored-looking receptionist that his flight back to London had just been cancelled. It wasn't just her then. At least she'd got in quick and would be able to stay in the hotel and not have the bother of moving somewhere else. She watched as the man fussed with his briefcase, attempted to make polite conversation, paid for his room, and waited for his keycard. A few minutes later, Jane had followed the exact same scenario with the bored receptionist minus the attempt at polite conversation about the weather. All in a matter of half an hour or so, she'd been booked in, taken her keycard, whizzed up in the lift, and put her bag in the room. Before she knew it, she'd showered, said a silent thank you that she'd popped an extra blouse and underwear in her bag, and made her way back down to the bar.

With a pink gin and tonic in front of her, tracing her finger around and around the gigantic rim of the glass, alternating staring into space and looking at her laptop, Jane contemplated her small little life. She peered around, wondering whether the people around her had big, full, happy lives. She wondered about the business people sitting with a laptop open at the table on her right; who would they go home to? What did they do with their life? She gazed to her left where a table of men in football shirts chatted over pints of beer. Did they have people on their side? Were their lives full? A lot less beige than hers?

Sitting sipping her drink with no one to talk to, she was checking her emails when a man rushed up to the table in a bluster. He pulled out the chair opposite her, plonked himself down, and looked over the table enquiringly. Jane blinked furiously, not knowing where to look first as she struggled not to drown in the bright blue eyes and the good looks peering at her. The man blurted out a rushed apology and leant forward on the table, shifting his weight in the seat. He fussed with an umbrella, placing it down beside him. 'Hello! Sorry about that. Absolute chaos out there! The traffic is at a standstill. The fog came down quickly. I left the cab in the end and walked the rest of the way, hence I'm a tad late. Apologies, again, sorry about that.' He twisted around to look at the bar. 'What can I get you before we get into it? Coffee, tea? Wine?'

Jane took the man in. Tall, a hint of a tan, short dark hair, blue striped button-down shirt, striking blue eyes. The smell was very nice, everything was very nice. Very, very, very nice. She didn't know what to say and surprised herself as a funny sound came out of her mouth and she felt herself sit up a little straighter. 'Err, hello.'

Hello. Who are you? What is your name? Where did you get those eyes from? Stay a while. Please stay. Yes, buy me a drink. Or six. Seventy-six.

Noting Jane's confused tone and the look on her face, the space between the man's eyebrows wrinkled into a question as it dawned on him that perhaps Jane wasn't who he thought she was. 'Jessica?' he questioned and then looked around to the table with the football shirts and to the people at the bar with the laptop.

'Nope. Not me,' Jane replied, smiling and shaking her head. 'Definitely not me. Sorry.'

'Oh. Right.' The man appeared confused as he looked around. 'Apologies, I, err, assumed you were Jessica...' He let his sentence trail off, perplexed, as he twisted around and peered over to the other side of the bar.

'Can't help you, I'm afraid,' Jane stated, thinking that she would like to help him. She would like to help him very much indeed. Or have a drink with him and get lost in the blue eyes. Or, really, do anything with him at all. She contemplated tying him to the chair and peering at him for the rest of her life.

The man brought her back to earth with a bump, as he shifted forward in his seat. 'You're kidding me, right? You're the only person in the bar who matches the description.' His face furrowed into irritation, and he stopped what he was about to say as his phone pinged and he looked down. Jane waited as he read a message and almost gasped at his eyes as he looked back up. He wiggled his phone in front of her. 'Yeah, so Jessica's not here. Fabulous. Not.'

'Right.'

'Still in Belfast. Also caught up in all this weather and strike stuff. She never made the flight at all in the first place.' He sounded more than irritated and tutted, the wrinkles on his forehead deepening as he frowned. 'You think she could have let me know that beforehand if she's supposedly been waiting at the airport all this time?' He made a low growling sound. 'Sometimes I really do have to wonder at the intelligence of some people.'

'Yep. Me too,' Jane acknowledged. 'Sorry, I don't mean the intelligence bit, I mean my flight's been cancelled too.'

The man looked over at the bar. 'Looks like my meeting is off then...' He trailed off.

'Jessica's not going to make it?'

'No. Quite annoying, really. I rushed here for this meeting.' His phone pinged again, and he looked down. 'Blimey, my meeting in the morning has also now been cancelled because of the backlog from the train strike. You've got to be kidding me.' He rolled his eyes. 'Great. Perfect. You can't really make it up, can you? I don't know, it's always something with the weather or someone or other striking while the rest of us actually try to do our jobs.' He made a funny little low growling sound.

Jane could barely string two words together in response. She was far too busy getting lost in the piercing blue eyes, the dark hair, the everything. 'Yeah, fog, apparently and the baggage is backed up everywhere because the airport staff were striking,' she said, trying to arrange her face into something very agreeable, less beige and small than usual. A super odd feeling had come over her. Her eyelashes seemed suddenly to be batting of their own accord, there was a very strange sensation in her stomach and she became aware that she'd pulled her hair over her left shoulder, twirling it as she spoke and was now holding her head at an unusual angle. Ludicrous.

The man shook his head and rattled on. 'I mean, really? In this day and age, can we not travel through a bit of fog and sort out a few suitcases? What a wind up. I'm up here all week and don't have time for things not to just, you know, go as planned.' He let out a big, irritated sigh. 'Nightmare.'

It was all Jane could do to nod in agreement as she felt the world do a strange thing in the presence of this man; it tilted on its side, wobbled a little bit, and left her hanging in the middle of nowhere, unsure about how to behave.

'Ahh, I've been in this situation before,' he continued and looked at his watch. 'Literally zero point in me being stuck here in this hotel all week if all my meetings are cancelled because no one else can actually get here.' He looked around at the bar. 'No point hanging around here all night, though. Not exactly much of interest on offer. Another night in the room with some rubbish on the TV for company, I guess.'

Jane answered, rolling her eyes at the same time. 'Yeah, how annoying. At least for me, I was at the end of my trip anyway.'

'Yeah, well, I'm booked in until the end of the week. At least I'm not stuck here like you, I guess.' He pushed his chair out and put his hand out to gesture goodbye. 'Well, sorry about that. Good luck with your travel arrangements and all that.'

Jane smiled, unable to rip her eyes away from his and answered cheerfully. 'No worries.'

'I don't normally go around plonking myself down in front of random women in hotel bars, just so you know. Not that I'm ever going to see you again, so it doesn't really matter anyway.'

Jane felt her eyes fluttering again, wishing fervently that she *would* actually see him again. *Ridiculous. Pull yourself together, woman.* 'Good luck. Hope you catch up with Jessica at some point.'

'Pah! I won't be up this way again for a while, so probably not.'

'Well, anyway, I hope the baggage thing gets fixed, so it doesn't mess up your plans even further.'

'Yes, same to you,' the man said as he hurried off without even so much as a glance back in Jane's direction.

Jane sighed. That was the end of that then. As she settled back into her chair, she felt the same old familiar tightness in her ribs, the little clutch of loneliness, the only thing accompanying her in her small, little non-existent life. Someone with not a lot going on, someone to be pitied alone in a hotel bar.

3

Following the incident with the man looking for Jessica, Jane had somehow managed to polish off two gin and tonics as she sat alone in the hotel bar. She hadn't been able to face going back to her room and had now moved from the table to a stool at the bar where she'd chatted to the woman serving drinks about gardening. They'd exchanged notes on ways to get rid of black spot on roses and what to do when the ground was so waterlogged it was tricky to get out in the garden. The hotel bar area had slowly begun to fill up and as she sat there alone, it buzzed with chatter and busy people talking into phones and peering at laptops.

Jane sat alone, gazing around, and thought that she could catch up with some work, but the gin was nice and she'd had enough of numbers. Idly staring into space, she then pulled over a menu and wondered if she could persuade the kitchen to make her a cheese, onion, and salad cream sandwich; her favourite humble sandwich, which had seen her through many dark times. It would go down very nicely after the two gins, that she knew for a fact. Just as she was ploughing through what was on offer on the menu and wondering if she could concoct her own sandwich version by ordering a cheese board, a couple of slices of bread, and a sachet of salad cream from the counter, she looked up as someone sat down on the stool beside her. The harried man with the piercing blue eyes from before turned to her and smiled. 'Hello, again. Still here?'

Jane nodded, returning the smile. 'I've not got anywhere other than my room and the TV to go. I did consider a long soak in the bath but decided that if I go back to the room, I'll end up doing work and I'm over that for the day. My head was swimming earlier.'

'Yeah, precisely why I'm back down here,' the man replied. 'Even though this has to be the dullest hotel bar I think I've ever had the misfortune to end up in.' He nudged his head towards the shelves full of bottles behind the bar. 'Drink?'

Jane swirled the last of her pink gin and tonic around the bottom of her glass. There was no way she should firstly, accept a drink from this man and secondly, have a third gin. Although the gin really had gone down rather nicely, in fact, it had done a magnificent job of taking off her edges. She felt her head cocking to the side again as it had before when the man had sat down in a rush. It rested at an odd angle, and she tried to control her eyelashes and swallowed. A little voice from somewhere inside sounded in her ear. *Do it, Jane! Why the heck not? It's not like you've got a lot else going on in your life. What harm would it do? One little drink with a hot man. Why ever not?* Another voice reasoned. *He was a bit rude earlier and there's no way you should be having another drink.* The other voice fired straight back. *But he has got very, very, very nice eyes.*

She looked at the man's expectant face as his right hand indicated to the person behind the bar. Before she'd had too much time to think further about it or listen to the voice inside, she felt herself nodding, smiling, and answering, 'Oh, go on then. You twisted my arm.' She got a whiff of him as he shifted his weight on the stool; fresh out of the shower, some kind of nice cologne, and something else she didn't know what, but it was divine. Could she bottle whatever the smell was and keep it beside her bed? She could inhale it every now and then. Rub the side of the bottle. It would add something to her small little life.

She settled back onto her stool. It wasn't every day a man asked her if she would like a drink. Indeed she couldn't remember a time when *anyone* had asked her if she would like an impromptu drink; it had been that long. Yes, she would sit here with this man with the dreamy eyes and enjoy it. Make the most of it until she got back to her small life. She observed as he ordered the drinks, his manner confident and waited until he passed over her gin. He smiled. 'There you go. Yeah, and also, sorry.'

Jane took the drink and looked confused. 'Sorry?'

'I was a bit rude earlier. I realised that as I was thinking about it when I was in the shower.'

'No, no,' Jane replied, thinking that he had actually been a little bit rude. 'Don't worry about it.'

'I was in a complete rush. I don't know why I do it to myself. You know what it's like when you're away, though? Always trying to fit that last meeting in. Always someone to see. Always so many people to see, actually.'

Jane nodded. She didn't know what it was like at all. Unless she counted the faceless grey suits she met every now and then in random business hotels in random cities, she never had anyone to see. Ever. 'Hmm, yes. I know what you mean,' she lied.

'You must think I'm a bit up myself. Charging in like that and making assumptions.' The man's eyebrows rose in question.

Up himself was far from what Jane was thinking about him. She was more preoccupied with his eyes. Or, to be quite frank, anything about him. 'It's fine,' she said, sliding the slices of strawberries attached to a little pink cocktail umbrella in her drink off the end and popping them into her mouth.

A smile crossed his face as she fiddled with the cocktail umbrella. 'In Edinburgh on business? Or pleasure?'

'Business. For my sins,' Jane answered, taking a sip of her drink, and enjoying the pink gin as it slipped down nicely.

'Right. What line of work are you in? Do you come here often?'

A chuckle came out as Jane continued to twirl the umbrella around. He frowned and put his hand to his forehead. 'Sorry. Yeah, that sounded like a right pickup line, didn't it?'

'A bit, yeah. Haha.'

He held out his hand. 'Sorry. How rude of me. I've realised I haven't even introduced myself. Oscar.'

'Jane. Though to my friends, I'm mostly Janey.'

Jane cringed inside as she repeated the words she'd said silently in her head. *Mostly I'm Janey. Really?*

'Lovely to meet you, Jane, Janey.'

'Likewise,' Jane replied as she felt her heart, already doing strange things, soar into the air. 'I had a day of meetings...' Jane let her sentence hang in the air, unable to think of anything interesting to say about her job. 'You?'

Oscar waved his hand about. 'Same. Pretty boring, if I'm honest. Same old, same old. I'm up here until the end of the week. It all looks fabulous from the outside when you're travelling, but it gets pretty old pretty quickly, flitting from this place to that and living out of a bag.'

Jane laughed. 'I was going to say the same thing. Work is work at the end of the day.'

'Too right.'

An hour or so later, the gin and tonic had continued to slip down very nicely. So had the next one. The conversation had flowed, and Jane had given up attempting to control her eyelashes. Oscar picked up the menu and then looked around. 'I assume the food will be awful. It normally is in places like this.'

'Expect so,' Jane agreed. 'It's more often than not a bit hit and miss in a business hotel. You never know, though.'

Oscar looked out towards the main hotel doors to a bustle of people who were still coming in after battling the elements outside. 'Probably better than attempting to go out and try and find something to eat out there.'

Jane nodded, twirling the little pink umbrella from her drink around and around. 'Just before you sat down, I was considering if it would be possible to just order a cheese and onion sandwich.' She flicked her hand across the menu and laughed. 'I'm not sure if that'll be doable by the looks of some of the things on here. I mean, hand-reared duck. Really?'

Oscar laughed as he scanned down the menu. 'Yeah. You're not wrong. Some of the things on here are weird.'

'How does one hand-rear a duck? Do you have any idea?'

'Hang on, are you telling me you've never hand-reared a duck?' Oscar laughed. 'You haven't lived. I've done it many times.'

Jane giggled. 'I am telling you that.' She pointed to the menu. 'At thirty pounds for a breast of it, I'm guessing it must be good.'

Oscar scanned his eyes down the menu and nodded. 'I can see why you contemplated a cheese sandwich. Some of this sounds way too swanky. It never ends well. I reckon you're best with something like the burger. You can never go wrong with a burger in a place like this. It's hard to cook a burger badly is what I've learnt over the years.'

Jane dipped the strawberry garnish into the last of her drink and then popped it into her mouth. 'Hmm, the problem is that it's not quite just a cheese sandwich that I'm after. It has to be cheese, thinly sliced onion, we're talking super thin, wafer-like, and salad cream. The salad cream is key. Lots of salad cream and when I say lots, I mean *lots*. Original, and if possible, in the glass bottle.' She pointed over to the end of the bar where bottles of vinegar, pepper mills, and baskets of sauce packets were stacked up next to jugs of water. 'I've already checked out the stash and they do have salad cream, not my favourite brand, but it'll do.'

Oscar followed her gaze to the end of the bar. 'I reckon I could sort you out with getting a cheese sandwich.'

Jane swallowed. As far as she was concerned, she would quite happily let him sort her out with anything, sandwich or not. She tried to keep her face straight as she answered. 'You do?'

'Yeah. How hard can it be?' Oscar reasoned.

'True.'

'Cheese, two slices of bread, onion. Surely they can rustle that up in the kitchen, you reckon?'

'You'd think so.' Jane nodded. 'If they can veer away from the hand-reared duck.'

Oscar slid off his stool. 'Stay right where you are. One cheese, onion, and salad cream sandwich coming up. In fact, more than one.'

Jane smiled and thought that there was no way she was moving an inch. She could sit quite happily beside him at the bar all week. 'I'll believe it when I see it.'

'I know I've only just met you, but don't doubt me. I make things happen.' Oscar laughed.

Twenty minutes later, Jane had a white bread cheese sandwich in front of her. On the side were a couple of pickled onions, on the bar next to her cutlery were four packets of salad cream.

Oscar indicated to the pickled onions. 'Are we still referring to this as a success, seeing as the onion is pickled and not freshly sliced?'

Jane peeled the bread from the sandwich and started to squeeze salad cream onto the bread. 'Just,' she joked.

'I think I did rather well, considering the waiter could barely speak any English.'

'Not bad,' Jane said as she struggled to cut the pickled onion into slices. 'I think we can mark this down as about seven out of ten. Hmm, actually, possibly a six due to the quality of the salad cream. No, no. Five and a half.'

Oscar tucked into his burger and chips. 'How long have you had this strange food fetish?'

Jane frowned. 'Err, I don't think it's a fetish but seeing as you are asking, umm...' She raised her eyebrows and looked up towards the ceiling, contemplating. 'I think since I was about ten.' She punctuated her comment with a little cough. 'Actually, who am I kidding? It's more like since I was five.'

'Right. Sort of weird, but each to their own.'

'Put it this way, I can't remember a time when I didn't have cheese, onion, and salad cream sandwiches in my life. My friends joke that I live on them. Come to think of it, I do.'

'A bit like some people and Marmite, I suppose,' Oscar noted.

'Hmm. Yeah. I guess it is.'

'You don't travel with it, then?'

'What? Salad cream?'

'Yep. Like that woman who does the cookery show on the telly who takes chilli oil in her bag when she goes away.'

Jane looked embarrassed and coughed. 'I may have done the same, yes. I also have emergency supplies of salad cream at home. Plus, it has its own cupboard.'

Oscar laughed. 'But you didn't bring any salad cream with you to Edinburgh?'

'I didn't, but I do normally have an emergency packet, but I must have forgotten to replace the last one.'

'Right, yes, of course. So, Jane, what does Jane do when she's not getting random men to order her cheese and onion sandwiches in hotels?'

Jane thought for a second. She had nothing really interesting to say about her small little life. Oscar continued as she paused, 'Husband, kids, hobbies, friends?'

'I've got a son and...' She stumbled over her words. 'I was married.'

'Oh right. Divorced?'

'Yeah, no, umm, my husband passed away, actually.'

Oscar stopped midway as he picked up his drink. Jane waited for the mixed look of sorrow and pity to cross his face, but it didn't come. His face remained the same. 'Must have been awful,' Oscar acknowledged.

'Yep. Pretty much,' Jane replied. She didn't, of course, tell him the real truth about what her husband had done. The state he had left her in. No one wanted to hear that side of it. She'd realised that when people heard that your husband had died, they wanted to just make sorry sounds and feel pity for you. They didn't want to hear the nitty-gritty of it. They wanted to tick the box that you were sad and they were sorry and leave it at that.

Oscar didn't go down the pity route at all. Jane waited for the inevitable sympathy-filled questions that arose when she told someone she was a widow and under forty, they didn't come. 'Must make you take life by the short and curlies.'

Jane nodded. He couldn't have been further from the truth. Her life had got smaller and smaller by the day.

4

The next morning, Jane sat in the business lounge at the airport with a coffee, a croissant, and a bottle of water in front of her. She watched as the grill on the engine of a plane went round and round outside the window and a little truck dragged piles of luggage towards the hold. A woman a few seats along from her who was squeezed into a spotty black and white top, made a big deal about being too hot and a teenager sat down at the next table with a plate piled high with food shovelling it in at nineteen to the dozen. Jane stared out the window, watching plane after plane land, lost in her own thoughts; an Aer Lingus plane with its green shamrock on the tail taxied past and a British Airways Boeing with a bright orange flashing light on top moved slowly to its parking spot.

Jane's mind whirred at what had happened the night before. Jane Le Romancer, woman with the smallest life in England, possibly the world, had ended up in the hotel room of a man she hadn't known from Adam. In said room, she and said man had not been talking about the weather. Thank goodness she'd shaved her legs and washed her hair that evening before she'd gone down to the bar. At least she'd been hair free and smelt good.

As Jane took small sips of her coffee, she wasn't sure what to think about what had happened the night before. All of it was a bit of a daze. All she knew was that it had been completely and utterly out of character for her, and at the same time, completely and utterly mind-bogglingly good. Amazing. Better than she ever could have thought. Stupendous. So good that as she sat in the lounge at the airport, it almost felt as if it had all been a dream. In the dream she had been dazzling and she had razzle-dazzled. Gorgeous and fabulous and interesting and happy. So very far from small.

She'd woken up that morning back in her own room to her phone alarm beeping in her ear and had stared up at the ceiling in disbelief at what she'd done. Mortified with embarrassment, in a frenzy, she'd collected her stuff from a pile on the floor, showered, put the same clothes from the night before on again, grabbed her things and bag, and scooted through the hotel lobby as quick as a flash. As she'd rushed to her taxi to the airport, all her bravado from the night before was long gone. She'd mused it and gone over it over and over again as she'd trudged through security and made her way to the lounge.

Who even was that person from the night before? The person who had ripped her top over her head, undone her bra and flung it across the room. She shuddered at the thought of it as her mind replayed what had happened, as if it was a movie showing on a screen inside her head. She'd actually flung her bra around! After which she'd cupped her breasts together and jiggled. What in the name of goodness had she been thinking? Jane and her small life had had sex with a man she didn't know! In a hotel!

As the airport terminal shuttle had jolted back and forth, she'd stood gripping onto the handle above her head thinking about it all and grimacing as her mind cast back to afterwards when she'd found herself lying in bed next to what was little more than a stranger. She'd laid there motionless, not knowing what to do. Not knowing how to act, not knowing what to say, not knowing what the protocol was. Not long after that, she'd mumbled a few things and bolted back to her room, overcome by a mixture of regret and embarrassment.

Jane came back to the moment in the lounge as her text pinged. Her phone showed a message from her friend Tally.

Hey Janey. Just checking in with you. How are things? What are you up to? Did you say you were away for work this week? Sorry, can't remember. xxx

Jane chuckled to herself as she contemplated what she was going to say in response. Should she give the same old response to Tally as she always did; that she was fine? Or should she tell Tally that actually she'd just had an amazing night? She fiddled with the cuff of her jacket as she stared at her phone. If she told Tally what had happened, there would be no doubt that Tally would tell the rest of their little friendship group. The five of them known collectively as the Hold Your Nerve girls had been friends since school and seen each other through thick and thin. She knew they all worried about her since her husband had died, though none of them really knew the truth. She shook her head to herself and decided not to tell anyone about what had happened in Edinburgh. She wasn't even sure what she thought about it herself yet. No one needed to know anything. It was all just a one off. She'd slip quietly back home, sidle on back to her small life.

I'm good, thanks. I got stuck in Edinburgh due to the weather. Just on my way back now. Xxx

Ahh. Nightmare. I heard it on the radio on the way to the surgery this morning. I didn't realise you were caught up in it!!! They were saying that a flight got turned back last night!

Yeah. It was fine actually. As soon as my flight was cancelled, I booked a room.

Jane reread the text as she sent it and continued to type. *I booked a room and then spent the night with the most amazing man!* Jane deleted the last sentence and pressed the little blue arrow.

You're a pro at going away on business now. Tally messaged back.

Jane chuckled to herself. If only Tally knew what had gone on. She would freak.

Unfortunately, yes, I am. Blooming weather!

Hang on a minute, I'll video call you.

Jane waited and then pressed to answer. Tally always loved a video call. She said she liked to look people in the eye, see what they were thinking. Jane rearranged herself in her seat and smoothed her hair as Tally came into view. Tally smiled and then squinted.

'Err, Janey? What's happened?'

Jane frowned. 'What? Nothing's happened.'

Tally rolled her eyes. 'C'mon. How long have I known you?'

Jane couldn't believe it. Surely one night of passion didn't show all over her face that much. 'Haha, too long, some would say.'

'You've had sex.'

'Don't be ridiculous!'

'Oh. My. Goodness!'

'Shut up, Tals.'

'When, where, how?'

Jane couldn't stop herself from beaming and chuckling.

'You blooming well have too! I knew it. You see, this is why I make a very good doctor, even if I say so myself. I can spot things.'

'You can diagnose whether or not someone has had intimate relations just by looking at them? Did you learn that at medical school? What module was that in?'

Tally hooted. 'I can where you're concerned. I'm gobsmacked.'

29

'I'm not saying a word.'

'You, my friend, need to spill the beans, and now.'

Jane lowered her voice, leaving a little deliberate pause to indicate she was serious before she continued, 'Don't tell anyone, Tals, I wasn't going to say anything.'

'So it's true! Wow. I need all the minutiae, I'm talking every single bit. And gosh, just let me add here how jealous I am.'

Jane laughed. 'I can't tell you in the middle of this place... all I'll say is it was, well, I don't even know how to describe it. Very good.'

'I'm flabbergasted! Janey, you don't do things like this.'

Little did Tally know how right she was. Jane didn't do anything much at all. Jane nodded. 'It was stupendous and a bit mad, really.'

'So, hang on, wait, who was it? Someone from work?'

Jane lowered her voice further and looked around. 'No.'

'Who then?' Tally frowned.

'I don't know!'

'What the? What do you mean you don't know? What?'

'Yep, I mean no, I don't know.'

Tally shook her head. 'No way! You're having me on.'

'No, no, I'm not.'

'Janey! I don't know what to say.'

'I know, right?'

'Are you seeing him again?' Tally's eyes widened. 'Sorry, I'm assuming it was a "he" yes?'

Jane rolled her eyes. 'Yes, and I don't know.'

'Well, I never...' Tally said, popping her glasses to the top of her head. 'I didn't see that coming on a weekday morning.'

'Anyhow, how are you?' Jane asked.

Tally sighed out through her nose. 'Ticking along, I suppose. Could be worse.'

'Have you come to any agreement?' Jane asked, referring to the state of Tally's marriage and her impending divorce.

'Not really. I don't know. I don't know my ass from my elbow at the moment if I'm honest, Janey. I'm just trying to keep all the balls in the air and get through one day at a time.'

'Must be tough.' Jane acknowledged.

Tally's voice dropped a notch. 'I don't know how I'm going to cope.'

'You'll be fine.'

'Yeah, sorry, I know you've been through worse.'

'You've always done everything on your own anyway,' Jane replied.

'I know. It's just financially and everything. You know?'

Jane nodded her head. She sure did know. She knew only too well what it was like to do it alone. Not that Tally or anyone knew just how badly her husband had left her up to her eyes in it. Up the creek without a paddle had been exactly how she'd been left. 'Tals, don't even doubt yourself. Take it from me, you'll be okay. If I can do it, anyone can.'

'I know. It's just a bit daunting. I never saw myself completely on my own with the twins.'

'No. I guess no one does, really.'

'The thing is, Janey, I've decided that life really is too short, isn't it? I could be dead tomorrow, right? I need to get myself out of this situation and move onwards and upwards with the actual life I want.'

Jane nodded. Tally was more than right. 'Yes, you absolutely could.'

'You have to take your life and do something with it if you're unhappy. That's how I started with all this. I just have to keep that front of mind when I think about being on my own and divorced. Anyway, sorry, got to go. Don't want to burden you with my reams of baggage! Hope you get back safely. I'll call you later in the week, and we'll have a proper chat about what went on in that hotel. Still gobsmacked. See you later.'

Jane smiled. 'Okay, look, keep it to yourself. I don't want all the girls knowing yet.'

Tally grimaced. 'Will do. But you know how much they'll want to know about this. Blimey, this calls for an extraordinary meeting, and a meetup, in actual fact.'

'I know, precisely why I'm not telling anyone yet. Anais will have it printed on the front page of The Telegraph.'

'Yeah, too funny. See ya.'

Jane put her phone back in her pocket, and as she checked the time and the board, she made her way to the gate. For the whole way back to London, her mind was a jumble of thoughts; it went over and over what had happened the night before. How she'd sunk the gin and tonics, chatted to Oscar about all manner of things, how as she'd sat up next to him at the bar, she somehow hadn't seemed quite as small anymore. How she'd felt all her inhibitions slip away as the gin had gone down. How she'd ended up back in his room.

Along with thoughts about the wild evening, what Tally had said kept playing over and over in her mind as if it was a news bulletin on the radio on repeat.

I could be dead tomorrow, right? I could be dead tomorrow, right?

She kept thinking about what Tally had said. Tally was more than correct. She could be dead tomorrow, and what had happened at the hotel highlighted that even more. It meant that she was alive, not quite as small.

Before Jane knew it, with her mind again reliving the night before, she was heading off the plane and tapping her card on the pad at the entrance of the tube. Pulling her jacket tight as a cold wind whisked around, she stood on the escalator as it carried her down to take her home. Take her back to her small little life where the next time she would see anyone properly would be at the end of the week when she went back into the office and the next person she would speak to would probably be Tally when she called again. Back to smallness. No gorgeous man to find her cheese, onion and salad cream sandwiches. No one to whisk her away on a tsunami of things she hadn't felt before. No one to make her life feel as if someone was there for her.

Thirty or so minutes later, she emerged from the underground at the station by the Common, a seven-minute walk from her house. She waved back as Sangeeta, the woman in the cubbyhole kiosk, waved to say hello just as she always had done for years. At least someone recognised her.

'How are you?' Jane asked as she slowed down at the kiosk and smiled.

Sangeeta raised her eyes and pushed her beanie back from her eyebrows. 'Not bad. You?'

'Yep, not bad.'

'Have you been away?' Sangeeta asked. 'I was only just thinking I hadn't seen you for a few days.'

Jane nodded. Sangeeta not seeing her trundling along to the tube was probably the only person who missed her. 'Yes, I've been away, and it got extended because of the weather.'

'Business?'

Jane chuckled to herself inside. Business with a whole lot of pleasure on the side as far as she was concerned. Not that she'd tell Sangeeta, or indeed anyone else, what had happened in Edinburgh. 'Yeah, another day, another case.'

Sangeeta rolled her eyes. 'You need to work a bit less, Jane.'

'Tell me about it.' Jane chuckled and pointed her finger. 'Hang on a minute, kettle calling pot black...'

Sangeeta laughed. 'Ahh, well, not any longer, miracles have occurred! Let me tell you, I've booked a month away. I'm so excited I can barely control myself.'

'Oh, really? Goodness, miracles have occurred, indeed! Where are you off to?'

Sangeeta couldn't keep the smile off her face. 'All over the place. Athens, then Rome, then down the coast to the bottom bit of Italy, Calabria.'

'Blimey! Jet-setting all over. What's brought that on?'

Sangeeta lowered her voice. 'Remember the cousin I was telling you about in Wolverhampton?'

Jane frowned. 'Oh yes, heart attack, wasn't it?'

'Yep. Gone.' Sangeeta sliced her finger across her throat.

'What? Oh my goodness! He died?'

'Yes.'

'Oh, dear, oh dear, I'm so sorry.'

'I know. Major shock. *Major.* I said to Lionel, "You know what, Lionel? Life's too short, I could be hit by a bus tomorrow." Yeah, so that was it; I booked the trip. Always wanted to go to Athens and Rome, and just like that, I'm there. I *cannot* wait.'

'Goodness. Impressive. That's the way to do it.'

Sangeeta beamed as she served someone a packet of Polos and then turned back to Jane. 'I haven't had a holiday in seven years, Jane. And from now on, I'll tell you one thing...'

'Righto, what's that?'

'No more standing here in the cold stomping my feet up and down all year long. No more looking out at this station for twelve hours a day, seven days a week. From now on I'm doing things with my life. Going places. I'm determined to make some changes. You know?'

Jane nodded. 'Good for you. Yes, good for you. Well, I'll get off. See you tomorrow.'

A cheeky look crossed Sangeeta's face. 'Will do, or you never know, I might be here or I might not.'

A few hours or so later, Jane was sitting on the sofa, showered, in her favourite dressing gown, her hair held back with an Alice band, a thick layer of very expensive face cream on her face. In front of her was a bottle of ice-cold wine, a cheese, onion, and salad cream sandwich, and her phone. As she scrolled through her groups and ate her sandwich, she stared around at the living room walls. Here she was again, same old, same old. Same walls, same sandwich, same wine, same laptop, same social media groups. No gorgeous men with blue eyes. Same small life.

She scrolled up mindlessly on social media as she polished off the last of the sandwich and swilled wine around in the bottom of her glass. Posts about spraying bugs in the garden with a solution of vinegar and one about getting men to wee on lemon trees to make them thrive. And then she was suddenly back at the house swapping post in the Darling Island group. She read through the post again and clicked to expand the comments. The poster had left comments saying that she'd had no luck, and she was going to look into renting an apartment instead. As Jane read through, Tally's words went through her mind again. *Could be dead tomorrow.* And then Sangeeta's. *Life's too short.*

And then she thought about what had happened with Oscar and how delicious it had been. How good it had felt to feel alive. How she had actually felt like someone. Not just small little Jane with no life at all. And suddenly, before she gave herself time to think about what she was doing, she started to type out a message.

Hi Catherine

My name is Jane. I've seen your house swapping post on the Darling Island page. My friend lives on Darling so I've a little bit of knowledge about the area. I've never done this before, but I think we might be a great swap. I live in a semi-detached Edwardian three-storey house in South West London. I'm a seven-minute (quicker if you muscle) walk from the tube station and a short stroll from two beautiful Victorian gardens and a Common. There are plenty of buses to hop on and off too. I think you might be comfortable in my house;

open fireplaces, a lovely Shaker style kitchen, a big old conservatory at the back, and the two main bedrooms have bathrooms and all the mod cons - plus fast internet, Netflix, underfloor heating, etc. I have a small but thriving garden with a lawn, a few apple and pear trees, some lovely old rambling roses, an undercover eating area and a gorgeous little office shed.

I'm not sure if you've found anything yet or you've decided to go for the hotel option. If you're still interested, I'd love to hear from you.

Jane read through the description. It sounded nice. It actually sounded really nice. She flicked on the lamps and walked around, taking a few snaps. She had to do a double take as she looked at the pictures. Her house looked lovely; the kitchen with its Aga, the copper pots and pans over the island, the conservatory, and the sitting room. All of it lovely; her comfy, pretty home. Attaching the pictures to the message she hit send, put her phone down, picked up her plate and glass, and cleared up the kitchen.

Fifteen or so minutes later, after spraying down the sides, loading the dishwasher, and flicking on the kettle, she was taking a bowl of Cornish sea salt ice cream into the sitting room. As she sat flicking through Netflix with her feet tucked up under her, trying to decide whether or not to watch a true-crime documentary about a serial killer in California, her phone pinged. Putting her spoon down, she glanced down and frowned at a notification that she had a message.

Hello, Jane. So nice to hear from you! Your house looks fabulous and just what I'm looking for. Thank you for sending me the pics. I'd just about given up on the idea of the house swap too! Maybe we could have a chat? Look forward to hearing from you.

Jane spooned more ice cream into her mouth, nodded her head, and before she had time to change her mind or think about it too much, she tapped out a reply.

I'd love to have a chat.

Great, me too. Have you house swapped before?

Nope. Have you?

Yes, I've done it a few times.

Ahh, right so you know what you're doing then?

Yep! It's worked out well for me as long as we're on the same page. Let's have a video call and we can discuss it further...

Okay, yes perfect. Let me know a time that suits you. Jane :)

A few minutes later, Jane had polished off the ice cream, arranged a time to chat with the house swapper, and as she sat and stared out the bay window onto the quiet London street, she couldn't help but feel a tiny bit of excitement in the pit of her stomach. A tiny part of her was feeling happy, fuzzy vibes. It was telling her that there was something good about the message, something good about Darling Island, something good coming up. The house swap was maybe a good thing on the horizon, something not quite as small.

5

Jane looked out at the back garden. She'd pottered with it over the years, and the time she'd put in showed all over the place; an archway of huge floppy pale pink old roses led the way to the lawn, a jumble of pots sat prettily by little steps to a sitting area surrounded by hydrangeas, and a few old apple trees she'd brought back to life when she'd first moved in now appeared healthy and happy. A wisteria she'd trained over a pergola and bench halfway down invited a sit to ponder, the herb garden planted on a whim and nurtured to life was always full of goodness, and the shed at the end was a place she liked to escape to after a busy week. Her mind flitted to the house swapper and the online post. What would it *really* be like to swap? Would the person care for her garden? Would she miss her small life? Would she miss the little slice of loveliness in her nice old London suburb?

What about her walks to the Common? The strolls in the fresh air at the weekend, watching the changes of the season through the weeks, the few nods of acknowledgement to people she recognised. Would she miss those? As she pondered, she reasoned with herself; she could swap her walks on the

Common for walks by the sea, couldn't she? She'd get to know people on Darling Island and be able to spend more time with her friend Lucie once she got back from her holiday. Yes, she'd be fine.

Her eyes wandered back towards the house; the gorgeous vintage bricks, the heavy sash windows, the louvre window in the attic looking out across the rooftops. She might have the smallest life in London, but she loved her house, loved feeling safe, loved coming home to her little sanctuary for one. Why in the name of goodness would she want to give it up and rock a small, safe boat?

A few minutes later, she was in the kitchen. She looked around and assessed it too. A Shaker kitchen she'd had hand built, a huge old vintage sink, a dresser filled with her bits and pieces. In the corner, the open fire she loved to sit by in winter evenings. The huge candelabra she'd found in Portobello Road market with its tiny little silk lampshades that when she flicked it on as she arrived home from work glowed and almost felt like a friend. She stood with her hands on her hips, analysing everything in her abode. It did look nice. It was nice. Sitting down, she slid her phone across the kitchen table, swiped up, and started Googling house swapping.

Home exchange is not for everyone. There are many pitfalls to be had. From horror stories of creepy men under beds and hidden cameras to hoarders' houses piled with filth... but get it right and you could open a door to a whole new world. Some people love to swap their houses with those on the other side of the planet and do it with much success multiple times a year. It provides them with the experience of living like a local and is a great way to get integrated into the life of a new place at the drop of a hat where exchangers are introduced to neighbours and new communities from day one. If you decide to swap your house with someone, get ready to enjoy the ride.

Jane swallowed as she continued to read the article on the pros and cons of home exchange. By the end of it, and after reading about some of the pitfalls, she didn't quite know whether to relish the idea of a new challenge and be champing at the bit to get started, or to message Catherine back right away and call the whole thing off.

Jane did another search and dived head first into a gigantic internet well of house swap stories. She read further and educated herself on the drawbacks and downsides of home exchange and felt a multitude of emotions; from a warm, fuzzy lovely feeling at house swaps that had changed lives, to a feeling of doom at tales of houses that, in reality, had been disaster stories where people had arrived with suitcases to dodgy houses in scary areas surrounded by filth. She smiled at the picture of a couple who had swapped and ended up getting married and another successful swap where it had gone so well that the swappers had kept the arrangement permanently.

She reread the message thread with Catherine. Part of her wanted to send another message saying that, actually, she'd changed her mind. Then she looked around her, blinking and shaking her head at her small existence, and she decided that her life was going to take a little bit of a turn. A turn away from small. The feeling had started the night she'd sat at the bar in the Edinburgh hotel; it had ignited something somewhere deep down inside. That night she'd decided to take a chance, live a little bit, and it had been brilliant, exciting, exhilarating. She would take that as her jumping-off point. An example of doing something with her life. There was no reason for her to continue as she had been for so long.

She scanned down through the message thread and nodded. Yes. She would do things to change her life. She would pash random men in random hotels and swap houses with people on the internet on little islands surrounded by sea. Jane Le Romancer was determined that her life would no longer be quite as small.

Sometimes we just have to take a deep breath in and not get stressed, she said in her head. Not that she was stressed, in trouble, or had anything wrong with her life. Perhaps that, indeed, was the problem. There wasn't anything in Jane Le Romancer's life much at all; no stress, no problems, not much to think about, and even less to do. If it wasn't for her friend Lucie's wedding planning, all she would have in her life was her job. Jane didn't need to worry about anything on the whole. She had enough money, comfort, a good job, a nice house, and a whole lot of small. She stared into her reflection in the glass on the back door and spoke to herself.

'Right. Time for action! Jane Le Romancer, woman of all things small, is ready. I am going to grow my life!' she said as she wandered around the kitchen and flicked on the kettle, and then found herself in the hallway staring into the mirror over the dresser, continuing to talk to herself. 'This opportunity has my name on it! Come on, Jane. Come on. If you can have wild, abandoned, totally amazing passion with a man in a hotel, you can do it. You can do this!'

Ten minutes later, she was sitting in the conservatory with her laptop open in front of her, tea, a notepad by her side, and a spreadsheet with a title, *Operation Le Romancer.*

Jane might have a small life, but she was an absolute expert in getting stuff done. It was why and how after her husband had died, she'd excelled in her job. She was prolific in her attitude and output and never left any stone unturned, ever. Unless, of course, it was something other than surviving after her husband had passed away, working, or looking after her son.

By the end of the pot of tea, Jane had a plan, a mission statement, three spreadsheets, four digital lists, two bullet point columns on the notepad, and an email documenting the whole lot sent to each of her different email accounts. Operation Le Romancer had begun.

Jane walked around the kitchen with one of the Operation Le Romancer lists open on her laptop on the kitchen island and started to look around at how her house would go down with a house swapper. She'd renovated the kitchen using a bespoke kitchen company from a very nice, thank-you-very-much, company in Kent. The stand-alone units had been beautifully crafted by a team of experienced carpenters who were passionate about their work. The whole thing had been painted in a carefully chosen eggshell white and slotted together for the look she'd lusted after on social media for a long time. It had cost an arm and a leg. Above the double butcher's block island, copper pans hung from a suitably aesthetically pleasing contraption. At the window overlooking the garden, a gingham café curtain hung from a brass pole and a double-width Butler sink displayed fancy soap from Melbourne, Australia with the matching hand cream, no less, nestled neatly by its side. Jane's eyes scanned the room for things to improve someone's experience in her kitchen and added new tea towels, nice mugs and 'clean out junk drawer' to one of her lists.

Next, she stood in the sitting room. The two huge sofas sitting opposite each other looked more than inviting; beautifully slipcovered in a pale duck-egg blue, piled with Colefax and Fowler cushions and layered with soft and cosy throws. The coffee table held a pile of books, a vase of silk hydrangeas, and a Penhaligon candle very much on its last legs. Jane added 'candle' to her list, and clutching her iPad, she continued walking through the house. The beautiful old bannister was scuffed and marked at the bottom and needed a repaint, a fine crack in the glass in one of the panels in the front door would need to be replaced, and the understairs cupboard needed a serious declutter.

She made her way up through the house, assessing. It was funny appraising your own space, analysing your own life. As she went through the bedrooms on the first floor, noting things down and peering around, it all seemed so very nice. Perfect, almost. Just as in her actual life from the outside, it all looked as if she was really doing rather well; like one of those capable, independent women on social media with a big white ivy-covered house, two well-behaved pedigree dogs, a wine cellar in the basement. The same women who seemingly actually enjoyed doing the washing up. Jane probably came across in the same way; her home was lovely, she had a very good career, nice things, a good education, classic taste, a healthy happy son, lovely furniture, and beautiful homewares. She had all of that. And not much else.

At the end of the day, Jane had nothing to want for, not a single thing to complain about. All the cogs were turning nicely, each doing their own little job in her small, but perfectly acceptable life. Why would she consider rocking the boat?

In her bedroom, she assessed her bed (super king), the linens (lovely high thread count sheets), the bedside tables (huge ginger jar lamps on either side), and her walk-in wardrobe (large and full of storage). She looked around the room and nodded to herself, just as everywhere else, it was more than tasteful; thick grey-white carpet, heavy tulip pleat, handmade bespoke curtains, floor-to-ceiling bay windows, a wicker trunk at the end of the bed. Everything lovely. Not a whisper or a hint of her husband anywhere; he was long gone. Not that anyone really knew it, but he was out of sight and very much out of mind. Her bedroom was a sanctuary, a place of comfort and loveliness, but as she walked around, she realised, nonetheless, it was also something else. A place to be lonely. A place where the tight little lonesome spot just behind her ribs stubbornly sat with her always like a sad little friend.

She opened her dressing room door, raised her eyebrows, and tapped on the list. Definitely in need of a serious clear-out. The room, designed for two but only ever used for one, was stuffed to the ceiling with way too many clothes, along with a more than healthy helping of junk. It was long overdue and always at the bottom of her to-do lists. She underlined it on her list and added bold.

By the end of the morning, Jane had assessed and documented the whole house in the tree-lined London street. The house would soon be in good order and she now had a list as long as her arm to make it just so. Operation Le Romancer had begun with a vengeance and Jane Le Romancer was raring to go.

6

In the short space of time that had passed since Jane had left to go to Edinburgh to sit with a couple of forensic accountants, lots had changed. Like a snow globe, it was as if someone had picked up her small life, given it a robust shake and put it back down again with everything having landed in a completely different place. She'd met a man in a bar and was now in the midst of arranging to spend a few months in someone else's house. The whole thing was quite surreal. The only thing that hadn't altered in the short space of time was the little daub of lonely tightness, always sitting just behind her ribs.

She sat at her dressing table, blending two different foundations into one another on the back of her hand, dabbed at the blob with a foundation brush, and began to tap the loaded brush expertly onto her skin. Taking a huge fluffy brush, she swiped it over a blusher pad and fluffed it generously onto her cheeks, and then picked up her phone and reread through the messages from Catherine at the house on Darling Island. There was a long message thread back and forth.

Hi, Jane. I was just wondering how long it takes from your place to

Fitzrovia where I'll be on the assignment for the three months? Do you have any idea?

Yes, I used to work over that way about ten years ago. It's about 25 mins or so. As long as no one decides to strike, lol.

Excellent. That would be great for my commitments. Do you ever drive into town at all?

Not really. The traffic and the congestion charge etc make it a hassle but you're free to use my car if you want to.

OK super. Thx.

Btw, before we have our chat, if we go ahead with it, I just wanted to clarify who will be staying in the house.

As I said in the post, just me. I'm single.

Ahh, OK. Same here.

Just checking on whether or not you are a smoker?

Gosh no! Never even tried it.

Excellent. Not being funny but I'm not open to smokers.

All good.

Look forward to our chat.

Same here! :)

Jane looked in the mirror. Did she look like an acceptable house swap candidate? She had no idea really, but with her face on she scrubbed up quite nicely. Not bad, at the end of the day. She finished curling the bottom of her hair, slicked on some lipstick, picked up her laptop, and headed downstairs.

In the sitting room, she placed her laptop carefully on a pile of books on the coffee table and analysed the background behind her; the pale blue sofa, a gigantic lamp placed just so, an oversized candle and a pile of books, which by their titles, she hoped would make her look a lot more interesting than she really was. Just as she was fussing with the cushions, her laptop sounded with the incoming call. As she clicked the button, Catherine came into view. She was sitting in her kitchen, a huge pitcher of white flowers beside her, a roll neck jumper, pearl stud earrings, a smiley, happy face. Pretty in a normal kind of way. An Aga piled neatly with pots and pans sat in the background and a candle flickered from a row of open shelving laden down with neatly placed dishes. Oh yes, Catherine was good. Jane might need to raise her game a little bit here.

'Hello,' Catherine said.

Jane made herself comfortable whilst inside feeling a bit nervous. 'Hi. How are you?'

'Very well, thanks.'

Jane took in the room behind Catherine. 'Wow, it looks like something out of a fairytale.'

Catherine turned around to look behind her at the Aga. 'Ahh, thank you. I'll give you a guided tour in a minute.' She made a little coughing sound. 'I, umm, tend to collect a lot of things as you'll see.'

'I'd love a tour, yes please.'

Catherine nodded towards the screen. 'Same goes for you. It looks lovely there.'

'Thanks, I've pottered with it over the years to get it to where it is nowadays. You know what it's like.'

Catherine rolled her eyes. 'Yeah, it takes ages to all come together, especially when you're doing it on your own, as I've mostly been.'

Jane nodded in agreement. 'So true.'

A few minutes later, she watched with her chin on the floor as, through her laptop screen, she was given a tour of Catherine's house on Darling Island. The lovely little sitting room with its multitude of lamps, the cosy snug with an old fireplace, the courtyard doused in pretty lights complete with chiminea and gorgeous outdoor seating, a tiny but comfy study. It got better the further up Catherine went, finishing with a freestanding bath squeezed into a small bathroom and an attic room with distant views of the sea.

'I'll take it,' Jane had joked.

Catherine sat back down at the kitchen table. 'Seriously?'

'Of course. I love it!'

'When can you be ready?'

Jane chuckled to herself inside. It wasn't as if she had any other pressing engagements to work around and not as if anyone would miss her. 'Umm, name the date. I can pretty much do whenever.'

Catherine paused, screwing her face up while she considered. 'Early next week, would that be too soon? My project starts then and it really would be good to get this sorted so I can settle. I'd all but given up hope and thought I was going to end up in some dreary business hotel.'

Jane hid her surprise. She wasn't sure if she was *that* ready, but then again, why not? She'd have a lot of scrambling around to do and possibly have to do a few runs to the recycling centre and the same to the charity shop, but that was all. She quickly assessed if she'd have time, if she was ready to swap her life for Catherine's. She hadn't even told her friend Lucie, who lived on Darling Island, anything about it. She hadn't told anyone anything about it. Before she could think about it too much, she heard herself agreeing. 'Yeah, why not? Let's do it. In for a penny...'

Catherine beamed. 'Honestly, you don't have to do anything special at all. We'll just slot into one another's lives, well, one another's homes as it were.'

Jane agreed whilst thinking at the same time that there was no way anyone was going to be seeing the inner workings of her wardrobe, under the stairs cupboard, or junk drawers in the current state they were in. 'Of course.'

'Right, well, I'll be in touch and I'll get the ball rolling down here. I'll tell the neighbours etcetera and put together an up to date document on what's what.'

Jane smiled, not sure what she had agreed to, but went with it anyway. 'Yes. Okay. Exciting! I'll do the same.'

'Definitely. I can't wait to get there now that I've seen just how lovely it is. It's really helped me out. I didn't fancy one of those extended hotel stays and the Airbnbs I looked at were all faux boho furniture and charcoal grey sofas.'

Jane laughed. 'Too funny. Let's do this thing!'

The conversation came to an end; Jane closed the lid on her laptop, and as she did so she started to feel an incy wincy bit of regret. What in the name of goodness was she thinking? Completely out of the blue, she'd decided to up sticks and live in a totally different place for three months, in a house she hadn't actually seen, in a place she didn't really know. Had she finally started to lose the plot?

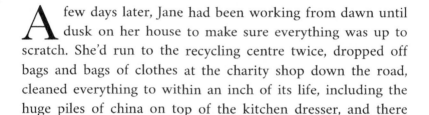

A few days later, Jane had been working from dawn until dusk on her house to make sure everything was up to scratch. She'd run to the recycling centre twice, dropped off bags and bags of clothes at the charity shop down the road, cleaned everything to within an inch of its life, including the huge piles of china on top of the kitchen dresser, and there wasn't a single weed to be seen anywhere in the garden.

Pottering around getting a few last few things sorted, she lodged her phone between her ear and her shoulder and waited for it to connect to her friend Lucie who lived on Darling Island, but was away on holiday. She could hear the happiness in Lucie's voice as she answered, 'Hi Janey. How are things?'

'Hello. Good, great in fact. Listen, you're never going to guess what.'

'What?'

'I'm doing a house swap with someone on Darling! Luce, I'm going to be your neighbour for a few months.'

'Sorry, come again. I'm not sure I heard you correctly. You're doing a what?' Lucie asked, the confusion evident in her voice.

'You did hear me right! I know it's all a bit random and out of the blue, but each time I've phoned you it's not connected and so I'm glad I've got through now.'

'Ahh! Yes, the reception is a bit dodgy here. It keeps dropping in and out. What, you're doing a house swap? Who the heck with? Where has this come from?'

'It all started in the community group I joined because of the wedding. Anyway, long story short, I answered a post and before I knew it I'd said yes and that was it.'

'Blimey. You haven't messed around. You're doing a house swap with someone on Darling. Wow!'

'I know. It's been a whirlwind.'

'Goodness! I'm so excited! Where is it on Darling?'

'Not far from the bay.'

'Oh, okay, cool,' Lucie replied, her phone signal dropping in and out.

'I'll send you all the details on WhatsApp. Sorry, I've been madly busy trying to sort it all out and working at the same time.'

'What brought all this on?' Lucie asked as the line crackled.

Jane sighed inside. Little did Lucie know about Jane's constant little companion of loneliness and her small life. 'Life's too short! I decided to go for my life when the opportunity came up.'

'Yeah, too true.'

'Listen, you keep breaking up. I'll love you and leave you and see you when you get home.'

'Yes, okay, wow, I can't wait to see you. Text me some pics and info.'

Jane put her phone down, pulled open the fridge, took out a bottle of wine, and then started to make a cheese and onion sandwich. As she was spreading salad cream thickly over the butter, her mind flitted back to the hotel bar where she'd eaten the same thing, albeit in quite different circumstances. In her head, she went over the evening and smiled. She wasn't quite as embarrassed now as she had been the morning after; maybe she'd do it again sometime.

She thought about Oscar. What was he thinking about it? Was he wondering about her? She remembered how, in a fit of giggles with the gin having taken away many of her inhibitions, she'd picked up his phone and wiggled it in front of him. She'd laughed and told him he was welcome to have her number if he liked. She'd added comically that he should count himself lucky because she didn't give her number out to any old Tom, Dick, or Harry. He'd taken the phone back and looked up at her expectantly. She'd giggled some more, tapped her phone, and he'd rattled off his number. She'd called his number, and he'd played along, answering it and laughing.

Thinking about Oscar and Edinburgh, Jane looked through the recent calls section on her phone and scrolled. There wasn't exactly a deluge of numbers there to trail through; a couple of calls from Tally, one from someone at work, and one from her neighbour down the road. Her eyes settled on Oscar's number. She held her phone in front of her, staring at it. Should she send him a message? Neither of them had said anything at the time about seeing each other again, and it wasn't as if she'd texted him the moment she'd woken up the next morning. But would he not have sent her a message if he was interested?

She mused it for a minute, wondering if she should consult any of her friends on what to do. She opened WhatsApp while the conundrum swirled around and around in her head and then closed it again. She'd have to go through the whole thing with them as it was only Tally who knew about Oscar. She knew anyway that her friends would be a mixture of opinions; two of them would say wait and see, the other two would say go for your life.

She peered out the kitchen window. What did she have to lose by sending one, short, how are you text? She didn't even know where Oscar lived or what he did, so it wasn't as if she'd be hassling him. He'd either answer the message and want to see her again, or not. Simple, right? Or not. She sat staring at her phone for ten minutes, typed something, deleted it, did the same again, and then continued to sit perplexed as to what to do.

After consulting Google, Jane had even less of an idea on whether or not to get in touch. The world wide web had a plethora of suggestions, scenarios, and advice to give on the matter of what to do in the aftermath of a one-night stand. At least by the end of her foray into the ins and outs of jumping into bed with someone in a hotel, she felt more normal than she had when she'd started. In the end, she decided to keep it short, sweet, and casual.

Hi, Oscar. How are you? I enjoyed the other night. Let me know if you fancy a drink sometime. Jane.

After a lot of subsequent deliberation on whether she should leave an emoticon or not, and grimacing at the memory of flinging her bra across the room, she hit send. In an instant, her screen told her that the message had been delivered. In an instant, there was regret. As she stared at the phone, nothing happened. No little dots flashing. No message. Nothing. Small.

Putting her chin on her hand and staring out the window, she sighed. Well, that was the end of that then. She could be waiting all day, all year, or for eternity for all she knew. So much for her mission to expand her life.

Later, as she was sitting in bed with a cup of tea reading a book, her phone lit up from the bedside table beside her. She glanced over nonchalantly and then snatched up her phone. Oscar had replied!

Hey, Janey :) Good thanks. Same here. What are you up to?

When Jane had first read it, she had beamed that he'd remembered her friends called her Janey, had taken ages to answer and considered calling Tally for advice. In the end, she'd decided that really it didn't matter at all what she responded. He was probably just doing it to be nice, to pass the time of day. She rewrote the text many times, trying to make herself sound a little bit more interesting than she really was. A little white lie didn't really matter when it was a text.

Busy! I've been to Clapham for lunch with a friend today. Then off out to a show in the West End. How about you? Jane had fibbed. Did watching Mamma Mia on her laptop count as going to a show? Maybe not quite the West End, but she was in South London. She'd wondered for ages about whether or not to add a kiss, but had plumped for a smiling emoticon. He'd sent a similar message back.

Yes, same here. I'm still up in Scotland. I finished off the working week, then I spent some time catching up with some old university friends in Banchory and I'm off to a race meeting. Ready to get home to be honest, strike dependent of course! I've had a lot on.

Jane had nodded. So he actually had a life, old friends and stuff to do. No mention of a partner, wife, or children or anything else, though. All very non-committal. Not really inviting any further communication either. He probably wished he hadn't given her his number in the first place. Jane couldn't stop herself from smiling, though. Operation Le Romancer had commenced; she was having a text conversation with a hot man she'd cavorted with without a care in the world, and she was swapping her small life and trying something new. As she sat in bed with her tea, there was a tiny little sliver of her that wasn't feeling quite as small.

7

It was the day of the house swap and Jane sat at the kitchen table with a mug of tea, her iPad beside her, laptop open in front, and scanned through the ticks in the checkboxes on various lists. She had the horrible pre-going away nagging feeling in the back of her mind that she'd forgotten something. As she scanned down the lists as far as she could see, she hadn't actually forgotten anything at all. Everything was done, and it wasn't as if she had to remember her passport and anti-diarrhoea tablets for her stay on Darling Island. She put her glasses on and cross-checked the lists for about the tenth time that morning. The only thing she now had to do was put her mug in the dishwasher and turn it on. She fiddled with the bottle of fancy red wine she'd left in the middle of the worktop and read through the note she'd left for Catherine again.

She'd spent all week getting everything ready for Catherine; all her really personal things were boxed up and in the attic, the house was spotless, and all the bills were up to date. She'd nipped to the deli down the road to add fancy cheese and nice bits and bobs to the welcome pack in the fridge, the window cleaner had just left, and she'd ironed the sheets and changed all the beds. There was nothing much else that she could think of to be done. The whole house sparkled and shone.

She yanked open the back door and as she took in her carefully tended roses, gazed at her pots full of lovely things, and smiled as the little birds who visited every morning turned around to say hello, she suddenly had a colossal pang of nerves. Her house was her sanctuary, the place where she could schlep around doing exactly as she pleased when she pleased. The place where she knew what was what. The spot where she was small and insignificant but comfy and safe. The place where she was quite happy to just be Jane. Would she miss the familiar smells of the garden? The lawn after it had rained. Her huge bed facing towards the window, where she could gaze up at the chimneys in the morning with a cup of tea. The sitting room sofa she sunk into at the end of the day. The kitchen island and window looking out over the garden where she'd sit and zone out.

She did a final check as she walked around the garden. There was hardly a hair out of place. She'd mowed the lawn the night before, jet-washed the terrace at the weekend, hung new bird feeders from the trees, weeded the beds until there wasn't a weed in sight and washed the chair covers on the chairs in the shed. Everything was as ready as it could be.

As she walked back through the house looking for anything she might have forgotten, she straightened a cushion in the sitting room and peered out the bay window at the front. A huge removal lorry inched down the road and stopped about halfway down. She wondered where the people were going. Were they going off on an adventure too? Were they also running away from small lives? Were they having wobbles about where they were going to go?

Jane put her chin up and watched as the beeping lorry reversed, stopped, attempted to back into a space, and then went forward again. She shook her head to herself as the juddering lorry matched the feeling in her stomach. There was no doubt about it, she was wavering, thinking that she was being really stupid, teetering on the edge of picking up the phone and calling the whole thing off. Nope, she couldn't do the house swap. She'd have to call Catherine and inform her that she was sorry and that there had been a family emergency, or make some lame excuse like that.

Trying to calm-breathe, just as her friend Lucie had shown her, Jane walked back into the kitchen to get her suitcase. The thing was that it had all happened so quickly that she'd not had a lot of time for second thoughts or cold feet, until now. Plus, it had been plain sailing without any hurdles along the way, which had meant she hadn't second guessed herself. When she'd advised work of her plans, they'd hardly even blinked. They'd just followed up the conversation with an email asking her to ensure she changed her contact details with HR. Her manager hadn't batted an eyelid and had informed her without barely looking up that it didn't matter where she worked from as long as she did the job. The whole episode had cemented what she knew all along; that no one was interested in her much at all. As long as she turned up, did the same stellar job and delivered on time as she always had done, no one gave an iota. And therein lay the problem.

It had been the same with her son. He wouldn't even be home for the three months that she would be away, so it didn't make much difference to him either. He hadn't blinked when she'd told him her plans. He'd bided his time listening to her, barely unable to conceal his eagerness to get off the phone. His head was more occupied with much more interesting things, like girls and beer and pretending to study. By the time he returned for the holidays, if he came back, she'd have been to Darling Island and come back again. So she definitely wasn't going to be missed there.

Jane plodded upstairs, flicking an imaginary speck of dust

from a photo frame. She knew the tread of the stairs almost as well as she did the back of her hand. Eleven steps up, three on the turn, along for three more and then hold on to the bannister for the second turn and then a few steps along to her bedroom. She tried to analyse her bedroom as if she'd just walked in and was going to be staying the night. As if she was Catherine arriving at the house for the first time. She nodded and smiled, pleased with her efforts; it looked more than welcoming. Better than a hotel room, whatever benefits and swish things they claimed to offer. Her room was gorgeous with its super king bed, plush rugs, nice lamps, and proposal of a deep, blackout sleep.

Jane sighed as she continued walking around and checking as the removal lorry outside still beeped away yet to get itself parked fully into place. Just as she was dragging her suitcase to the front door, the doorbell went. She frowned and looked through the porch onto the step where the local delivery driver, known affectionately as Springer due to his propensity to spring down the road delivering parcels, stood with a plastic post satchel and an expectant look on his face. Jane pulled open the main entrance door, stepped onto the mat, and pushed open the porch door. Springer, who delivered most of Jane's oft-arriving packages, held out a parcel and beamed.

'For you, Madam,' he joked, brandishing the parcel with a flourish.

'Oh, hi, how are you? Ooh, thank you. I didn't think these would make it in time,' Jane said, looking at the branding on the outside of the satchel. 'Espadrilles.'

'That's meant to mean something to me?' Springer joked and held out a machine. 'Give me a squiggle here if you don't mind.'

Jane took the parcel, the stylus, and the machine. 'Ahh, you're an angel. I thought I was going to have to get these forwarded.'

Springer had delivered many of Jane's late-night, wine-fuelled shopping sprees over the years. 'Yeah, I remember you said you would be away for a stint. I veered off from the other side of the main road to get it to you before you left.'

'Aww, you're too good to us, you know that, Springer?'

Springer chuckled. 'All in a day's work and all that. Count myself lucky to have a job, you know, Jane.' He rolled his eyes and shook his head.

Jane chuckled. 'I feel very lucky to have a good job too.'

Springer nodded towards Jane's huge case. 'Yeah, I think we'll leave it at that. All packed and ready to get going?'

'I am, indeed.' Jane shook her head back and forth and stepped forward. 'Truth be known, I'm beginning to question myself. I've definitely got the jitters. What was I thinking?'

Springer shook his head as he started to step back down the path. 'Get away with ya! You'll have a whale of a time. If you don't go, you'll never know. You only live once. We'll all be here when you get back. As I said, I'll watch out for the place,' he replied, looking up at the house.

'Thank you. Yes, you're right, I suppose. When are you going away? Turkey, isn't it?'

'We're off next month. Can't wait. Cannot absolutely blooming wait, Jane. You see, this is what I mean; you work hard all year and you go off for sun, sea and relaxation. No time for standing around striking and messing up everyone's plans.' Springer rubbed his chin. 'The state of the airport situation? Don't even get me started on that. Need stringing up those gaffers at the top.'

'Yeah, true. Maybe I'm going the right way by getting away from it all.'

Springer opened the gate. 'I should say so. Bon voyage. Have a wonderful time and see you when you get back. It'll be over before you know it. You'll have loads of tales to tell me about what you got up to living by the sea for a few months.'

Jane smiled, waved and watched as Springer hot-footed it

towards his delivery van. She closed the door behind her and looked at her case. Hopefully, Springer was correct. Hopefully, she would as he had said have a whale of a time. She clicked up the handle on her case - the wobbly bits in her stomach weren't quite so sure.

8

On the train, Jane had read and reread the instruction document from Catherine detailing the ins and outs of the house and Darling Island. According to Catherine, and her friend Lucie too, it was best not to use a car on the island if you could get away with it, and so Jane, weighed down by her suitcase, ginormous backpack, tote bag, and satchel across her body, had made her way via public transport. Catherine was doing the same, and they'd sorted out insurance on each other's cars, just in case. Arriving at the approach road before she got to the Darling Island floating bridge, Jane was faced with row upon row of cars whose owners had decided to leave their vehicles on the mainland, with a sparkly blue estuary as the backdrop.

As she struggled with her luggage, she looked over towards the ferry. She'd recently been to Darling Island a few times since her friend Lucie had moved there, but now everything appeared in a different light. Now the place surrounded by hazy blue was going to be her home for three months, it looked that little bit less holiday, a lot more daunting.

Making her way along the path towards the water and

shifting the tote bag to her other shoulder, she took in a big deep inhale of sea air. Nice. Very nice. As the breeze hit her, she remembered how she'd thought before as a visitor to Darling, how fresh the air smelled compared to London air. She continued her way to the floating bridge, dragging her suitcase behind her and squinting over to the island. A short line of cars sat bumper-to-bumper on a slip road down to the sea and a small queue of foot passengers was standing waiting for the ferry to arrive. Taking a spot by the barrier, Jane stood her suitcase up, wriggled her backpack straps from her shoulders, and rubbed the back of her neck. She'd not really noticed the little things before when she crossed over onto the island to visit Lucie. Everything looked different now as the floating bridge ferry made its way towards her. On board, a man in thick navy-blue cargo trousers and a white uniform shirt called out towards the waiting queue of passengers.

'Darling Bay! Foot passengers keep to the left! Wait for the gate to board!'

Jane squinted as the floating bridge clanged and banged, and looked up at a sign overhead she'd never noticed before. She stood with her head up and hands kneading into the small of her back as she read.

Darling Floating Bridge is a vehicular chain ferry crossing over to Darling Island, nestled just off the dazzling blue waters of the south coast.

Family-owned, wholly operated, and still privately run by The Darling Floating Bridge Company, it is one of the few remaining chain ferries in operation today.

First established in 1871, some of the original ferries can still be seen at our boatyard. The Darling floating bridges remain the only way to cross to Darling Island. The Pride of Darling crosses the narrowest point to Darling Bay.

7 days a week. 365 days a year.

*First ferry runs continuously from Darling Bay 5.30 a.m. Last ferry at
12.55 p.m.*

With everyone else seemingly oblivious to not much but
their phones, Jane observed as the ferry made its way to land.
Water splashed on the slipway and two heavy chains disap-
peared down into the water. Getting ready to get on, she heaved
her backpack and tote bag back into position and followed the
people in the queue in front of her as they shuffled in single file
closer to the gate. As the gate went back and people filed on,
another crew member whose reflective strip on his shirt flashed
in the sun approached her. He tipped the cap of his hat and
smiled as he tilted his head up in greeting.

'Morning. Looks like you've got your hands full there.
Darling Bay?'

'Yes, thank you,' Jane replied, fiddling with the clasp on
her bag.

The man's tanned, wrinkled skin creased into a frown as he
looked at her enormous suitcase. 'Staying on the island by the
looks of it, are you? Got the kitchen sink in there with you too?'

'Yes. I am,' Jane replied, whilst rummaging for her phone. 'I
do seem to have rather a lot of stuff with me now.'

The man's eyes shifted to her backpack and then back to her
face. 'Resident?'

Jane went to hold her phone out to pay as she narrowly
saved her suitcase from toppling over. 'Sorry, what?' She tried to
hide her irritation. She just wanted to pay and be done with it.

As the man's eyes twinkled, Jane remembered the strange
question from her last trip over to see her friend Lucie. 'Funny
old place is Darling. We run on a different clock to everyone
else with our own byelaws. Even though I'm aware you're not a
resident, I have to ask, see?'

Jane didn't really see. She remembered before that she'd

found the question a bit odd, a tad on the rude side, but today, weighed down by luggage and apprehensive about what she was doing, it irritated her. The man, however, seemed unperturbed. 'Hang on a minute.' He shook his head back and forth and tutted. 'Yes, silly old fool I am. You must be Jane.'

Jane frowned. How on earth did this man know her name? He continued with a chuckle. 'Catherine. She said you'd be crossing about this time on foot, laden down with bags. She's gone the other way. You're going to the mews. Correct?'

Jane nodded. It all made sense. However, she wasn't sure whether or not she wanted this man to know where she was going or to impart the knowledge that she was on her own, but it was clearly too late now. She was a little bit annoyed with Catherine. It felt all sorts of upside down compared to where she was from to be broadcasting a woman being on her own. She shook her head. There was a law for residents, was there? She racked her brain to try and remember what Lucie had said about it. She wasn't really sure what to answer. The man, still unfazed, did it for her and continued, 'Officially, you're not an actual resident, no.' He scratched his chin. 'I mean, officially, I'm not sure if the house swapping thing is included...' He paused for a bit. 'No doubt someone at the council has discussed it, or Mr Cooke is all over it. Anyway, on you go, no charge for residents. Need some help with your bags?'

Jane gazed up at this jolly man and went to say no, then changed her mind. What harm could it do? The bags were killing her, and he already knew where she was going. In for a penny, in for a pound. 'Yes, that would be lovely, thank you.'

As the man picked up her case, he smiled. 'Looking forward to it, are you?'

'Sorry, what? Am I looking forward to what?'

'Staying with us for a bit. Getting your fill of Darling. You'll love it. Does wonders for the soul, it does. They don't make 'em like this anymore. Good things happen on Darling. Amazing things.' He patted the barrier and looked around affectionately.

Jane followed his gaze to the surroundings. 'Yes. I needed a bit of a change. Do something a bit different.'

The man sucked air in through his teeth as he nodded. 'Yeah, we heard that. A break from old London town?'

Jane couldn't stop herself from frowning. This man seemed to know an awful lot about her. It unnerved her somewhat. She wasn't sure if she liked him, how it made her feel, or what to make of it. It seemed borderline creepy. It had ruffled her feathers slightly. She had no recollection of feeling like this when she'd got the ferry over to see her friend Lucie. 'Yeah, something like that.'

The tanned lines on the man's face creased even further and wrinkled at the sides of his eyes as he laughed and he continued as if reading her mind. 'Don't worry, you're safe here, but you'll have to get used to our ways, see? And this floating bridge here, the Darling Punt, well, this old thing knows all the ins and outs of the place. You want to know anything, you'll find it out on here. It all gets to here one way or another.'

Jane nodded. This man knowing her had thrown her a bit. She'd already felt anxious about being in a new place completely on her own, and now those concerns had intensified. She covered her feelings with a smile. She decided to try and not think about it as they got to the middle of the ferry; after all, she was only staying for a few months. What could happen in that short time? The man parked her suitcase beside her and tipped his hat. 'Enjoy the ride and welcome to Darling Island, Jane. Be careful how you go. You might never leave.'

Jane nodded, heaved the backpack to the floor, perched her bag on top of it, and looked out across the hazy blue sea and thought to herself. *I very much doubt that.*

~

J ane held her phone in her hand and peered out over the water, her eyes focused on Darling Island. The gate noisily banged shut to her left as the front of the ferry was slowly hoisted into place, and the man she had been speaking to pressed a few buttons on a little panel by the barrier. She watched as the floating bridge lowered down into the water and seemed to glide across the choppy sea. Every now and then, seagulls swooped down to the water, where little dancing spots of light glinted on top of the waves.

As she stood staring out at sea, her mind drifted to Edinburgh and Oscar again. She opened the cover on her phone and read through the last of their text thread. She scrolled back up on her phone and put her glasses on. As she read through, she had second thoughts as to her initial feelings; maybe he hadn't been binning her up or off or whatever it was her son called it, after all. She reread what he had messaged.

Hey, Janey :) Good thanks. Same here. What are you up to?

When Jane had first read it, she'd been really happy with his response and had taken ages deliberating on what to reply. She'd told a few fibs and as she reread them, she chortled. There was no way her life was as interesting as her text had implied.

Busy! I've been to Clapham for lunch with a friend today. Then off out to a show in the West End. How about you?

As Jane stood on the ferry and reread what she had sent, she gulped at the little white lie - she'd watched Mamma Mia snuggled up on the sofa with a cosy drink, not quite gone to see a show. She scanned through his reply.

Yes, same here. I'm still up in Scotland. I finished off the working week catching up with some old university friends in Banchory and then I'm off to a race meeting. Ready to get home to be honest, strike dependent of course! I've had a lot on.

Jane focused on the approaching Darling Island as she

thought about the messages and then flicked on the calendar app and counted the days since the night in the hotel. Had it really only been such a short time? In the time since Edinburgh, she'd swapped houses with a complete stranger and now found herself on her way to live somewhere new for three months. She decided to send Oscar another message. 'Oh stuff it, stuff it, stuff it, stuff it. I'm going to text him,' she said, speaking quietly to herself as the waves crashed into the ferry below. 'What harm can it do?'

What did it really matter? She'd never see him again anyway. Yes. She'd use texting Oscar as a little testing ground for Operation Le Romancer. Throw caution to the wind, put herself out there, invite further communication and see what played out. Him not replying after that initial post hotel room text would get her used to being rejected by people. She tapped out a message, held her phone out in front of her and nibbled on the side of her nail before she sent it.

Hi again, Oscar. You just popped into my head and I thought I'd message to see how you are.

Jane pressed send, squeezed her eyes shut and then hugged herself as she could see that Oscar was immediately texting her back.

Good! Busy, busy. How are you?

Same here.

Yeah, look, sorry I'm tied up in a work thing at the moment. Chat soon.

Jane smiled, she wasn't quite sure what to think of that, but she had made contact and was way too happy that Oscar had replied. She slipped her phone back in her pocket with a buzzy feeling inside and just under ten minutes later, the ferry had made its way to the other side. Foot passengers bustled towards the front, drivers sat ready to get moving, the man made his way down from a hexagonal tower in the middle, and Jane gripped the handle on her suitcase just that little bit tighter.

As the ferry docked, Jane was ready to go; ready to make her way to the house she'd seen from the screen on her laptop, ready to settle into a break from her actual life for a bit. To start the journey into making her life less small. To cement Operation Le Romancer into place.

9

Stepping off the ferry, Jane scanned down the instructions from Catherine. She'd been over on the ferry a few times previously, so she wasn't completely in the dark, but her friend Lucie had either been waiting for her or she'd simply strolled to Lucie's house around the corner. This journey involved a ride on the tram and was a little bit more convoluted. According to the directions, she had to get onto the tram and make her way over to another part of the island. She followed the handful of foot passengers hustling along, and as a loud beep sounded, the man with the satchel's face creased up into a smile as he tipped his hat and called out goodbye.

Jane yanked her suitcase behind her, squinted down at her phone, and then looked up. The instructions told her to continue on the pavement to the left of the ferry for a short walk until she got to a tram bay, where she would see trams coming and going, tram shelters, and various stops labelled with letters. She'd been there before with Lucie, but weighed down by what felt like the kitchen sink, she was a little less certain of the way to go. She needed to follow right around to the far left and wait at stop 'B' where trams came every seven to twelve minutes. Resisting the urge to phone Lucie on her holiday, she shifted her backpack and made her way along the pavement.

As people rushed past going the other way heading for the ferry now loading to go back, she huffed and puffed along until she could see a tram in the distance and the tram bay ahead. Smiling to herself, as she got closer, she tried to ignore her heavy baggage and focus on her destination. Lovely old-fashioned carriages liveried in the same blue and white as the ferry passed her as she shuffled along to stop 'B' and stopped alongside an old timber tram shelter. Hunched uncomfortably over by the backpack and tote bag, she stood waiting and looking up at a small digital destination board. As she looked around at an approaching tram, she could just make out the front destination as it trundled along, making its way to the end. She watched as another tram hissed down the tracks, passing white four-storey houses packed in next to the pavement and observed as the front sign began to flicker and change. The tram then started up again and made its way to stop 'B' and a woman smiled from the window as it pulled up. Jane heaved her suitcase in front of her up the steps and the woman walked along from inside, smiled and pointed to the case. 'Need a hand?'

Jane took the woman in and dismissed the notion that she looked vaguely familiar. 'Yes, please.'

'Are you on the right tram before you get on with all that?'

'I think so. Is this one going to Darling Main? That's what it says on the front.'

'Indeed it is. All the way along Darling Street. First stop is Darling Fire Station. You get to see all the delights of our little island on this one. Never gets old as far as I'm concerned, but I'm biased.'

Jane shoved her suitcase in front of her. 'Excellent. Thank you.'

The woman nodded towards Jane's luggage as Jane slipped her backpack straps over her shoulders and rested it on a seat.

'Staying with us for a bit, are you?' the woman enquired as she squeezed in beside a seat to let a pensioner sit down.

Jane nodded. Strange, the people here actually spoke to you as if it was part of their job. She hadn't remembered that from her previous visits. It had been the same on the ferry. She couldn't stop herself from thinking that it was nosy. Someone had even said hello to her as she'd dragged her suitcase along the road, and a man had actually stopped his car and let her cross the road. 'I am, yes.'

'Lovely. Best time of year on our Darling, I think I say that all the time! When it starts to warm up, that is. Not that it's not nice at any other time of the year. You want to be here if we're lucky enough to get snow.'

'Yes, I hope the weather stays like this.' Jane smiled.

'Resident? Sorry, I have to ask. It's the law. I presume that's a no,' the woman said as she tapped the little payment machine in her hand.

'I think I am, actually. If staying for three months is considered being a resident.' She gestured over her shoulder. 'They said so on the ferry.'

The woman smiled broadly and put the machine back in its holder. 'Right you are, then, if that's what they said, that's good enough for me. Okay, hold on tight and enjoy the ride. Welcome to Darling Island.' The woman leant forward and pointed further up the carriage. 'Have a little pew, my love. Trust me, best seat in the house for a first-timer on Darling.'

Jane didn't bother to tell the woman she'd been to Darling before or that her friend Lucie lived down by the ferry. From what she'd witnessed so far, that might involve interrogation. She looked at her luggage and the woman batted her hand. 'Don't you worry about that, it'll be fine there. Park yourself up the font, and I'll look out for you.'

Jane was flummoxed at the kindness. She sat back in her seat, poked her head into the fresh air coming in the window, and looked around at the carriage. A bell with a braided rope shone at the front, gleaming timber seats lined either side of the old carriage and sliding paned windows with old-fashioned brass catches were open along the top. She settled back into her seat as the woman walked back towards the front of the tram yanking on the rope, rang the bell and called out at the same time. 'All stops Darling Main! Main! Fire Station, Angel, then all stops Darling Main.'

As the tram cruised along, the sun peeked in and out from behind white clouds, catching the tramlines, and as Jane got lost in new things, she felt hopeful. She had to keep doing double takes at things she'd never noticed when she'd been to Darling before. A line of three-storey houses with pale blue windows, a cosy corner pub's door was propped open to the street, and a little coffee shop showcased a striped awning blowing in the breeze. The old fire station came into view, the tram passed alongside a war memorial, and a group of mums with prams stood chatting outside a Temperance Hall. A little row of shops bustled with shoppers, someone was polishing the door of an old church, a restaurant on a corner looked pretty covered in window boxes and ivy, and every now and then in the far distance, the sea flicked in and out of view.

Lost in her surroundings as the tram skimmed along Darling Street, Jane watched as the people of Darling went past the window going about their business. Not long after, she found herself stepping off the tram and peering down at her phone. The conductor rang the bell and called out the upcoming stops as the tram prepared to pull away and Jane felt herself almost go to wave. Surprised at herself and tutting at the same time, she pressed the arrow on the map app and waited for the pulsating blue dot to appear. As it did so, she put the address in and pressed walking directions; they told her the way and as far as she could see, it was more or less a straight road with a few veers left along the way. With her luggage piled up beside her, she looked all the way down Darling Street at the rows of blue and white shops with bunting strung in garlands above, and as the tram rumbled away with its bell ringing, the sun filtered through a canopy of trees. Shoppers pottered here and there, a group of pensioners with matching bags were waiting at the pedestrian crossing, and two young mums with buggies peered up at the tram timetable. From what Jane could see, so far so good.

As she took it all in, her earlier nerves had all but dissipated and standing holding her suitcase handle, she almost hugged herself at the prospect of being somewhere different. Now she'd done it, it felt good to be away from the regularity of the same old same old in the humdrum of her life. As she stood there in the centre of Darling, she suddenly realised she was buzzing. Excited, almost. Looking forward to three months with new things and different experiences. Rolling out the first steps of Operation Le Romancer. Hoping that in the not too distant future, she and her life would not be quite as small.

10

S topping to take a breather from the weight of her bags, Jane inhaled deeply with the intention of calming her butterflies and opened the pictures of the house on her phone again. She wasn't sure what that would achieve, it was too late now, she'd made the decision. Plus, right at that moment, Catherine would probably be walking up the path of her house, getting on with her end of the bargain. She looked down at the pictures and smiled. Yes, she most definitely still loved them. She'd studied them so many times when she'd first seen the post in the Darling community group that she felt as if she'd already been there. Now, as the house swap reality loomed, its enormity staring her in the face, she felt nervous about whether or not she'd done the right thing.

The short, supposedly pleasant walk from the tram seemed to take forever, and with her suitcase bumping over the cobblestones, it was as if she was on a roller-coaster of emotions; one minute high as a kite at trying something new, the next despondent at what she'd done. As she turned fully into the road, she strained to try and see her destination, parked her case and stopped. What looked back at her was really rather nice; on either side of the cobbled road lines of flat-fronted mews houses were painted in white. She peered up at the only one a few down encased in a layer of pale aqua blue. At the house nearest to her, on either side of the door huge planters held clipped olive trees and a little cat peered from the front window without a smile.

Jane continued to amble along the cobblestones, gazing at the houses; one groaning in ivy with the windows open to the breeze, another wearing a heavy coat of wisteria and sporting brass harbour lights to the front. As she ventured further down the street, her case bumping along behind her, wondering what she was doing and why she'd ever thought that a house swap was a good idea, she finally made it to the house she'd seen so many times in the photos. She gasped as she stood looking at the front door. In the light of day, the *actual* house itself made the pictures look mediocre. Oversized, galvanised dolly planters filled with shrubs stood by the front door, a vintage Mini was parked outside a set of double timber garage doors, and flowers in window boxes seemed to dance in the fresh coastal air. A pale aqua weathered old door sat squarely in white vintage brick-work and on two tiny steps, a jumble of pottery planters were brimming with blooms. Jane couldn't stop herself from beaming; it was more than gorgeous. She felt the little butterflies in her stomach come to life again and the feeling somewhere inside that this three-month jaunt might bring good things to her life.

For a minute or two, she just stood there gaping, taking it all in; to the left honeysuckle hugged a paned window and a horse-shoe-shaped knocker sat plum in the middle of the front door. A cruiser bike was perched beside the garage door and a small café table and chairs fit snugly under one of the windows.

Now, yes, I think I can do with some of this. Let Operation Le Romancer begin, Jane cooed to herself as she looked up at the windows on the first floor. Just as she had punched the code into the keypad to the right, a woman in a floral dress, denim jacket, scarf, and boots with a basket over her arm strolled past from a few doors down.

'Hello! You must be Jane.'

Jane smiled in return. Another person who seemed to know her name. She wasn't quite sure whether she liked it or not, but she was getting used to it. 'Hi! Yes, I am.'

'I'm the neighbour. The one who is here to help. I'm on the list of numbers to call, though you can just knock, obviously.'

Jane remembered the comprehensive instructions Catherine had sent and her note that all the neighbours were lovely. 'Ahh, yes. Well, here I am.' She gestured around to the mews. 'What a spot. Much, much better than I thought it was going to be, if I'm honest.'

'Well, our Catherine doesn't leave a stone unturned, I do know that for a fact. A real asset to this little row of mews. She's a neighbour worth having.'

'I think I've got a notion of that from our chats.' Jane chuckled and nodded inside the house. 'I can only assume it's just as nice inside.'

'Oh, yes, indeed. I think you'll love it. A little bit of a retreat for you?'

Jane paused, contemplating. There was no way she was going to tell the woman that actually she had no life and was on a mission to grow it somewhat. 'Err, sort of. Just a bit of a change, you know?'

'What is it they say? A change is as good as a rest, or something like that anyway.'

'Yes, I hope so.' Jane didn't add that anything would be less boring than her previous bland existence. That her main companion in life was a lonely tightness in her chest.

'You'll love it here. Most people do. Plus, you never know what will happen on Darling, that's what they say.'

'Thanks. Yes. I've actually visited a few times before. Over at the other mews houses,' Jane replied.

'Rightio, well, you've got a head start then. We have our own strange little ways on Darling; you'll probably have seen some of them already if you've been here before. Some people just don't fit in at all. You either get it and just kind of put your feet under the table or, well, you really don't. It's tricky to explain it to, well, umm, to someone who isn't actually a resident.'

Jane nodded, unsure of what to say. The woman continued, chuckled and joked. 'It all starts on the punt, you know, the floating bridge. Little do you know it, but you're being checked out from there. Then of course the same thing happens on the tram and then in Darlings if you venture there. Anyway, sorry, I'm rambling. Just give me a knock if you need anything.'

'Thanks. I certainly will.'

'Enjoy your first few nights. The weather's warming up. It's a lovely time of year on Darling. Oh, and if Catherine didn't tell you about our new bakery, you need to go there.' She lowered her voice. 'The buns are to die for. That's if you can actually get hold of any, of course. Right, well welcome.'

'I'll keep that in mind,' Jane replied, not bothering to mention that she'd actually had the infamous buns at her friend Lucie's place. She watched as the woman strolled away down the road and then pushed open the front door, lugging her case over the step behind her. As she looked around, she felt her shoulders untie themselves from her ears and she smiled. This wasn't half bad at all.

The heavy blue door creaked as Jane closed it behind her and she stood in a small entrance hall. She balanced her backpack on a chair and stood with her hands on her hips taking it all in. There was an open-plan kitchen and dining room leading to a sitting room. Every which way she turned, everything seemed to have been exquisitely chosen and carefully placed. Large paned sash windows sat in exposed brickwork, a bank of vintage French doors looked over a courtyard, and along the windowsill a plethora of herbs brimmed from pots. As she peered through the old panes, another bike was stored on the wall and she could hear but not see a burbling of running water. In the sitting room, two huge sofas were layered with reams of white throws, vintage reading lamps were perched on every available surface and one wall lined with shelving was weighed down in a jumble of colour-coded books. Shabby it was not.

In the kitchen, a long, wide butcher's block island displayed vases of white flowers, together with a cluster of candles, and an old shabby unit repurposed for the kitchen was stacked with vintage preserving jars. On a little shelf, a cream tagine was stacked on top of a Persian cookbook alongside a row of antique glass teapots. Tucked in the corner, an Italian vintage fridge was asking to be opened for a bottle of chilled wine and to the side of the Aga, a dresser housed jugs rammed with wooden spoons and cooking utensils. Battered Baccarat coffee makers were lined up over the top of the double-width cream Aga, and a large whistling kettle looked ready to make tea. A jumble of white linen napkins was stacked in a basket and dozens of white and cream plates looked out from an old-fashioned plate rack.

Jane plonked herself down at the long dining table adjacent to the island and gazed around. She spoke aloud to herself. 'Well, Ms Le Romancer, you've really fallen on your feet here. If nothing else, it looks the part.'

She peered from the dining table down to the sitting room where a slipcovered sofa layered with pale creamy throws invited a snooze. Everything induced calm; little lamps with pale floral fabric shades, a coffee table piled with books, a vase stuffed with flowers, and a Bentwood chair used as a side table holding a candle. Jane's eyes wandered further to an old dresser where small coffee bowls were stacked up carefully. Jane remembered that coffee bowls were a Darling thing and her friend Lucie served coffee in the same little vessels.

Wandering around, Jane felt as if she'd entered some kind of fairytale; seagrass striped rugs gave the place a warm cosy feel, a huge shallow bowl offered fresh fruit, a stack of logs filled an alcove, and a small potbelly stove was laid and ready to be lit. Jane let out an enormous sigh and held her hands up towards the ceiling in prayer. 'Whoever got me here, thank you, thank you, thank you.'

She could quite happily make a milky coffee, top it with something strong, light the fire, draw the curtains, snuggle up under a cashmere throw, and not surface for... oh, something like three months.

After a few minutes of gaping, she dragged her suitcase past linen shopping bags by the French doors, an antique lifebuoy hanging on the wall, and an assortment of huge market baskets. A gallery wall showcased an assortment of botanical prints and paintings of the Darling coastline and by the stairs, a table was piled with cloches displaying things washed up by the sea.

Heaving her suitcase up a narrow set of steep timber stairs one bump at a time when Jane got to the top, she squealed in pleasure. A beautiful brass bed dressed with pure white linen sheets and carefully placed dress cushions was begging to be slept in, and an enormous gilt-edged mirror on an old dresser bounced coastal light around the room. Jane continued to explore, finding more and more reasons why the house swap so far had been a success; a clawfoot bathtub with copper taps, a sparkling fancy mirror over a pedestal sink, an antique Union Jack hung on the wall. All of it delightful and inviting a sit down.

Jane made her way downstairs to retrieve her backpack and whipped out her phone and messaged Lucie.

I've arrived. Blimey, Luce, this place is unreal!

Phew, thank goodness.

It's much better than the pictures. Like, MUCH better.

Lucie sent a grinning emoticon back. *Always a good thing, lol.*

I'm panicking now that my place isn't as good.

Haha, you're a joker. I'd move into your place tomorrow.

What, and leave your precious Coastguard's??? Jane joked.

Haha, well not quite but you know what I mean.

Yeah. Anyway, it's fab here. I love it, thank goodness.

Wish I was there. Can't wait to get back now tbh.

Same here. How is it going over there?

Very well. I can't complain. Bit too hot for me, though.

Doesn't sound too shabby, sunbed, cocktail and warmth.

Yeah, would be good if I could actually do that & I wasn't working.

True. Jane acknowledged adding an eye-roll emoticon.

How was Edinburgh btw? Tally said you got stuck in that storm.

Jane smiled wryly to herself; that was one way of putting it.

It was fine. Just boring old business.

And wild sex with a very, very handsome man. One I'll probably never see again.

Ha! I get you.

Anyway, you better hurry up and get yourself back to Darling... we have a wedding to plan.

Indeed we do. So pleased I've got you, Janey and I can't believe you're going to be on Darling for the next three months. Woohoo. We've got some catching up to do.

Jane replied, finished the text thread, slipped her phone into her pocket, and made her way up the stairs. Lucie wasn't the only one who couldn't believe it. Perhaps on Darling Jane Le Romancer's life wasn't going to be quite as small after all.

11

J ane had had a thoroughly nice day. She'd unpacked her stuff, enjoyed a slap-up lunch sitting in the sunshine in the courtyard, tied on her trainers, and gone on a deliciously long walk around Darling Bay. The coastal air had been incredible, the feeling of freedom as she'd looked out to sea almost unfathomable, and whatever it was that she couldn't put her finger on about how refreshing a walk was when shoreside, she'd loved it.

However, as the sun had quickly gone down, the early evening had rolled in, and the light had faded as quick as a flash, Jane began to feel terribly alone. All of a sudden, the rose-tinted glasses she'd been wearing since she'd agreed to the house swap had most definitely fallen off. Only a few hours prior, she'd been almost ecstatic as she'd walked around Darling Bay, gulping in the sea air and drinking in the hazy blue, but now, as she sat alone in the house, the euphoric buzz that had seemed to carry her an inch above the ground had fizzled out and died. She was no longer hovering above the ground; in fact, Jane Le Romancer had come back to earth with what was referred to as a mighty great bump. A jolting horrible blow that had left her with a sad look on her face and a shaking head. Here she was, again alone.

What had she done? Stretching ahead of her were three long months where she didn't know what was what. It had all felt so deliciously exciting when she'd thought about it in the comfort of her own home. From the safety of her cosy sofa with a cup of tea, the idea had sounded like a fabulous one. A bit like the hot man in the hotel bar. She'd sailed along on a dreamy idyll that all would be delightful; she would float around Darling in white linen dresses and her espadrilles, a sun hat on her head, a baguette in her summer basket, a contented little smile on her face, pottering around with a bit of work, strolling out for coffee. Now that she'd arrived, the bump she'd come down with had been brutal. And the ground was rock hard. Darling was nice; she had enjoyed the sea air, the ferry ride, the friendly residents who'd greeted her so far and the bay. But she didn't really know what she was doing there. Even having her friend Lucie on the island when she got home wasn't doing much to make her feel better. Lucie didn't know anything about Jane's smallness. Nor did any of their other friends. They all assumed that Jane was fine. Good old Jane, trooping along, getting her head down, always there. Jane the Widow. And, at any rate, Lucie had her own life, a new love, a wedding to plan, a business to run, and a lot on her plate. No time for Jane and the smallness of her life. Jane sighed as she felt the familiar lonely tightness in her chest. In the little mews house it had not only come back, it had roared back with a vengeance.

Jane tried not to think about it. She was being ridiculous! Twelve short weeks. Three quick months. It would be over in a flash, and she would be back to her old life where everything was in its place. Cosy. Nice. Safe. Small.

She stood by the window with a glass of Chardonnay in her hand and peered down the road. She had nothing to worry about. Far from it. Everything around her was divine; a floral wreath hung on the front door of the house opposite, a coach light pooled gold onto the cobblestones next door, and a few houses along fairy lights lit up a window with their twinkling. She watched as a car bumped slowly over the cobbles and parked. A family bundled out of the car; a woman in a pretty dress and trainers, an equally nicely dressed man, two point four children beautifully turned out. Yes, everything was just so very nice. She would be okay.

As she stood with her wine resting in the nook of her left arm watching the family gathering things from the boot, she knew that she would be fine for the three months on Darling. Because Jane was always fine, wasn't she? The wobbles were more because, plucked out of her other life, she realised with a gnawing sadness how very lonely she was. Her house and the routine of her life did a splendid job of masking the loneliness very well. Normally her life simply turned as one continuous wheel that she never had to get off, cosseting her in not having to think too much, keeping the little knot of lonely tightness in her ribs right where it always was. But the house swap brought into perspective just how the loneliness was with her every day. And a house swap, though a fabulous find promising all sorts of things, couldn't offer her a companion or provide her with something to make her life less small. It would always be there wherever she lived. Beautiful old mews house with an Aga or not.

As she watched the family go into their house, Jane shook her head, resigned to the fact that nothing would change. She turned and smiled as little fairy lights flickered to life on a timer and the kitchen was bathed in light. It couldn't be that bad. She would just have to pull on her big girl pants and get on with it. Just as she always did.

Putting her arms into her cosiest cardigan, she grabbed her bag from the hooks by the French windows and sat in the kitchen surrounded by light. She would work on Operation Le

Romancer. See what she could muster up. There must be something she could do. She looked down at the bucket list of things that she'd plucked out of nowhere to supposedly grow her life. She shook her head as she read down. The thought of doing much of anything at all on her list now seemed foolish. She wasn't up for trying to meet people. She wasn't really interested in joining an evening class, and the thought of striking up a conversation with someone and 'seeing where it went' almost made her want to gag. At least with her small life she didn't have to bother with all that. Now it was as if she *had* to make an effort. She had to make an attempt to follow through with her stupid plan. Before, she could have just stayed being quietly small.

Jane let out a huge sigh, and stood by the island in the beautiful kitchen. She eyed the old plate rack and ran her fingers along a couple of vintage floral plates, wondering where Catherine had found them. Then she opened the fridge and stood there, umming and ahhing. Another glass of wine? Perhaps she'd make herself some pasta. Nice buttery pasta with loads of Darling salt, whatever that was, and watch a movie. Or maybe a cheese, onion, and salad cream sandwich. *Oh, go on then.*

As Jane lined up the three bottles of salad cream she'd brought with her in her bag and started to slice off some cheese, her thoughts wandered back to the cheese sandwich at the bar in the hotel. Oscar was there in her head too. Her mind then slid, ever-so nicely, to what had happened in the room. In the bed. She puffed air out in a funny little sigh. Ooh, that had been nice. Shame it hadn't come to anything. Jane sniffed. She could but hope.

Jane took a sip of her wine and popped in another bite of sandwich. 'I'm going to text him again. Just one more time and then I'm done,' she said, speaking to her laptop. 'It doesn't really matter. It's just a text.'

She put her wine down, wrote out a message, put her phone beside her and drummed her fingers on her top lip before she sent it.

Hi again, Oscar. I was just having a sandwich (salad cream, haha) and it made me think of you. Funny night. Funny good night.

Again, there was the debate about a kiss. 'To leave a kiss or not to leave a kiss, that is the question,' she said to her laptop and giggled at the end. She tutted. She'd clearly had too much wine. Was this even a good idea? Probably not. She checked the message again, picked up the last quarter of the sandwich and, with her heart hammering, clicked the blue arrow.

As soon as she saw the message had been delivered, she was filled with regret. What was she thinking? She was staring at the big old forty date of doom in the not too distant future and here she was sending desperate texts to someone she knew almost nothing about except for his first name. Although she'd had quite the bird's-eye view of various (very nice) parts of his anatomy.

With the little flashing dots sorely missing in response, she pulled over her laptop and put Oscar's phone number into the search bar and hit return. Nothing. She then added his name and still nothing came up. She thought back to the hotel bar. What had it been about this Oscar that had prompted her to act so out of character? She remembered the blue eyes. But, yeah, whatever. The sort of air about him. What even was that? He'd been handsome, yes, very, but there was something else. The broad chest she'd explored when she'd got to know him better hadn't been too bad. The strong jaw, very nice. Nah. She tried to kid herself that she didn't know. She knew exactly what it was. It was the prettiness of him. She'd never been able to resist it over the years, though she'd always been able to hide it. There'd been a guy Marty at work a few years before, he'd had it too, and of course, her husband, who was now dead. Not that Marty had really known about her, but she'd definitely known about him. Oh yes, indeed, had she seen him. She'd learnt quite a fair bit about him too, thanks to social media. He'd worked on the next floor up and had the same pretty look as Oscar. She'd not even let herself go there, but she'd been tempted. Not that he would have been tempted by plain Jane from the next floor down. The one who was mostly invisible most of the time.

Jane flicked a few crumbs from her trousers and glanced at her silent phone. Of course there wasn't a reply. Oscar was probably seriously regretting the alcohol doing the talking and reeling off his number for her to key into her phone in the first place.

As she sat there with the empty plate and wine glass in front of her, the lack of reply on her phone and the noises of a strange, not hers house, she rested her elbows on her knees and chin on her hands, and forced the tingling at the sides of her eyes away. She pressed really hard and pulled her skin back so that her eyelids closed. She would not cry over this, it was ridiculous. She hadn't cried for so, so long. She couldn't even remember the last time. She was determined not to let a single drop of tears, or anything else for that matter, roll down her cheek. But as she sat there amongst the cashmere throws on the house swap sofa, a fancy three-wick candle flickering beside her, Jane Le Romancer had never felt more alone in her life.

12

Jane had gone to bed the night before, after sending the text to Oscar, in a blur of loneliness. The same constant gnaw, always there just below the surface of a half-hearted smile. She frowned as she woke up remembering the fog horn going off in the middle of the night. It had awakened her from her sleep in the cosy bed, and she'd thought that she'd be tossing and turning for the rest of the night. What had actually happened was she'd slipped out of the covers, gone to the loo, pushed up the old sash window to let in some fresh air and hopped back into bed. The next thing she'd known, daylight was peeping in through the gap in the curtains, she was under the cosiest quilt ever and was wondering if she turned over and snuggled up, she'd drop back off to sleep. Nothing quite to get up for, that was for sure.

In the end, she'd padded downstairs, made a cup of tea, brought it back up to the bedroom with a packet of Digestives and was sitting with her knees up and dressing gown on, flicking through a magazine she'd found downstairs. Her phone vibrated, and she frowned as she picked it up and looked at the notifications on her screen. Five messages in the WhatsApp group she was in with her four friends, plus three text messages. She opened the WhatsApp group chat first and scanned through the conversation. Their little group with its nickname 'Hold Your Nerve' had seen it all over the years, and now here was Tally in a pickle calling a video meeting that evening. With her cup of tea balanced precariously on Catherine's luxurious bedding, she typed a message with her thumbs to say that she would be there and sent a separate one to Tally asking her if she was okay.

She then clicked on the green button for her messages and shuddered in delight. A number she didn't totally recognise and hadn't added to her contacts yet, but by the first line, she could see it was from Oscar, sent at 8.06 a.m. He'd replied! Woot woot. Get the flags out.

Yes. It was a very good night from my end.

Jane closed her eyes in happiness and felt herself light up. He'd added three winking emoticons at the end. She knew it was quite pathetic, more than pathetic, but it had made her spirits soar. She mused what to type back as she dipped her biscuits methodically in her tea. Eventually, she chastised herself for reading way too much into a solitary little text message and fired one back. He was probably just being friendly after what had happened.

Haha. Glad to hear it.

She hugged herself as she sat there and, to her surprise, saw the little lights start to flash, indicating that he was typing a response. Ooh, it was going to be a text conversation in real time. Excellent.

I enjoyed chatting...

She shot back straight away. *Same here.*

He sent back a smiley face which made Jane grin. Deciding to take the bull by the horns, she sent another message.

We should meet up for a coffee some time.

Even though she wasn't sure what she would do if Oscar

wanted to name a time and place, she knew that ultimately she would be there like a shot.

Great idea! Sounds good.

She couldn't believe it. It sounded like he was up for meeting up. Maybe Operation Le Romancer was actually beginning to work!

What's on the agenda for today? She quickly messaged back.

Busy as usual. I'm heading home and meeting up with a cousin I haven't seen for a while. How about you?

Jane still didn't like to ask where home was for Oscar, but boy did she want to find out.

Same here, doing a bit of work from home and then I'm playing wedding planner for one of my best friends.

Sounds busy. Anyway, nice to chat.

Yes. Absolutely.

We'll have to make that coffee sometime.

Yes, let's lock in a date.

~

Jane floated around for the rest of the morning on the pink cloud that had appeared after the text exchange. She'd pottered in the house, had a quick few messages with Catherine on how things were going from her end, and had given all the plants in the courtyard a good soaking.

After a late shower with Catherine's divinely exorbitant shower gel, she'd pulled on white jeans, a blue button-down shirt, threw a navy-blue jumper over her shoulders, slung a basket over her arm, and was heading down Darling Street. She might not quite be in the white linen dress... yet, but the melancholy from the night before had faded. It had nothing to do with a little text thread on her phone that morning. Nothing at all.

It was a gorgeous day on Darling with the hint of warm, longer days in the air and as Jane made her way down Darling

Street, all was good with the world. A tram trundled past as she walked along, heading away from the bay area, and a couple of people said good morning. She'd almost had to stop the second time it had happened to turn around and see if the person was looking at her or someone else. By the time she was walking past Doctors on Darling, the local GP surgery where even a teenager with headphones on had smiled at her, she was beginning to understand that on Darling as you passed by you said hello, raised your eyebrows, or made some kind of acknowledgement. It was clearly the only way to behave.

As she arrived at the next tram stop and after being informed that the trams came along every seven or so minutes, she waited. Hopping on as she had done the day before, she sat up the front and looked out onto the street as her new little town for the next few months went by. Lost in thought, she was jolted back to the present by a friendly greeting.

'Hello again.'

Jane looked up to see the same woman in the tram uniform as before standing in front of her. Jane went to get out her phone to pay. The woman continued with her chat. 'Morning. How are you today? How was your first night on Darling?'

Jane, of course, didn't tell the woman the truth that she'd been hit by a monumental bout of self-pity and had never felt as lonely in her life. She slapped on the same smile as she always did despite the lonely tightness in her chest. 'Yes, good, thank you.'

'How was the house?'

Jane nodded and smiled. 'Lovely. I don't think I've slept like that for a very long time.'

'Fog horn wake you up?' the woman asked as she rang the bell and the tram continued on its way.

Jane chuckled. 'It did, actually. I thought I'd never get back to sleep being woken like that and then bam, before I knew it, the sun was up.'

'Yeah, that'll be the air. It sends you off into a deep old sleep, at least that's what they say. It's always worked for me. Where are you off to today? A nice walk around the other side of the island, is it?'

Jane pointed out the window. 'My friend Lucie lives down past the floating bridge there.'

The woman frowned and then held her hands up in exclamation. 'Oh! Yes, yes, of course! Honestly, brain like a sieve half the time. I didn't put two and two together properly.'

Jane didn't want to be rude but she couldn't place the woman at all really, though she was wearing a hat and glasses, but as she took her glasses off, Jane remembered her from Lucie's engagement party. 'Shelly.'

'Ahh, yes, hi, sorry I didn't recognise you in your uniform.'

'Popping down to check on the house, are you? When are lovely Lucie and George back? I thought it was around about now. Have you heard from them? I bet they're having a lovely time.'

Jane smiled. 'Yes, they are. I'm going to be video chatting with her soon - myself and the others, that is,' Jane said, referring to the little group of friends and the WhatsApp conversation regarding the state of Tally's divorce.

'Lovely,' Shelly replied and waved away Jane's phone as she gestured to pay. 'You're doing all the wedding planning too, aren't you? Lucie was telling me all about it when we were at Leo's a while ago before they took off.'

'I am, yes, for my sins,' Jane joked.

Shelly adjusted the collar on her shirt as she chatted. 'She's so grateful to have you she was telling me. You're very good at planning and organising, she said. It's what you do for a living, is that right?'

Jane chuckled inside. All the Hold Your Nerve girls loved that she was good at planning and she was, it was definitely a skill and she enjoyed it, but a lot of the time over the years she'd done it because, unlike everyone else, she had nothing much else going on in her life. 'Goodness, no, not my day job, but I seem to be the one who ends up doing all the organising. I quite enjoy it. I like a list or three, ha.'

'Right, I see. Well, you've got your hands full there with that wedding. Sounds like it's going to be quite the bash,' Shelly remarked.

'I think so.' Jane agreed with a nod.

'What a spot it is at the club down there. There aren't many places that can beat it for a wedding, especially if the weather is nice.'

Jane nodded. 'Yes, I think the weather is going to be key. It's a shame we can't plan for the nicest British weather for the day. That would really help me out. It is what it is though.'

'We'll have to start praying for Lucie.' Shelly laughed. 'Start a hashtag or something.'

'Haha, yep.'

'She was telling me she wants the same sort of look and feel as the engagement party; an English country garden fête kind of thing.'

'She does, which is a whole different ball game with the club because it's a lot bigger than a marquee in her garden.'

'Hmm.' Shelly nodded and turned back to the front as the next stop approached. 'Good luck with that. Looks like you're going to need a lot of people whipping up tissue paper pompoms. Give us a shout if you need anything.'

'Will do. Thanks, Shelly.'

About half an hour later, Jane had walked past Lucie's house. She smiled at how lovely it looked backed with the hazy blue of the estuary, and was walking towards the Sailing Club where Lucie and her partner George were getting married and she was wedding planner extraordinaire. She stood and stared for ages as the flags on top of the club flapped in the wind, a flock of seagulls messed around above the deck and the sun dipped in and out of a bank of grey-white clouds. She slipped her glasses out from her bag and squinted her bottom eyelids to crisp things up. What a place for a wedding. When she'd been to stay with Lucie for the night and they'd started to brainstorm wedding ideas, she hadn't taken a huge amount of notice of the club. But now, examining the old building properly with the sea in the distance, she could see just why George and Lucie had wanted it as their venue.

As Jane turned off the pavement and made her way towards the club nestled down on the water, she nodded to herself at its beauty; in a similar coastal style as her friend Lucie's house, it was fully clad in white timber. From the top, winding white-washed stairs led down to a silvery-grey expansive deck, and sitting on the main section, a turret with a weather vane stood to attention. Jane's mouth gaped open the closer she got. This was going to be some wedding. Climbing up the deck stairs at the front, she pushed open the heavy white door into a small reception lobby where the lovely vibes kept on coming. In the corner, two huge wingback chairs slipcovered in a pale blue gingham invited a sit down. Old ship's wheels and sailing para-phernalia decorated the walls and she could just about make out Ella Fitzgerald playing somewhere in the distance. Running along the far side porthole windows looked out to sea and an old-fashioned oak counter was topped with a huge goldfish bowl vase full of flowers. Hanging perilously over the counter, a majestic brass ship's bell gleamed in the light flooding through the windows.

A woman in a white Darling Sailing Club uniform and neat hair was sitting behind the counter looking at a screen. She looked up as Jane came in the door. The woman's face was friendly with a little hint of 'what do you want, I'm busy' on the side. 'Can I help you?'

'Err, yes, I hope so. My name's Jane.' Jane pointed over in the direction of her friend Lucie's house. 'My friend lives down there.'

The woman hadn't yet smiled, surprising Jane from what she'd so far seen on Darling. 'Yes?'

'Lucie Peachtree, that is.'

The woman nodded and clicked something on her computer giving Jane her full attention. 'Yep, I know Lucie and George as a matter of fact. Sorry, what was it you wanted?'

'Sorry. I'm not making much sense. I'm Lucie's best friend, or should I say one of Lucie's best friends... and I'm the wedding planner.'

The woman's face suddenly opened up, and she batted her hand in front of her. 'Ahh, yes. The penny's dropped. Course you are! I remember you from the party. We did some of the drinks. In fact, we were probably on the same email chain. Apologies, I've been up to my eyes, I've a pounding head and think I might be on the start of a migraine.'

Jane smiled, not recognising the woman at all. 'Sorry, I'm a bit hopeless with names.'

'Gosh no! You must have had your hands full organising that party. Talk about decorating delight.'

Jane laughed. 'Hmm. I put a lot into it.'

'I'm Annabelle, Hannah's sister. Hannah's the manager here you were liaising with.'

Jane smiled. 'I see, all slotting into place now.'

Annabelle got up from her chair. 'What can I do for you?'

'I was hoping for a little bit of a look around. Actually, scrub that, I do want to scope it out but I thought I might come down and sit on the deck for a bit with a drink. According to Catherine, at the house where I'm staying and her recommendations, the cauliflower steak special at the moment is out of this world.'

Annabelle's eyebrows shot up. 'Catherine?'

'Yes.'

'Ahh, right you are. You're not staying at Lucie's. Ahh, the house swap? Blimey, small world.'

'I'm beginning to realise that and I've only been here a day.'

Annabelle burst out laughing. 'Yes, our little island is so very far from care; it also knows everything about you and you can't quite work out how or why.'

'I'll have to watch what I get up to,' Jane joked.

Annabelle chortled. 'I wish that was a joke - you do have to watch your back around here.'

'Ooh, crikey! I'll be careful.'

Annabelle tapped a couple of buttons on the keyboard, paused for a second, and handed over a piece of paper. 'They'll have my guts for garters if I don't give you one of these. Guest pass. It's a Darling Municipality requirement for guests in the club. There's a funny old byelaw down this way,' Annabelle said, rolling her eyes. 'They're all over the place, as it goes. Drives me a bit batty. We're not in the dark ages any longer. I mean, we're all tracked by our phones anyway.'

Jane took the receipt and stuffed it inside the cover of her phone and laughed. 'Gosh, residents, guest passes, it's like there's some secret little club you have to be part of... Lucie did mention a few things. I half thought she was making it up, if I'm honest.'

Annabelle wiggled the mouse and walked around the counter. 'Yes, indeed. You'll get used to them, though.' She shook her head. 'Or you won't and you'll get completely sick of it and leave us to it. That's how it normally goes.' She raised her eyebrows and nodded knowingly at the same time.

'Makes sense. I'll see how I get on,' Jane replied.

'Okay, yes, back to the cauliflower steak, it's amazing. I'm not really sure why they call it "steak" but there you go. It's so, *so* good. I'll pop out and check if there are any left. I know there was a big batch there earlier, but it doesn't usually last long.' Annabelle gestured for Jane to go through some doors towards a room further down the entrance hallway. 'The old ballroom is just through there. Have a little nose, it's gorgeous, I'll be back in a sec.'

'Thank you,' Jane replied.

As Annabelle went to disappear down a corridor, she looked over her shoulder. 'What about crumble? Do you like that, too?'

Jane nodded. 'I love it. I wouldn't say no.'

Annabelle made a kissing lips gesture. 'It's the bomb with proper homemade custard; let me check if there's some of that left. I'll be back.'

Jane peered through another long hallway corridor where old-fashioned brass pendant lights softly lit the way to a bustling bar area with windows overlooking views directly out to sea. She walked through and arrived at the old ballroom. Cupping her hands over her eyes, she peered in through the panes on the huge, old, white doors and stared. What looked back at her took her breath away; thick timber beams ran under a vaulted ceiling in a white room the size of a village hall. Showcased all around the top what Jane assumed were some sort of nautical flags. Floor-to-ceiling paned windows encased a view out to the estuary and a mismatch of framed pictures formed a gallery wall. Jane tentatively pushed open one of the heavy old doors, stepped over the herringbone parquet flooring, and stood staring at an exposed brick fireplace running all the way along the wall at the end. She whispered to herself as she slowly spun around, nodding her head, and did a low whistle.

No wonder Lucie had earmarked the ballroom for her wedding. It was nice enough as it was, but with Lucie's old English country fête vision and Jane planning the decor, it would be spectacular, that much was obvious.

'Dukkah spiced cauliflower with pistachio, chilli, dried currants, and walnuts,' Annabelle said with a laugh as she poked her head around the door of the ballroom.

Jane spun around. 'Ooh, yes, it does sound delicious. Thanks.'

'It is. I'm not one for all this vegetarian malarkey myself, but I'm telling you even I have chosen it over a good old-fashioned sirloin and that's saying something. Your luck's in, we have a few left.'

Jane smiled in appreciation. 'Lovely, thank you, and this is amazing,' she said, sweeping her right hand around, taking in the view of the coast outside.

'It definitely is if you can get it.' Annabelle agreed.

Jane frowned in alarm. 'I'm not with you. I thought Lucie and George had the date locked and loaded as far as I was aware.'

'Yes, yes, they most definitely have. What I mean is this room is only available to hire for the likes of them.' Annabelle giggled. 'The elite who live on this side of the island, that is.' Annabelle made a funny little sound. 'Then again she's marrying a Darlingdown, so, more or less, she and they can do what they want.'

Jane didn't know what to say, not being au fait with Lucie's partner's status. She laughed noncommittally. 'Haha.'

'Anyway, yep, so this is the ballroom and there's a cauliflower steak with your name on it.'

'Thank you,' Jane replied.

A few minutes later, Jane was sitting at one end of a cane sofa with a navy-blue and white striped seat pad with a Cosmopolitan in her hand. Taking in the view, she was lost in thought as she stared out to sea and thought about the plans for Lucie's wedding and her time on Darling. It was looking up. Maybe she was going to like it after all.

13

Jane was pottering around getting ready for a video chat with her friends Anais, Libby, Nathalie (Tally), and Lucie, also known as the Hold Your Nerve girls. The five women had been friends for a long time with a multitude of ups and downs along the way. Thirty-five or so years of friendship, many a laugh, a lot of gatherings, and every one of them always available at the end of a phone with a listening ear. Today was no different albeit that Jane was in a new spot, and for once, not that she was sure if she was going to divulge or not, she actually had some news. As she straightened the sofa and folded up a cashmere throw, she was looking forward to a chat and a glass of wine.

Over the years, since they'd all met at school, the group had moved this way and that, always fluid and ever changing. All of them going through the various stages of life at different times but always there for each other when the highs and lows hit the fan. Jane being the focus of a meeting had been few and far between over the years, the last one not that long ago when she'd had a few problems at work.

Jane thought about their 'Crisis Talk' meetings as she gathered her bits and bobs together and mused why she'd never fully told them the truth about what had happened when her husband died. The aftermath of it had been a deep well of shock and despair that everyone around her had always assumed was pure grief. Only it had been far more than that. She wished she knew herself why she'd never fully relayed any of what had really gone on; it was like a dirty little secret strapped around like her like duct tape, always there taunting her from the corner. She couldn't get her head around it, even after all these years. She didn't even know what it was; a vile mix of shame and embarrassment intertwined with a massive layer of sadness at the reality of what she had found out. That her husband had gambled a lot and that the times when she'd thought he was away on business, he was actually in casinos and had not ended his nights alone. That the women he was with were being paid. No one really needed to know was what she had always said to herself, so she'd kept it quiet until it had become something she rarely thought about. She'd just let people conclude that she was sad and save herself the embarrassment of the truth.

Jane lit one of the large candles on the coffee table, tucked a huge plate of pasta with chilli oil beside her laptop, and made herself comfortable. As she flicked through her phone, she waited as one by one, the Hold Your Nerve girls came onto the screen. Libby was in her pyjamas and dressing gown, Anais had her hands cupped around a steaming mug, Tally had a gigantic glass of red wine, and Lucie's hair was tied up in a ditsy print scarf.

'Evening all,' Tally joked. 'How are we?'

'Evening,' Jane responded first. 'I'm good.'

Anais interjected, 'Ooh, look at you, Janey! It looks lovely there. Jealous!'

Jane nodded. 'I know, right? How nice is it? I've come up trumps. It's so nice here. I've been walking around the island just like Lucie and doing all sorts. The views are phenomenal. I can see why people love it here.'

'I'm coming to gatecrash,' Libby joked.

'Get in the queue behind me,' Tally commanded. 'I'll bring my divorce papers, too.'

Lucie turned the conversation more serious at the mention of Tally's divorce. 'How are things, Tal?'

Tally let out a massive whoosh of air and shook her head. 'Ahh! I don't know. I wish I hadn't called the meeting now. It's actually the last thing I want to talk about after the day I've had. I've had a gutful of work, a gutful of home, a gutful of the girls. I know I shouldn't say that but...' she trailed off, her voice catching and took a huge gulp of wine. 'You know what? I've had it. I'm officially cream-crackered.'

'It sounds like you've had a gutful of life,' Jane noted.

Libby nodded her head in agreement. 'Yup, sounds like it to me. You need to hang in there. This is probably the worst bit.'

'That sounds about right, I have. I'm so over it. No one tells you divorce is so complicated and so, I dunno, messy. Maybe I was just naïve.'

Anais laughed. 'We need to cover Lucie's ears up, considering she's just about to take the plunge with the delectable George. We don't want to put her off or anything!'

Tally nodded. 'Yeah, sorry, Luce. I must sound like a miserable, jaded, old battleaxe.'

Lucie shook her head. 'Err, you're looking at the woman who got left by her long-term partner via a note and a message that he was having a baby with someone else. The fact that I didn't have a ring on my finger didn't change anything.'

Jane nodded. 'Too true, that.'

Libby addressed Jane. 'Janey, let's talk about wedding planning. How's that going now you're on Darling?'

Jane shuffled forward on the sofa edging closer to the screen. 'As you may or may not have gathered, I have a lot of lists going, some of which I've shared with you.' They all chortled as she continued, 'I've now properly vetted the ballroom.'

Anais raised her eyebrows in question. 'And? What's the Janey verdict? Good or not good?'

Jane, with a glass of wine halfway to her mouth, paused and widened her eyes. 'Good is an understatement. It's going to be some wedding party, that's all I can say. I hope you're ready.'

Lucie blushed. 'Thank you again, Janey. I wouldn't be able to pull it off without you in charge. I'm so grateful to have you in my corner.'

Libby rolled her eyes. 'How many of those blimming paper fans will we be making this time? We nearly suffocated in them for the engagement party. I went to sleep dreaming about them!'

Tally grinned. 'Hundreds, no, thousands.' She held her hands up in the air. 'Ahh, girls, thank you for this. I feel better already and we haven't even talked about my stuff. It's so nice to just chat and think about something else. It always makes me feel better. Priceless therapy you can't buy.'

Anais smiled from her screen. 'Yeah, thank goodness we have each other. What else has everyone been up to?'

Everyone chimed in, reviewing what had been going on in each of their respective lives. They discussed a story about Lucie's extended work holiday, Libby's run-in with a woman at work who she'd found looking in her bag in the staff room, and Anais who'd had a palaver after she'd left her tablet in the back of an Uber.

'Janey, what about you? Apart, of course, from taking off to some island in the middle of nowhere swapping houses with randoms,' Tally said with a funny look on her face and sound to her voice.

Libby interjected, 'What? Janey? I know that Tally voice. She knows something. What have you been up to?'

Jane attempted to keep her face straight. 'Nothing at all. Just as she said, coming here for an adventure for a few months. That's all I've been up to.'

Anais squealed. 'Janey! You're up to something. I know it! Now I'm looking at you, I can see it. I thought earlier that you looked different. You do! Oh my, have you had something done? Is that what it is?'

'What? I don't know what you're talking about.' Jane tried to shrug it off, thinking that she knew exactly why she might appear a bit different to the women who had known her for the majority of her life. Men in hotel bars and bedrooms tended to do that for a girl. Whatever it was that they could, or could not see, there was one word and one word only for it: Oscar.

'Tally did the voice she does when she knows something. It's the same one as when she introduces herself as "Nathalie" to someone she likes the look of,' Libby stated. 'Come on, spit it out, Janey.'

Tally started laughing. 'I did not do a funny voice, and I'm not saying a word.'

Anais wasn't going to let it go. 'So there is something! What? Tell us.'

Jane couldn't hold back the chuckles either, and Libby waved her hands in front of her screen. 'Come on! Spill.'

Jane took a big sip of wine and decided she would tell them about her little incident in Edinburgh. 'Well...' She paused dramatically.

'Oh my goodness! Come on,' squealed Lucie.

'Shall you tell them, or shall I, Tals?' Jane laughed.

'You tell them. I don't think they'll believe me if I tell the story,' Tally stated mock seriously. 'It's borderline unbelievable for you.'

'Okay.' Jane nodded and took a sip of her wine.

Tally hooted and tossed her hair back. 'Strap yourself in, girls, you're not quite going to believe what our Janey has been up to. It's big for her, huge in fact. Gigantic.'

'Oooh! Hang on,' Anais instructed with wide, baffled eyes. 'Let me make another cup of tea, and I'll be back.'

A few minutes later, all four women were waiting as Jane stared into the tiny circular spot in the top centre of her laptop. 'Actually, I'm not really sure where to begin.'

'Crikey, I'm about beside myself! This involves a man. I know it,' Lucie said. 'I can't believe you've kept it to yourself! And here I was thinking that the sea air had done you the power of good.'

Jane swallowed. 'Okay, the other week when I went to Edinburgh, the weather was really awful as you may have seen plastered all over the news. That, combined with the baggage handling thing and the strikes, meant chaos in Edinburgh. Meaning that at the last minute when I should have been coming home, I had to get a room.'

'Flipping heck!' Libby exclaimed with a shaking of her head. 'Where is this going?'

Tally held her hand up. 'Don't interrupt her. Ladies, this is gold.'

'Yeah, so anyway, this man came in and mistook me for someone else. He thought I was someone called Jessica. He arrived at my table as I was sitting there with a drink.'

'What do you mean?' Lucie asked, screwing up her face.

'Get with the programme, Luce!' Tally yelled. 'Listen!'

Jane continued, 'We got chatting later at the bar and had a few drinks. Sorry, I need to backtrack a bit. Before that, he'd plonked himself down at my table assuming that I was someone he had a meeting with, but she was stuck in Belfast or Dublin or somewhere.' Jane let out a whoosh of air. 'And then we, umm, sort of ended up in his room.'

'Oh! My! Goodness!' Anais repeated over and over.

Libby chuckled. 'Janey, you had a one-night stand in a hotel? I'm flabbergasted. I did not see that coming, not at all. Talk about surprising someone.'

Jane drained the last of her wine. 'You and me both!'

'Goodness, our Janey doing all the things.' Lucie chuckled.

'What was he like?' Anais asked.

Jane couldn't stop laughing. 'Hot!'

'I would think he was if you ended up in his room!' Libby squealed.

'It's mind-blowing, isn't it?' Tally said, shaking her head.

'Hang on. How come you know?' Anais asked, addressing Tally.

'I happened to call when Jane was in the airport the next morning, and I could see it written all over her face.'

Jane nodded. 'She did! Haha. She guessed it right away.'

'So, what happened next?'

Jane proceeded to fill them in further on what had happened; how she'd sneaked out of the room and bolted from the hotel the next morning, how she'd texted him, and how it was now moving onto them possibly seeing each other again. All five of them had dissected and reiterated and given their opinions on what had happened until Jane didn't know what to think. She asked for further clarification. Do you think I did the right thing by texting? Maybe I should have waited until he texted me?'

'Absolutely, you did the right thing,' Anais stated. 'Why wait?'

'Yup.' Libby nodded. 'You did. You've got nothing to lose.'

Jane screwed her face up in confusion. 'But what now, though?'

Lucie rolled her eyes. 'Gosh, don't ask me. I'm the last person to give relationship advice. The first one didn't go too well in the end. I'm far from experienced,' she joked. 'Though I'm pleased to say that the second one is turning out to be quite nice. Hopefully he'll hang around...'

'Maybe I should just have left it as it was?' Jane pondered.

'Nope,' Libby replied. 'It's good to be proactive or you might never have known.'

Anais agreed, 'You might be hit by a bus tomorrow, anyway.'

Jane wrinkled up her nose. 'I suppose so. Too late now, it's done. I'll never know if he was going to text me first, but I do know that we're going to sort out a date to meet up again.'

'This is very exciting, Janey!' Lucie said.

'You know what's coming next, don't you?' Libby asked.

They all laughed, and Tally held her glass up to the screen. 'Hold. Your. Nerve.'

Anais chuckled. 'Exactly! Janey, you are to continue with the light text chatter with this man and quite simply, you need to do one thing and one thing only. The thing we have been doing for many a year. Hold. Your. Nerve.'

14

In turned-up white jeans and a cosy cream jumper, Jane slipped her feet into her new espadrilles with a wry chuckle as she bent down, tied up the straps, and opened the side door to the courtyard. It was hardly espadrille weather, but there *was* sunshine and a blue sky, albeit with not quite espadrille temperatures to match. She didn't care. The shoes were going out for a little bike ride. She wrinkled up her nose and nodded as she stepped out onto the block paving; she was darned if a little bit of good old British weather was going to stop her. Even if she did have to wear espadrilles with a scarf.

Studying the sky, she contemplated the rest of her day and what had happened since she'd arrived on Darling. Firstly, she was very much enjoying Catherine's house. There had been so many things to discover and new things to learn; she'd had a bath filled with gorgeous charcoal bath salts that she could have sworn did actually make her muscles relax, she'd read a book about Margaret Thatcher, had a good look at Catherine's crafting stash, and had a go at cross stitch. She'd even made something in the tagine which had been sitting on a shelf by the Aga in the kitchen. Secondly, she'd chatted to a few people here and there and didn't feel quite as alone. Thirdly, after seeing the ballroom at the Sailing Club, she'd got well stuck into Lucie's wedding planning. All in all, things were very much on the up.

With a brighter outlook than when she'd first arrived, she found herself humming as she opened the garage door and wheeled a pale blue bike with a basket on the front around to the front of the house. With a few days of intensive work lined up where she was planning to lock herself in the little room just off the kitchen, she was determined to get out and about on Darling and make the most of it. As she was pushing the bike over the cobbles, wondering if perhaps the espadrilles' first outing and a bike ride were a good idea, the neighbour she'd chatted to when she'd first arrived waved and crossed the road.

'How are you getting on?' the neighbour called out with a smile.

'Good, thanks. You?'

'Not too bad, thanks. It's not quite as warm as it looks down by the bay. Good to blow the cobwebs away, though.'

'I'm just off now to get a bit of the Darling air.' Jane laughed, looking up at the sky and pointing down to her feet. 'I'm probably in completely the wrong attire, but I couldn't resist. I've got that new shoes feeling.'

'Ha ha, we live in hope. I had thick woolly tights under my dress the other day, but the shoes are nice.'

Jane smiled. 'I'm hoping the sun will stay for the day as I'm back to working from home tomorrow.'

'Ahh, I see. Where are you off to now, then?'

'Darlings café. It's the place to go,' Jane joked.

'Certainly is! Lovely. Well, enjoy your coffee.'

'Will do. See you later.'

As Jane toddled along in the espadrilles and then popped herself on the bike, the air was chilly in her hair, but she felt as if nothing much could dampen her spirits. After cycling in and out of a web of narrow lanes and alleyways, she arrived at

Darlings, the coffee shop where her friend Lucie worked part-time. From her view on the bike, it was ticking a lot of boxes. Whatever the actual food and coffee may be like inside, from the outside it rocked. Darlings was right up her alley. She took it all in as she approached; a tiny bow-fronted shop front wholly covered in climbing foliage. Window boxes spilled over with plants next to coach lights hung on either side of the door. On a glass panel above the window, 'Darlings' was engraved and a little brass door knocker in the shape of an anchor was wedged into the centre. Small café tables laid with gingham tablecloths and topped with pot plants were jammed outside by the windows, outdoor heaters stood by the tables, and cosy pale blue rugs were neatly folded onto the backs of the chairs. Lace half café curtains were at the windows and just adjacent to the door, a small glass box displayed a handwritten menu. Next to a well-used umbrella bucket by the front door, a door mat covered a half step, and a small sign tucked in the bottom of the front window told customers to ask for dog treats.

A bell tinkled as Jane pushed open the door and raised her eyes at what greeted her. As she stepped into the tiny coffee shop, she was surprised to see it not only bustling with chatter but absolutely stunning. Floor-to-ceiling shelving loaded with china lined the walls, small bistro tables were squashed into every inch of space and right down at the end, a unit suspended from the ceiling displayed all manner of kitchen paraphernalia. A coffee machine whooshed and hummed constantly from behind the counter and a throb of bustling staff, clinking of spoons against saucers, and chatter added to the buzzy atmosphere.

Taken by surprise at how busy it was behind the door, Jane hovered in the espadrilles. Unable to spot a free table, she was just considering turning around to leave when a woman with glossy hair arrived at the entrance with a friendly smile. With an unsure look on her face at whether there was a table for her,

Jane smiled hopefully. She recognised the woman as Lucie's boss from Lucie's engagement party and as the woman, Evie, got closer and focused, she recognised Jane and cracked into a beaming smile. 'Hi! Jane, Lucie's Jane, isn't it? Lovely to see you again,' Evie said warmly.

Jane's chest almost swelled up in pleasure at Evie's friendly greeting. It felt nice to be known and remembered. 'Hello. Yes, it is. How are you?'

Evie's silky, tawny-brown eyes rolled a touch as they flicked around at the café. 'Good, good, busy. I think I always say that, though! And we're run off our feet without Lucie here. Not that I'm complaining, of course. It's always good to be busy. I'd be complaining if it was the other way around. You can't win, can you?'

Jane looked around. 'No, you can't. Yes, it *is* busy in here. I was hoping to sit down, but it looks like you don't have any free tables at the moment. Never mind.'

Evie flicked her hand down to the end near the counter. 'If you don't mind squeezing in, there's one right down there. Always room for a friend of Lucie's in Darlings. We know which side our bread is buttered, haha.'

'Aww, that's nice. Anywhere works for me. Thanks.'

Evie turned, beckoned for Jane to follow, and whisked a couple of empty coffee bowls from a table as Jane followed her to a small spot tucked down the end by a dumb waiter. Evie pulled out a chair. 'Here we go. It's a cosy little spot here. Just you, is it?'

Yes, Jane thought. *Just me. Mostly just me wherever I go.* 'Yes, it is. Perfect. I'm fine anywhere. Thank you.'

Evie handed Jane a menu from the pocket on her apron as Jane sat down. 'Would you like a coffee?'

Jane nodded, tucking her bag under the table and joked, 'I've been told the coffee is amazing from someone in the know.'

Evie's eyes flicked to behind the counter. 'Yep, especially when Piper is working her magic on the machine.'

'Sounds like just what I need,' Jane replied as she wriggled in the chair and made herself comfortable. Evie tapped the order into an iPad, raised her eyebrows in greeting to another customer, and looked directly back at Jane. 'What are you up to for the day? Busy? Have you got a lot on? Lucie's been telling us all about your wedding planning and all your ideas. It sounds like you've got everything more than under control.'

Jane nodded, thinking to herself that she probably hadn't ever been as busy as this pint-sized woman who seemed to do six things at once and scooted around almost as if she was on skates. 'I've got a day of exploring Darling ahead and then tomorrow I'm back to the reality of work.'

The woman called out cheerio to a customer and flicked her eyes back to Lucie. 'I see. So what's on the agenda for the rest of your day?'

'I thought I'd just go with the flow on the bike and see where I end up.'

'Do you want a little resident's tip?' Evie asked and chuckled, her silky eyes glinting in humour.

'Sounds good to me. I'd love one, actually.'

'Head over to the old pier. It's lovely on a blustery day like this. Climb down onto the beach and mooch around underneath. There are all sorts of beautiful seashells and sea glass down there. If that's your sort of thing, of course. Always nice to while away an hour or so. At this time of year, there'll probably just be a few ramblers down there and it'll be fairly quiet.' Evie turned and pointed to a shelf near the window where three gigantic glass preserving jars were stuffed with sea glass in an array of turquoise blues. 'I've found some beauties over the years.'

'Okay, right, yes, thanks, I think I might have a go at doing that. Sounds like my cup of tea.'

With a whoosh, Evie turned and then zipped in between the tables as she made her way towards the coffee machine. Jane observed as Evie multi-tasked in the small bustling café; delivering coffee, plumping gingham cushions as she went past, and chatting to customers. Propping her menu up by a little vase of flowers, Jane gazed around in awe. The place oozed welcome; stacks of fluted cake moulds were piled up on shelves behind tables, mountains of little coffee bowls were arranged in descending sizes, and a hotchpotch of teapots were lined up neatly on a dresser. She looked around at the other customers with their little white wicker baskets in front of them and smiled at the loveliness of it all.

Jane continued to people watch in the café and shivered as a group of women in wetsuits with the tops rolled down, beanies, and jumpers made her feel cold as they piled in the door. Evie, seeing them enter, gathered piles of baskets in one arm and a tray of coffees in the other and greeted them at the door. The women laughed and smiled at Evie, there was a quick exchange of words as they took their coffees, and a few minutes later they were all standing back outside strolling over the cobbles, coffees in hand. Jane watched as the little café did its thing; a girl in the same apron as Evie balanced on a ladder on wheels stacking up the bowls in colour order, in the corner, a group of pensioners were playing chess and a younger girl was behind the counter pulling sheets of buns out of the oven. Lost in people watching, Jane was jolted back to reality when a small fluted bowl filled with frothy, milky coffee arrived on the table. Evie smiled and winked. 'You're good with a bowl? I can get you a mug if you like, but seeing as you're here for a few months, I thought I'd get you started on it.' She rolled her eyes. 'One of many of our odd Darling customs.'

Jane waved her hand, she had been served coffee in bowls at Lucie's. 'All good, thank you.'

'What are you having?' Evie asked, looking at the menu.

Jane chuckled. 'If I remember rightly, Lucie instructed me that the way to go is to ask for a basket.'

Evie nodded and whipped the menu from the table. 'Done. Ha, seeing as you're a friend of Lucie's and I quite like the look of you, I'll get you one.'

Jane went to ask what was in the basket, but clearly, that wasn't an option in the funny little place. She tried to remember what Lucie had told her about the baskets but for the life of her, she couldn't. A few seconds later, Evie placed a white basket with a gingham napkin knotted at the top in front of her. Evie smiled. 'A breakfast basket for you. Luckily we had some cinnamon buns from the bakery left.'

'Lovely, thank you.'

Evie whizzed off again as Jane untied the knot, pulled the fabric corners aside, and peered in. Tucked inside the basket were three mini doughnuts, a small cinnamon bun, and a glass jar with a ceramic lid filled with what appeared to be apricot jam. Jane took a bite of the cinnamon bun, held the bowl to her lips and sipped on the coffee as she gazed around the café. A couple of ladies with white hair beside her were chatting animatedly over their coffee bowls and dipping the little plain doughnuts into their coffee. Jane followed suit and chuckled to herself. She'd only been in the place a day or so and she was already feeling quite the local. As she sat sipping her coffee, her phone pinged. She smiled at a text from Oscar. Ooh, this was becoming quite the thing.

Janey, did you see the stuff from the airports again in the news this morning?

Yes. Nuts!

You never know what's going to happen when a flight's cancelled. Oscar added a surprised emoticon at the end.

Jane nodded her head. Little did Oscar know it had been the best thing that happened to her in a very long time.

15

Jane definitely felt good as she propped the bike in a bike stand, consulted her map, and stared along the beach to see if she could see the old pier Evie had mentioned. She could just make it out at the end, its location perfect for a long walk, a potter around underneath looking for shells as Evie had recommended, and a short stroll back. All of it, of course, espadrille dependent. She checked the bike was locked properly, popped her bag over her shoulder and as she started strolling along, she stopped and looked up at a noticeboard by the side of the road. It seemed Darling had no shortage of societies; the Darling Horticultural Society met once a week (she wasn't sure how that differed from the Gardening and Coffee Club), the Darling Variety Club (founded in 1982) performed annual shows, highly popular pantomimes and Shakespearean comedies and the chess club was looking for new members. She stood with her hands on her hips as she read through the goings-on of Darling. A picture of a market basket brimming with daffodils, hyacinth and poppies right in the centre of the noticeboard made Jane smile. She moved closer to read the flyer, and as she took it in, she realised she'd seen the poster in her peripheral vision here there and every-where on Darling; it had been tucked into the window in Darlings earlier that morning, on the information board by the floating bridge, and she'd seen the posters in windows all over the place.

In beautiful calligraphy surrounded by a trail of watercolour pastel flowers, the poster promised lots.

Darling Twilight Market is here. All your favourite secret Darling Island produce will be joining us. Enjoy a limited batch of DJ's Twilight sausages, Darling Bay Preserves (special blend for residents), Darlings will be providing food baskets (first come, first served) and yes there will be Josie's eggs available (get here early for first dibs). Stalls will include homegrown plants, cards, gifts, the Darling beer tent and an assortment of handmade homewares (Fleur & Follie has donated!). As usual and weather permitting, braziers will be on the beach. Do join us if you can at 5pm in the Coronation Pier Village Hall.

As Jane continued her walk heading along towards the pier, she could suddenly see the Darling Twilight Market posters everywhere: tied to lampposts, tucked in windows, and taped to the inside of cars. As she got closer and closer to the pier, the village hall on the other side of the road couldn't be mistaken; flags and bunting adorned the old building, a large blackboard easel stood by a white picket fence where another poster listed stalls, and alongside it a huge printed list documented what volunteers were doing what for the market. Jane again stood and read all the way through. It sounded more like a party than a market with no shortage of alcohol. After reading that basket donations were to be placed under the porch, she put her glasses on and squinted to see a pile of baskets filled with goods just by the door. Nodding and thinking that she wouldn't mind trying a special Darling sausage, she continued walking. The basket thing seemed to be nearly as serious as the question about her residency status when she'd boarded the ferry and the guest pass rule at the Sailing Club. Jane shrugged to herself; it was a funny little place, that was for sure.

As she continued on her walk, the day had certainly stayed sunny, but it was bracing and chilly by the sea. She pulled her soft grey pompom edged scarf from her basket, wrapped it around twice, chuckled that it didn't quite go with her footwear, and slipped on her huge sunglasses. The air was salty, chilly, and clear, the sky blue, the sunshine the sort that promised warmth in the months to come. Jane Le Romancer loved a good, bracingly chilly day walking the gardens near her London home and it was the same story on Darling as she made her way to the pier. What she hadn't quite reckoned for was the glorious added loveliness of coastal air. As she strolled along, she took in huge deep lungfuls of the stuff, raising her head to the sky and smiling. Darling Island, funny little byelaws or not, was feeling rather good.

Gazing towards the shoreline, she wished she'd brought a flask. A cup of tea and a sit down tucked up in a sheltered spot down by the pier would go down well with the chilly air whipping around her head. As she got closer to the pier, a tiny little timber clad kiosk with blue and white bunting strung across the top caught her eye. She approached intending on ordering a cup of tea and stood in a queue with two people ahead of her, a gaggle of ramblers in walking gear to the right and a couple with a rugged-up toddler in a pram were staring up at the menu. As she got to the front of the queue, a man with a bushy grey beard, twinkly green eyes and a big wide smile leant over the timber counter and bellowed down to her, 'What can I get you? Nice day for it!'

'Just a tea, thanks.'

'Sugar?' he roared again.

'Not for me, no.'

'Sweet enough, are you?' he hollered, adding a snort at the end.

Jane laughed and did a double take that the man in the kiosk was quite as jolly, although she was quickly getting used to the fact that Darling-ites spoke to you whether you were lining up for a cup of tea or getting on the tram. This one, though, seemed particularly jovial. 'I think that might be debatable, actually,' she joked with him.

The man laughed as a woman appeared from the back of the tiny kiosk, and nudged him on the arm. 'Take no notice of him. He's always losing us customers. On a day trip to Darling? Nice and brisk down here by the sea today; sun's out, though, just the way we like it. Beats all that recent fog.'

Jane shook her head. 'I've been told it's a good place to do a bit of treasure hunting underneath the pier.'

The woman sloshed tea from a gigantic old-fashioned teapot into a takeaway cup. 'Right you are. Who would be informing you of that then?' she asked without looking up.

'Evie in Darlings,' Jane responded, ridiculously pleased with herself that she was in the know.

The woman smiled and laughed again. 'She must 'ave liked the look of you, my lover. Giving away our secrets!'

'Hmm, I don't think so. I'm a friend of Lucie, Lucie Peachtree, you might know her, she lives over the other side there near the ferry.' Jane gesticulated behind her.

The man held his hands up. 'Of course! Ha, we all know Lucie for taking on that house.' He lowered his voice. 'And for taking on George. That was an undertaking and a half.'

The man got a nudge on the elbow again for his comment. Jane smiled, wondering what he meant about Lucie's partner, George. 'Yes, it was in quite the state when she arrived.'

'That it was, indeed. The same could be said of Mr D.' The woman winked and passed over the tea and a lid. 'I thought they were away at the moment?'

'They are, yes,' Jane agreed with a nod and took the tea, fitting on the lid and cupping her hands around it.

'Oh, I see, right, you're house sitting. Not a bad idea these days, I suppose. You never know, not that anything ever happens on Darling. Good luck to anyone attempting to burgle a house here. It's not so easy to get off this island. They'd be strung up and left for dead.'

'No, no. I'm not house sitting. I'm staying here for a few months.' Jane surprised herself that she was imparting her whereabouts to these random people in the kiosk she'd never clapped eyes on before. Her mouth seemed to be working on its own as she continued telling them what she was up to. 'I'm doing a house swap, actually.'

The man bellowed again. 'There we go, not much that goes on around here without it being two degrees of separation! Must be the bay mews, yes? Our daughter and son-in-law live down there and our grandchildren. We heard Catherine was swapping with someone from the big smoke.'

'Yes, that's me.' Jane beamed.

'I'm Vanessa.' The woman smiled and extended her hand across the counter.

'Jane, nice to meet you.'

'You'll have to come along to the Twilight Market. Have you seen the posters?' Vanessa asked and pointed to a poster taped to the outside of the kiosk. 'You couldn't really have missed them.'

'Yes. I've seen them all over the place. It's down there in the hall, is it? What sort of things are for sale?'

Vanessa rolled her eyes. 'All sorts. It's a bit of an excuse for us lot over this side to get together and have a few drinks, to be quite frank, but don't tell anyone I told you that. I'll be lynched.'

'Should I be interested in the eggs?' Jane chuckled, referring to the poster and looking at Vanessa as she took a sip of her tea.

'You most definitely should,' Vanessa replied. 'They'll be fighting over 'em. Shelly from the tram one year had a right old ding dong with who was it again?' Vanessa put her fingers to her chin. 'Can't for the life of me think who it was now. Anyway, come along. There'll be all sorts, plus it's to raise funds to repair the roof, so all in a good cause.'

'Thanks, I'd like that,' Jane replied.

'If anyone asks, just say Vanessa from the kiosk invited you to the bit afterwards.' Vanessa did an odd little cackle and tapped the side of her nose.

Jane frowned. 'I didn't realise it was invite-only. All the posters and everything everywhere...'

'Officially, it's not, but, the bit on the beach, well, you know...'

Jane didn't know what she meant at all, but she left it at that. 'Rightio, thanks for the heads up and for the tea.'

Vanessa lowered her voice. 'Anyway, enjoy your stay with us. Be careful what you get up to. The old Darling chit-chat will be all over you.'

'I think I'm beginning to realise that. I'll keep it in mind.' Jane smiled and waved as she walked away from the kiosk with her tea in her hand. As she strolled past the gaggle of ramblers and got closer to the pier itself, she wondered what other residents she would make acquaintance with on this sweet little island with its weird and wonderful customs and what they would be chit-chatting about her.

With her tea in her hand, she clambered down some steps onto the beach, bent down to take off her espadrilles and let her feet sink into the sand. It felt cool and damp between her toes and as she walked over the beach and sipped on her tea she bent down to pick up a shell and smiled to herself. Exploring on Darling was really rather good for the soul. Perhaps it also worked its magic on those with a small life.

16

A fter her long walk by the sea, and with her pockets full of treasure, Jane made her way through the back streets of Darling on her bike with the wind in her hair. Arriving back at the mews, pushing her bike over the cobbles, she couldn't quite remember having had such a nice day for a very long time. It clearly was the little things. All she'd done was have a little sit in a café, ride a bike, and then have a cup of tea by the sea. There hadn't been much to it at all, but then again, maybe there was something in the different pace of life by the coast. She shook her head. Ridiculous, surely it had nothing to do with that. It was just that she wasn't working, that must be it.

After parking the bike back in the garage, she stopped as she got to the front door. Perched neatly on the doorstep were two baskets. A small oval basket with a handle and a lid was propped beside a flower pot, beside it, a small rectangular white basket edged with a pale pink gingham liner. Frowning, she hooked the oval basket over her left arm and wedged the other one in the crook of her other arm, keyed the number into the keypad, and pushed open the heavy, faded aqua blue door.

Once she was in and settled in the kitchen, she lifted the lid of the oval basket and peered in. As she opened a neatly taped white paper bag, the scent from a batch of small buns filled the air with vanilla. Alongside the bag, a tin of artisan loose leaf tea was tucked in beside a white mug with matte gold spots. Pulling out the mug, Jane turned it over, read the branding underneath, and picked up a little card nestled at the bottom of the basket.

Welcome to the loveliest little island on the coast. Enjoy your morning tea with a vanilla bun. Love, Holly, Xian, and all at Darling's little bakery.

Jane decided she'd try the buns and the loose leaf tea right away and after flicking on the kettle, she peered up to the shelves above to the glass teapots. Clambering precariously on top of a stool, she pulled one down, sloshed it out with hot water and after spooning in some tea, she put the other basket on the worktop by the window. Waiting for the tea to brew, she smiled to herself at the deliveries on the doorstep. She'd read about the Darling baskets as one of Darling's funny little customs and heard about them from Lucie, but hadn't thought for one minute as a visitor she'd be included in the strange little ritual. Maybe it was because she was looking after Catherine's house? It wasn't as if she was your regular holiday maker. She vaguely remembered Lucie telling her that when she'd first arrived on Darling, the baskets had appeared and multiplied almost daily.

Opening the second basket, Jane smiled again. Inside sat three little jars of homemade jam with handwritten labels stuck to the front. A note was tied to the basket with a silky white ribbon.

Lovely to have you on Darling, Jane. Welcome. See you at the Twilight Market... come along and join us afterwards sitting around the fire on the beach. Best, Vanessa (from the kiosk) and all at the Darling Coronation Hall committee.

Jane thought to herself that Vanessa hadn't wasted much time, opened a jam jar, stuck a teaspoon in, and closed her eyes at the taste. The raspberry jam was delicious; if the produce at the market was as good as the jam, and everyone was as nice as Vanessa, maybe she would make an effort to attend. She nodded. Yes, she would make her attendance at the fundraiser part of Operation Le Romancer and see where it would take her. She made a mental note to ask Lucie if she'd be back in time and maybe they'd pop over there together.

Ten or so minutes later, Jane poured the tea out and went to sit in the courtyard with the paper bag full of buns. As she pushed open the paned door and was surrounded by plants, she felt some of the tension she'd been carrying around for years gently lift from the top of her shoulders. The tension sliding away had occurred a few times now on Darling; subtle little shifts within her aching body and an easing of the strain built up inside. Walking across the courtyard, she felt another tiny bit of long-held stress and perhaps a smidgen of the loneliness wedged just behind her ribs slightly slip away.

She'd read in Catherine's information notes that a small sliver of late afternoon sun landed right in the corner of the courtyard at a particular time of the day. The notes informed her that she'd find two comfy chairs angled perfectly to catch the rays. Spying the chairs, she put her tea down on a round outdoor table topped with pottery planters, plumped up one of the cushions and sat down. After sending a quick text to Lucie with a couple of pictures of the baskets, Jane continued to let the tension ooze out of her body. She revelled in the scents of the courtyard and the far away sound of the sea as she sat with her head resting back on the chair and her feet up on a piece of driftwood from the beach.

Lost in the calmness of the moment, she silently went through Operation Le Romancer in her head, methodically ticking off what had she done so far and, more importantly, trying to analyse if anything had changed. She considered the house swap first and pursed her lips together in contemplation.

Yes, the move had most certainly opened her eyes to different things. The journey alone and doing something out of the humdrum of her day-to-day life where she knew every little nook and cranny had changed her perspective on lots of things. Then there was the actual house itself. All of Catherine's things, all with their own stories and tales to tell. Not some horrid little generic place with everything painted in grey, but a house with wee foibles and stories every which way; the worn away dip in the top of the steep stairs hinting at previous inhabitants, the wonky leg on the table that wobbled ever-so-slightly as she sat down, the piles of books she never would have ordinarily picked up inviting escape to other lands, and in the courtyard, an array of botanical gatherings some of which she'd never seen. Yes, Jane nodded, the house swap could definitely be ticked as a successfully completed part of the Le Romancer plan. No doubt with more to come.

Of course, then there was actual Darling Island itself. She thought about the baskets by the front door and the friendliness on the tram. Then there were the sweet old shops on Darling Street where people had actually smiled and nodded in acknowledgement and the loveliness of Annabelle as she'd shown Jane around the ballroom at the Sailing Club. There was another nod at all of this; doing something different had opened Jane's eyes to a little community of friendliness, opened her eyes to new things and so far it felt very, very nice.

Making her way back inside, she put her cup in the dish-washer, opened the fridge door, and just as she was pondering whether she could sneak in a cheeky cheese, onion and salad cream sandwich as a little mid-afternoon snack, her phone buzzed from her pocket. Pulling it out, she felt her heart jump. Oscar. Again! This was getting good.

The funniest thing happened in the supermarket & I thought of you! I heard a woman ask for vegan salad cream. It made me laugh.

Jane didn't really know what to think about the text, but she did know that the blood rushing in her ears pounded around out of control. She put her phone on the worktop, leant the palms of her hands on either side of it, and read through a couple of times. She had to laugh that the mention of salad cream had reminded Oscar of her. The most interesting thing about her was salad cream! Marvellous. She was sure other women were full of interesting stories, had tales to tell from travelling to far-off lands, had fabulous rich lives. Jane Le Romancer had met a man in a bar, flung her bra at him after a few too many pink gins, and he remembered her salad cream fetish. Fantastic.

She thought about what was going on with the messages for a bit while she pottered around the kitchen and decided at the end of the day she didn't really care. Stuff it. Who even was he to her anyway? In the short while she'd been on Darling it had taken her out of the regular old humdrum just enough to realise that Jane was Jane and though she might not have that much going on, actually, she didn't mind it too much at all. She quite liked her funny little ways. From now on she was just simply going to be Jane. She nodded and typed back a message as she waited for the kettle to boil.

Hope you told her it has to be Original and a glass bottle???

Oscar responded immediately with a laughing emoticon. *Nope! But I thought about it.*

There is only one type of salad cream. It's always good to remember that. Jane joked.

I know now. You enlightened me about a whole new world I didn't even know existed. We don't even mention the word "mayonnaise." Correct?

We do not, lol.

Who knew that I was so in the dark about this before?

Jane smiled; she was loving the texting with Oscar and wondered where it would go. They had got on really rather well in the bar and, ahem, the hotel bit afterwards had been positively luscious. And it seemed to be continuing via their fledg-ling text relationship. She nodded to herself and wondered. There had been a lot of back and forth with texts now, so perhaps it would go somewhere. People had text communica-tion with people all the time, who knows what could happen? Where it might go.

17

I t was a gorgeous day on Darling and as Jane whisked along on Catherine's bike by the sea, with the fading sunshine glinting on the top of the water, everything around her made her smile. Her friend Lucie was now home from her working holiday, and Jane was on her way over there for supper. After a day cooped up in the study with numbers swimming around her head, she'd decided to ride the long way around via the coast, taking the back roads, and then cutting back into Darling Street at the end. It had been a lovely ride where she'd seen all sorts going on in the sunshine; people on boats coming back into the bay, daytrippers with backpacks strolling towards the floating bridge and along Darling Street locals were bustling about enjoying the sunshine.

Everything looked different from Jane's bike top view as she whizzed along and drank in the loveliness of Darling. She smiled as things passed; the domed roof of the town hall, the pretty little church adjacent to the mini roundabout, a blue and white gift boutique squashed in beside a curry house. Funny higgledy-piggledy chimneys peppered the skyline, the tram bell dinged as it zipped past, and houses with crooked windows sat directly on the pavement.

As Jane got down to the end of Darling Street, she cycled past the tram station and watched the retreating back of the Pride of Darling ferry as it made its way over the other side of the water. Zipping along, the sea breeze whipped against her skin and she pinged the bell on the handle of her bike just for the fun of it. As hazy natural hues where the sea met the sky flashed by, Jane couldn't remember feeling as free for a long time. Riding her bike around Darling had catapulted her back to days long before the little bit of loneliness had arrived and had sat stubbornly wedged just in front of her heart.

She could just make out Lucie's house in the distance and as she pedalled along she was swaddled in the loveliness of Operation Le Romancer and the doors that were opening little by little in her life. Arriving at Lucie's place, she squeezed her brakes, came to a stop, and balanced with her feet on the floor looking up at Lucie's house.

When Lucie had bought the property after a horrible relationship split, Jane and all the other HYN girls had gasped in horror when they'd seen the photos. The house named the Coastguard's House had been in a grim, unloved state. The garden had been left for dead, old cladding painted a murky green suffocated everything, and a stripy flag at the top had been ripped and torn. Now as Jane gazed up at it from her bike, the house stood tall to attention, its cladding now brilliant white, the flag flapping proudly in the wind, the garden well tended and smiling in the sunshine. Jane pushed her bike up to the front door, took a bunch of flowers from the basket on the front, and as she was flicking down the bike stand with her foot, her friend Lucie opened the door.

'Hello, stranger. How are you?'

'I'm well,' Lucie replied with a big smile, stepping onto the path and hugging Jane hard.

'You look it,' Jane said as she stood back and took Lucie in.

'Right back at you,' Lucie replied. 'We both clearly need to get away more often. I'm so pleased I'm back now and you're here.'

'Me too. Who would have thought, eh?' Jane replied, handing Lucie the bunch of flowers.

'Thanks, yes, I know, the house swap thing sounds so exciting. You never know where you might end up I imagine,' Lucie said brightly. 'You were a bit of a dark horse about this one!'

Jane gesticulated around to the coastguard's house. 'Imagine if you put this place up for a swap. There would be so many takers. You'd be inundated.'

'Gosh, you reckon? We could go all over the place. It really would open up the world, wouldn't it?'

Jane nodded in agreement. 'It would. I don't know, though, I've sure read some horror stories. I think you have to do your due diligence, otherwise it might not be all roses.'

'Yeah, I bet,' Lucy replied, swishing her hair behind her. 'Come on in and I'll get you a drink.'

Jane followed Lucie through the hallway with its gorgeous off-white cladding, jar lamps, and fishing basket light fittings a far cry from the way it had looked when Lucie had first moved in. Proceeding down the little steps to the kitchen, scents of cooking and a plethora of copper saucepans hanging on a rack overhead greeted Jane. It smelt amazing; lemon, garlic, and something she couldn't put her finger on. 'Ahh, it smells delicious,' Jane said as she ran her finger over the kitchen table, peered out the window to the garden and looked around at the creamy white kitchen. 'The place is looking better and better. It's lovely, Luce. You're so good at all the little touches and everything.'

Lucie took a vase from a shelf and started to fill it with water for the flowers. 'Thanks. It was a complete dump before, remember? It's scrubbed up well, right?'

'I should say so. That awful burgundy paint colour! I thought you'd lost your marbles to take it on.'

'Ha! Yes, I think I was in a strange sort of post-relationship break-up induced mania.' Lucie laughed. 'I never want to go there again.' She dished out two huge wine glasses and grabbed a bottle of rosé from the fridge, cracking open the screw top. 'It's lovely to have you here to just pop over for supper on a whim. I miss having that.'

Jane nodded. Little did Lucie know how much it really *did* mean to her. It caused the stubborn, lonely spot in her ribs to shove out of the way for a bit. 'Yep, and I cycled here with the wind in my hair. What a way to live.'

Lucie laughed. 'We'll have you moving to Darling yet!'

Jane shook her head. 'Don't know about that. Work was okay for a few months but I don't know if they'd be okay with it full time.'

'They'd let you do anything from what I've seen. They sure get their pound of flesh out of you. You don't really need to go to the office that much, do you?'

'I suppose not, really.'

Lucie passed over a glass of wine and as she lifted the pot on a Dutch oven, a cloud of lemon and garlic hit the air. 'Hope you're hungry. I've made enough for an army. I never like the idea of under catering and then I end up going the other way. George and I will be having this all week long. You'll need to take a doggy bag home with you.'

Jane nodded and inclined her head to look in the pot. 'I always do the same. Never knowingly under-catered. Ooh, what have we got? It looks and smells delicious.'

'Lemon, garlic, and mustard chicken with white wine, and I'll shove in a load of cream at the end. Super easy and super tasty,' Lucie replied as she pulled a wooden spoon from a jug and stirred around the pot.

Jane inhaled. 'Fabulous. Goodness, don't you just love a cosy kitchen dinner?'

'Yeah, I do. I must say though, I was wondering if I should just do you a platter of cheese sandwiches, with salad cream of course. It would have been done and dusted in minutes.' Lucie chortled a warm, indulgent laugh. 'I know how well they would have gone down.'

Jane raised her eyebrows and took a sip of her wine. 'You're correct. I'm always happy with that. At least I'm easy to please.'

'Do we have a round of sandwiches accompanying us in the basket for emergencies?' Lucie joked, nodding over towards Jane's bag.

Jane hooted and shook her head. 'You know what? As I was getting ready, I thought it's the one place I can go without one in my bag. I can trust you to feed me well, Luce, that I do know for a fact.'

'Ahh, says a lot coming from you.' Lucie smiled. 'It's a shame the others aren't here. We must lock in a date. Before we know it, the wedding will be here and we won't have seen each other. Time seems to be flying by so fast at the moment.'

Jane nodded. 'Yeah, we must.'

Lucie opened the pantry door, chose a platter and popped it on the table. 'So, tell me. How's the text relationship progressing?'

'Well, funny you should ask because he messaged me earlier. Looks like we're going to meet up, sorry, I need to clarify, we *are* meeting up,' Jane replied, unable to stop her face from cracking into a huge smile.

Lucie whipped her head up from the salad she was arranging on the oversized platter. 'Goodness! Excellent. This is starting to turn into something. This is definitely going somewhere.'

Jane tapped her phone and turned it around to Lucie showing her the text thread. 'Yep, he messaged me earlier and we've got a date locked in.'

'Right, I see. This is so exciting!'

Jane tried to downplay it. 'Ahh, not really.'

'Not really? Are you actually kidding me?'

'It's nothing,' Jane said, dismissing it with a bat of her hand.

'It is not nothing!'

'It probably won't go anywhere.'

Lucie started vigorously shaking a mason jar containing vinaigrette. 'We'll see. Hang on, so where are you meeting him? He's coming over here, is he?'

Jane shook her head. 'No. I haven't told him I'm over here. I figured we'd meet in the city. We haven't sorted out the actual details yet, just locked in a date. It hasn't really come up that I'm here, either.'

Lucie wrinkled up her nose. 'It hasn't come up that you've house swapped for three months? Why not? That's a bit weird, isn't it?'

Jane shook her head. 'Nope. I just thought that if he wanted to meet, I'd get on the train. So no, I haven't actually mentioned I'm staying here at the moment. Not sure why, really. It's sort of different when you're texting someone, if you see what I mean. It hasn't come up.'

'Fair enough. It's all a bit more off the cuff I guess.' Lucie grabbed two white bowls and put them together with salt and pepper grinders at the other end of the table and laid napkins on top of the plates. 'I wonder where this is going to go. What do you think?'

'I've no idea, if I'm honest.'

'I'm still reeling in shock at what happened in Scotland.' Lucie chuckled. 'So out of character for you, Janey.'

Jane smiled, thinking inside that little did Lucie know how small Jane's life actually was and for her it was more than huge. 'Ahh, well, things are changing with me.'

'What does that mean?' Lucie replied with a frown, as she

slid a loaf of bread out of a white paper bag onto a breadboard. 'Changing for you?'

'It means I'm making the effort to...' Jane stopped mid-sentence, not wanting to admit to Lucie the truth that she had not a lot going on in her life '...to just try a few new things. You know? Like the house swap and stuff.'

'Like jumping into bed with someone you don't know?' Lucie quipped. 'That was certainly trying new things. Ballsy is what I'd call it.'

'Something like that,' Jane agreed.

'Well, it's worked well.' Lucie put the lid back on the Dutch oven and leant onto the worktop and sipped her wine. 'Yeah, it's obviously working. You've done a big thing with the house swap and you've clearly got a text relationship going on with a potential love interest. Not only that, he's moved it to the next level by locking in a date to meet up with you again.'

Jane smiled as Lucie held her glass up across the table and clinked her drink. 'Yes,' she replied. 'I suppose I have done quite a big thing, for me that is.'

Lucie chortled. 'Now all we have to do is sit back and see what happens next.'

18

On the afternoon of the Twilight Market, Jane stood in the bathroom looking in the antique mirror over the sink. A little glass shelf held all manner of Catherine's lotions and potions. She'd happily dipped into a large pot of cleansing balm, followed the instructions to massage it into her face with lymphatic strokes and now stood with the accompanying muslin cloth wiping the expensive ointment from her face. After rubbing a thick layer of expensive-looking serum into her face which promised to do all manner of things for her skin, including imbuing her with plump, hydrated layers, she turned each of the old copper bath taps to full, poured in a long stream of bath salts from an oversized glass jar, and once the tub was nearly at the top, allowed herself to sink down into the water.

Luxuriating for an hour or so in the deep, bubbly bath, topping up every now and then with hot water, and with a book from the sitting room bookshelf propped on the bath caddy, Jane had totally relaxed. Since the day she'd been out on the bike ride to Lucie's, she'd been shut away in the tiny study just off the back of the sitting room locked in a labyrinth of work. After long days with her glasses on, laptop open and a continuous stream of cups of tea, she'd finally emerged a few days later with another of her work spreadsheets ticked off, a brain saturated by numbers, and a back needing not just a long deep bath but a professional massage.

She reached over the side of the bath, plucked the little bottle of spritzer she'd brought up in an ice bucket, poured it into the accompanying wine glass and then sat back in the bath. As she rested her head back over the edge, her elbows resting on the side and every now and then taking a sip of wine, she contemplated her evening at the market. Another occasion where she would be attending something on her own; Lucie was meeting her, but overall she would be arriving, as she always did, alone. Her mind went back and forth over whether or not to bother. What, really, would be the point? She didn't know anyone; she wasn't that into making small talk with strangers despite what Operation Le Romancer said, and the weather forecast was predicting it to be a clear, but chilly night. She wondered whether to text Lucie and tell her it was off.

Squeezing her eyes together, she thought about Operation Le Romancer and the promise she'd made to herself after the hotel room escapade. She gave herself a lecture then that she would make the most of the opportunities that came her way. She would open little doors here and there to see where her life would go. The Twilight Market was precisely one of the opportunities she'd mused back in London that might come along, one that she needed to grab hold of.

Jane ran the conundrum over and over in her head as she stretched out in the bath and sipped on her drink. In her small life at home, she wouldn't have even glanced at a poster advertising a market and there was no way she would have made an effort to attend. No, the other Jane would have stayed being small, much preferring to walk home from the tube, kick off her ridiculously high work shoes, drop her coat over the end of the bannister, make a cheese, onion, and salad cream sandwich, and sit at her kitchen table with a glass of wine. Alone. That's how her old life rolled. No room for opening doors of opportunity at any turn.

But things possibly felt a little bit different now. A little glimmer of hope on the horizon and perhaps her life, already, had grown. Or maybe it was her imagination. As she got out of the bath, she eyed her dressing gown hanging on the back of the bathroom door. It was so tempting to just pull its softness over her arms, pad downstairs to the divine sofa layered with throws, light the little wood burner, pour a Baileys, and snuggle down for the evening with a pile of books. It did sound very nice. Much nicer than walking around a silly cold market attempting to open imaginary doors and talk to people she didn't know. She reasoned with herself that she would soon be meeting up with Oscar for dinner and that if she'd kept that door closed, she quite possibly never would have seen him again. It was all about grabbing opportunity by the horns and seeing what happened, she reiterated to herself. How was she to know what might happen at a market with a beer tent and special sausages?

She looked in the mirror as she dropped the towel into the laundry basket and spoke to her reflection defiantly. 'No more small.' She nodded, trying to muster up the enthusiasm to get dressed, put a bit of make-up on and stroll to the pier end of Darling to the market.

Five minutes later, determined not to be swayed by the incessant calling of the warm, safe dressing gown, she was standing in her underwear wondering what to wear. It was that funny time of year when one day it could be quite warm, the next a completely different ball game altogether. Deciding on jeans, with a t-shirt under a cosy cream roll neck jumper, she decided she'd take a jacket and scarf in her basket just in case she did end up staying for a sit around the fire. Half an hour later, with a bottle of wine in her bag to donate, white tennis shoes on her feet, and her basket over her shoulder, she clicked the front door shut and made her way over the cobbles in the direction of the market. Strolling along, Jane's hair was whisked around by a breeze coming in from the sea; the sun had dipped down, and she luxuriated in the twilight. A deep purple pinky-blue etched the sky, an orange glow nipping at the edges and the sound of the waves crashing on the beach, in out, in out accompanied her walk along by the sea.

A few minutes or so later, the hall came into view. She stopped for a second as she looked on. All the way up the path, garlands of little gold lights flickered towards the entrance. Jane raised her eyebrows to the porch where a garland swag of silk flowers cascaded around the double doors. A canvas domed marquee twinkled to the left and a sign in the shape of an arrow announced in calligraphy 'parking this way.'

Jane side-eyed to herself. She'd been expecting a dusty old village backwater hall, a cluster of sad-looking plastic topped trestle tables displaying a few pots of jam. This clearly was a market done Darling style. As she got closer, she joined a throng of other people heading through the gate to the hall. Standing in a small queue at the entrance, she fiddled with the neck of her jumper and waited until she got to the top where she recognised the man with the deeply tanned skin from the ferry. He wore a navy-blue butcher's apron and stood behind a little table topped with a blue and white gingham tablecloth. He looked up with a smile, the same bright eyes twinkling as before.

'Evening, my lover. Jane, wasn't it?'

Jane had to stop herself from shaking her head, bewildered that he'd remembered her name. 'Yes. How are you?' For the life of her, she couldn't remember if he'd told her his name or not. She recalled with a wave of embarrassment she'd thought he was erring on the side of creepy at the time.

He lowered his voice. 'I'm marvellous. I hear you're joining us on the beach.'

By his tone, Jane realised this was significant and stopped

herself from shaking her head. Her first reaction was to say that she wasn't sure if she was going to bother. By the look on his face, she decided against that line altogether. 'I am, yes.' She thought it wouldn't matter if she didn't end up there, no one would even notice whether she was there or not anyway.

He held out a little dongle for her to pay. 'There you are, then. A contribution to go in for our fund and then you're all set. It's going to be a lovely evening out there tonight.' He frowned and flicked his eyes towards her basket. 'Have you got a jacket with you? Might get a bit chilly down there on the beach.'

Jane tapped her basket. 'I'm well prepared; jacket, scarf, and hat, all present and correct.'

'Looks like you're sorted. Right you are.' He nodded to the hall. 'Enjoy. A little tip; head straight through, around to the marquee, get yourself a tipple, then get straight in line at the barbeque, the sausages won't be lasting long. Before you know it, they'll be sold out and everyone will be complaining that they didn't get here earlier. Happens every single time without fail. Follow my process and you'll be laughing.'

Jane smiled. 'Thank you. I'm very grateful for the advice.'

As Jane strolled into the hall, she didn't know where to look first. Dusty old village hall it most certainly was *not*. A vaulted ceiling was doused in liberal garlands of lights and dangling from invisible wire, an assortment of Moroccan lanterns hung from right to left. Together with the garlands, the lanterns with their differing lengths and flickering flames gave the whole hall an ethereal feel. Jane took in the hessian covered tables all beautifully accessorised with little blackboard signs, each volunteer standing behind in the same pale blue shirt and apron as the man at the front.

Deciding she'd follow his seriously delivered advice, she walked through the hall and exited via a set of double doors in the centre, did a left and followed other people heading out to the beer tent. Ten minutes later, she was standing with a plastic glass of locally brewed ale and waiting in the growing queue for the sausages in rolls. She scrolled through her phone as she was waiting, inwardly sighed after reading an email about her current work project and chuckled as she enlarged some pictures from her son drinking beer from a glass bigger than his head. As she was nearing the top of the queue, a text from Lucie arrived.

Hi. I'm running late, we had a bit of a problem with Darce. Soz. I'll see you there for a drink and a mooch. I need one lol. Xxx

No dramas. I'm just lining up to get something to eat. Is she okay?

Yeah, she's fine. Nothing bad. There was a mix-up about who was picking her up from her friend's place. It's sorted now, but that means I'm a bit late. See you soon x

Okay. I'll have a potter around the stalls. Don't stress. x

As Jane put her phone back in her basket, she got to the top of the queue. A man with a huge barbecue tool was standing at the back turning three lines of sausages, a woman in an apron was taking orders, and Vanessa, the woman from the kiosk, was standing next to a gigantic stack of buttered rolls wrapped in gingham napkins. Vanessa smiled as she picked up a roll. 'You made it! Lovely to see you.'

'I did.' Jane smiled. 'This is my kind of market. I, umm, didn't quite think it was going to be like this.'

Vanessa laughed, a knowing look crossing her face. 'Not quite what you were expecting? I bet you thought it would be some dodgy, old, dusty place with multicoloured disco lights. No, no, we know how to do it on Darling,' she said, waggling her index finger back and forth.

Jane burst out laughing. 'True! Err, not meaning to be rude, but I was anticipating a jumble sale feel, somewhat. It's a bit far from a dingy old village hall here...' Jane stopped, concerned that she'd come across in the wrong way.

Vanessa chuckled. 'It's all just a ploy for us to get down to the beach later and have a drink. We get to raise some money for the new roof at the same time. We're not stupid on Darling, ha!'

'I'm beginning to realise that more and more.' Jane held her glass of ale up. 'This stuff is delicious. I was told to get in there first, I think it was a very good move.'

Vanessa nodded. 'A special batch just for this event. Right you are, what will we be getting you? There are two choices, DJ's special sausage in a roll with butter, or DJ's special sausage in a roll without.'

Jane laughed. 'There's only one answer to that as far as I'm concerned.'

'Butter?' Vanessa answered, her eyes smiling.

'Oh yes. Is there any other way?' Jane was going to say that she had a trusty bottle of salad cream in her bag, but thought better of it.

'Not in my book,' Vanessa replied as she opened a roll and the man beside her deftly plonked in a sausage. Vanessa handed over the roll in the napkin and winked. 'There you are. See you later on the beach.' She pointed to Jane's drink. 'There'll be more where that came from and if it's anything like last year, there may well be some silliness. I hope you've got your dancing shoes on. It'll be a fun night.'

Jane chuckled as she moved to the right. 'Thank you. I'll see you over there.'

As she stood on her own under a tree, Jane remained gazing back towards the beer tent as the light began to fade further. People stood in little groups chatting, a couple with two huge teddy bear dogs sipped on pints of beer and a woman with a newborn baby in a sling stood swaying from left to right in the queue for the sausages. As she finished her roll and drink, dropped the napkin in a massive fisherman's basket and went to pick up her bag, she suddenly felt all alone. The atmosphere was more than amenable, the place looked the part, but from Jane's stance, nothing had really changed. She was still saddled with the same old spot of horrible loneliness in her ribs. Perhaps she was kidding herself about everything in her plan. Everyone around her slotted into something else; part of a family, part of the community, part of *something*. As if a tonne of bricks had just dropped on her, Jane felt engulfed by loneliness. Attending the market as part of Operation Le Romancer was doing the complete opposite of what she'd hoped, and she certainly couldn't see any open doors. All she could see were other people chatting and enjoying themselves while she stood alone. It was just a romantic notion that being on Darling, trying new things, going to meet Oscar for dinner, making changes, would alter anything at all. Here Jane was, yet again, standing somewhere, wondering at what point she should go home. *Just go home*, was more often than not the conclusion she came to when she attended things on her own. She adjusted the neck of her jumper and made her way to the hall. She'd have a quick mosey around, and then text Lucie to say that she was heading back to the mews.

Jane had been standing at a stall selling candles making a big deal out of choosing which delight to take home with her. The candlemaker had recommended one that she'd designed that reminded her of the smells of crossing on the Darling ferry and another which was wild fig taken from her holidays in France. Jane finished chatting, tucking the candles in her basket, and headed through the centre of the now bustling, twinkling hall. As she was heading to a cake stall, she saw her friend Lucie in a beautiful ditsy floral dress and oversized scarf making her way through the throng of people towards her.

Spying Jane, Lucie hugged her in greeting. 'Hello, Janey. How are you?'

Jane buried all her low feelings of loneliness and injected a bright, happy tone to her voice. 'I'm great, actually. This is a very lovely market. I don't know what I was expecting, but it wasn't this.'

'Sorry about the delay.' Lucie rolled her eyes.

'Not a problem. Everything good now?' Jane asked.

'Yeah, yeah,' Lucie replied, shaking her head and looking around. 'Flipping heck, Janey. You're right, this is gorgeous. Ha, I thought it was going to be a glorified jumble sale with a load of old tat when they contacted me about donating to it,' she whispered. 'I feel a bit mean thinking that now.'

'Tell me about it,' Jane replied and pulled back the top of her basket. 'I've got chilli and orange chutney, two candles, and I nearly bought a heat pack too.'

'Goodness. Yes. I could be relieved of a lot of money here. I'd better watch myself.'

'I thought the same!'

Lucie stood back and gripped onto Jane's arms and nodded. 'Blimey, Janey, you're looking so well! It was the same the other night. Clearly one-night stands suit you to a tee.'

'Don't be ridiculous! It's just because I'm not at work and I'm chilled.' Jane shushed Lucie and took her arm. 'Let's go out to the beer tent. Do you think George will make it?'

Lucie checked the time on her phone. 'I doubt it. I told him to head home. He's shattered and the Darcy thing pushed him over the edge. Plus, I thought it might be nice to have a bit of girl therapy. Just you and me and a lot more catching up.'

Jane laughed. 'Sounds good to me.'

~

Lucie looked at Jane as they got to the front of the beer tent where Lucie's friend Mr Cooke was standing serving glasses of beer. He chuckled as he saw them and Lucie gestured to him. 'Remember Jane from the engagement party?'

Mr Cooke smiled. 'How could I forget the person who organised that party down to the last tent pole? How are you, Jane?'

'Very well, thanks.'

'And how's your stay on Darling going?'

'So far so good, thanks. Everything has been lovely. The weather's certainly been on my side,' Jane replied as she remembered a conversation with Mr Cooke, his penchant for walking by the sea and love of seaside treasure. 'I actually had a gorgeous afternoon walking down by the pier here and found some of the prettiest things. I think you'd be impressed with my efforts.'

Mr Cooke laughed as he passed over two small glasses of craft beer and inclined his head towards Jane. 'I see you're training her well already,' he joked to Lucie.

Lucie held her hands up. 'Nothing to do with me, actually. Not guilty. She did it of her own free will!'

Jane interjected, 'It was Evie who told me about under the pier.'

Mr Cooke's eyes widened and he joked, 'I'll have to have a word with her for giving away my trade secrets.'

Jane joined him in chuckling. 'I was told I should feel very privileged to be let in on a bit of Darling insider info. That's correct, is it?'

'Indeed you are.' Mr Cooke nodded. 'You must promise to keep that knowledge under your hat. Guard it with your life.'

As they walked away from the bar, Jane took a sip of her beer. 'Is everyone always quite as jolly?'

Lucie nodded. 'More or less. Surprising, isn't it?'

'A bit. Does it ever get on your nerves?'

'Strangely, no.' Lucie shook her head.

'Do you think it's something to do with living here? Being on this little island with the coastal air.'

Lucie frowned. 'What do you mean?'

'C'mon, Luce. It's not like this in a lot of places. Have you forgotten that already?'

Lucie screwed her lips up in contemplation. 'Hmm. I guess I have. I've got used to people being nice, saying hello, being interested.'

'Is everyone always so welcoming and friendly?'

Lucie lowered her voice. 'They have been to me, but actually no. Apparently, if you're not liked, it's really not very nice.'

Jane's eyes widened in astonishment. 'Really? I can't believe that. Are you sure?'

'I know you wouldn't think it, would you?' Jane continued, 'Up there over the other side, just near George's house, a couple bought one of those old houses looking out to sea. She had a name of a fruit. Something weird. Daughter of that pop star from the seventies. Porcupine or something. No, no, that's not a fruit. Plum, that was it. She called herself Plummy and the partner - he was Higgy. Anyway, they built a huge yurt thing right up the back of their property and didn't get permission from the council.'

'I see. I'm guessing by the sound of your voice that didn't go down well with the residents.'

'That's an understatement. The whole municipality thing is taken very seriously according to George, according to every-one, really. Leo, next door, said he pooh-poohed it a bit in the early days and made a sore mistake he nearly didn't recover from.'

'Funny little place, isn't it? Funny and lovely. Really lovely.' Jane sipped her drink. 'It would be good if people were a bit more, what's the word, respectful everywhere like the old days, wouldn't it?'

Lucie chuckled. 'Hark at you, sounding all old school.'

Jane shook her head and batted Lucie on the arm. 'I'm not. It's just, I don't know, people here are lovely, and it's nice to see that.'

Lucie nodded. 'You're right and that's why I liked it when I first arrived here. You sort of forget it when you've lived here for a bit. It becomes a way of life.' Lucie turned as someone came up behind them. 'Ahh, hello stranger, how are you?' Lucie's friend Leo, an Australian who lived a few doors down from her, was standing with a pint of beer. 'I was just talking about you.'

Leo smiled at Jane. 'All good I hope! Hi Jane, I heard you were coming to stay. How are ya? What's going on?'

'Great, thanks,' Jane replied, taking in Leo's lovely bronzed face and big cheesy grin.

Leo stepped back and frowned, peering at Jane's face. 'You look really well. Have you done something different since the last time I saw you? Changed your hair or something like that?'

Lucie interrupted and jogged Jane's elbow. 'See! It's not just us, you're glowing at the moment. It must be something you've done or somewhere you've been.'

Jane felt herself blushing at Lucie's knowing smile. Maybe everyone was right and the thing with Oscar and subsequent occurrences in her life had been a good thing. 'It must be something to do with the sea air.'

'Yes, yes, it must be, or maybe it's something else altogether,' Lucie replied, laughing.

'What have you got planned while you're here?' Leo asked. 'It's quite the break you're having.'

Jane shook her head. 'Oh, no. I'm not on holiday. I'll still be going into the office now and then, though mostly I'm working from home. I just have to lock myself away for the day and get my head down when I'm working so I can more or less do it anywhere. It's not quite rocket science.'

'Ahh, I see. A bit of a sea change for a bit then.' Leo nodded. 'Sounds good to me.'

Jane smiled. If only Leo and Lucie for that matter knew how

much Jane had needed a change of scene. 'Yes, I'm enjoying it so far.'

Leo looked over to the middle door towards the beer tent. 'Okay, well, I'll love you and leave you and see you on the beach later, will I?'

Lucie nodded. 'Yep, see you over there.'

Leo lowered his voice. 'There's a special brew and I've heard there are some of Shelly's cocktails. Lethal.'

'Ooh, I might have to have a little taste of that.' Jane laughed. 'Give it a go.'

Leo rolled his eyes. 'Oh, dear. We'll be dropping her off home a bit worse for wear.'

'Ahh, don't you worry about me.' Jane laughed. Little did Leo know she was well used to looking after herself and had done for many years.

Leo tipped his hand to his forehead. 'See you later, ladies. Have fun.'

Jane followed Lucie out of the village hall and smiled at the silhouette of the old pier juxtaposed against the evening sky. As they made their way closer to the beach, the temperature dropped significantly, the salty, pungent scent of the sea filled the air, and Jane's hair whipped around in the breeze. She pulled her scarf out of her basket and as she wrapped it twice around her neck, she looked down towards the water. A cluster of basket-shaped braziers was surrounded by a circle of director chairs and every now and then spiked candle lanterns were stuck into the sand. Lights from the pier lit the area in a soft glow of golden light and between the chairs, old tea chests held drinks. Lucie pulled on her denim jacket, turned around to Jane, looked out towards the sea and as the wind whipped around them, she did a fake little shiver. 'Brrr. Bit of a nip in the air this evening,' she said as they arrived at the chairs and the woman Jane recognised from Lucie's engagement party, and the tram came up to them and smiled.

'Hey, ladies! How are we this evening?'

Lucie kissed Shelly on the cheek. 'We're good, thank you, how are you?'

Shelly gesticulated around towards the chairs. 'Oh, we've had fun setting these out this evening! All a bit of a bluster. It took ages and getting the fires going was a bit of a job, but now we're ready to go. Everything is done and dusted. All we need now is the infamous cocktail to arrive.'

Lucie looked over at the chairs. 'It's a lovely evening for a bit of stargazing around a fire.'

Shelly nodded her head to the far end and pointed towards two seats nearest to the promenade. 'It's a good spot just there. A little bit sheltered and looking out to sea,' Shelly noted.

As Jane followed Shelly's eyes to the chairs, she pulled her jacket on, and as they stood chatting about how much money was likely to be raised from the market, Jane wasn't sure whether the spot was good or not. She didn't want to say anything, so she stood listening wondering whether she would last the evening in the cool temperatures. As they walked to the chairs, it felt chilly to her as the cold, damp sand squeezed between her toes and the wind whipped Lucie's dress around. Jane filled her lungs with the salty sea air and wrapped her collar a bit tighter around her neck. Maybe these sea-dwelling folk were a tad more hardy than she was in her secluded, townie life.

As they got closer to the fire, Jane's worries went out the window as she felt the warmth hitting her in the face and she let out a little sigh of pleasure. The flickers from the fire danced around, filling Lucie's face with shadows as Jane turned to her. 'It's much warmer than I thought it was going to be, thank goodness. I didn't think I was going to last long at all!' Jane exclaimed.

Lucie patted her on the arm. 'Trust me, Janey, you'll be fine. Please, Darling party people know what they're doing and they'd never see you get cold. Remember that dinner I went to when I hadn't been here long? Every single detail was perfect, and it ran like clockwork. Just wait until they bring out this cocktail everyone's been talking about. I've heard it's very good... we might even have to have it at the wedding if it's really as nice as it's cracked up to be.'

Jane shook her head. She had never heard of a rhubarb cocktail before and she wasn't sure it sounded nice at all. She decided to keep her mouth shut as everything so far on Darling had proved to be lovely. She decided that she would commit to a lovely evening by the sea and see where it would take her. She would give the cocktail a chance and put into play a part of Operation Le Romancer and see what transpired.

As they sat down and got comfy in the chairs, Lucie turned to Jane, and with her eyebrows raised, asked a question. 'So, Janey, tell me more about the guy in the hotel. I want loads more juicy details than what was said in the group chat. We ended up side-tracked the other night over supper.'

Jane laughed with an embarrassed look on her face and shook her head. 'There's not much to tell, Luce. There isn't much more than what you already know. It was all over pretty quickly.'

Lucie shook her head. 'You're not getting off that lightly with it. I can tell something is going on with you. You seem so happy and, I dunno, light, yes that's it, you seem so chilled out.'

Jane dismissed it with a flick of her hand. 'No, I don't. You're imagining it.'

'Janey, even Leo noticed and he doesn't even really know you! It clearly suits you.'

'It was one night, and it was ages ago now.'

'How many times have you heard from him since then?' Lucie asked.

Jane pulled her phone from her pocket and waggled it in front of Lucie. 'I told you all this the other night! It's just a silly few messages on my phone. Honestly, I don't even know anything about him,' Jane replied, wishing wholeheartedly that she knew a lot more about Oscar. 'I just text chat with him every now and then, and we're meeting up next week. That's all.'

'There is such a thing as a text relationship.' Lucie chuckled. 'And may I please let it be noted that the fact that you have any kind of relationship at all is, well,' Lucie cleared her throat, 'it's a step forward.'

'It's nothing like a relationship,' Jane insisted.

Lucie shifted in her seat. 'Maybe not, but we do have something here to discuss, so there's that.'

Jane shook her head and rolled her eyes. If only Lucie knew how much she did want to be talking about a relationship. 'It's hardly a relationship, Lucie! I can't even believe I'm saying this, but I had a bit of a thing with him in a hotel in Edinburgh. I've not set eyes on him since, I don't really know where he lives or what he does and I've exchanged a few texts with him here and there. Plus, I'm meeting him for, well, I suppose you could call it a date.'

Lucie nodded. 'It doesn't sound much when you say it like that, I will admit.'

'I wouldn't exactly call that a life-changing relationship.'

Lucie shook her head. 'Well, you never know. Big things start from small things and everything has to start somewhere. When you say only a few texts, how many exactly? Are we talking reams of the things? Or what?'

Jane navigated to Oscar's messages on her phone, turned it towards Lucie and started scrolling down. Lucie squinted in the light and as her eyes focused, her jaw dropped open. 'Oh my! So, we *are* talking about a text relationship! There are loads.'

'You think so?'

'By the looks of that little lot, yes!'

'Anyway, it doesn't matter, it's nothing. We'll see how I get on when we meet up next week.' Jane wanted to close the conversation and was pleased when Shelly came up to the tea chest beside them to add in bottles of rhubarb cocktail and the subject was forgotten.

'Rhubarb cocktails going right in here beside you.' Shelly put her hands on either side of her head, wiggled, and laughed. 'These are mind-bogglingly good. All I'm going to say is that they go down very easily. The rhubarb is grown on the allotments, so I'm guessing we're calling that organic.'

Lucie chuckled. 'Ahh, I could down a few bottles.'

Shelly frowned. 'That's not like you! Haha, I'm the one who can pack them away.'

'Don't worry, I'll only have the one.' Lucie smiled and joked. 'Wouldn't want to upset the residents with my tipsy behaviour or anything like that.'

Jane shuddered as the wind whipped around. 'Me either. We'll have to limit ourselves.'

Shelly was back two seconds later balancing a pile of baskets in her arms. She passed one to Jane. 'Here you go, share one of these. Also very nice, but they do come with a health warning and don't even think about one if you're counting calories - if you are, don't sniff one of these.'

Jane laughed. 'They sound good already.'

Lucie peered inside the basket and pulled out what looked like a little parcel of filo pastry. 'Aww, what are these? They smell fabulous.'

'Goat's cheese parcels. Darling made cheese. Honestly, you won't want to stop eating them.'

Lucie handed one to Jane, who joked, 'I'm glad I walked here, what with all the goodies that have been on offer tonight!'

Shelly patted her stomach. 'Tell me about it. I'm booked in for a spin class tomorrow to burn this evening off.' She turned her head and looked back towards the pier. 'Okay, see you in a bit. I'm off to get another load of drinks.'

Jane watched as Lucie took a bottle of the rhubarb concoction and poured its contents into two plastic glasses. 'Cheers then, Janey. This is the life, eh? You, me, the sea air, lovely lights, nice surroundings, a basket full of delicious things to eat and a very special cocktail.' She held her glass up. 'Cheers, to you, Jane, and to a few months on Darling doing all the nice things.'

Jane tapped Lucie's glass in response. 'Cheers to wedding planning and the most gorgeous wedding Darling has ever seen coming up in the not too distant future. Plus, a beautiful bride.'

'Yes, here's to my wedding! Wahoo. I still can't quite believe I'm saying that, but there you go. I'm doing it! I'm actually going to be a bride.' She rolled her eyes. 'It blooming well took long enough!'

'Lucie Peachtree's getting married. I'll make six toasts to that.'

'Me too.'

'I'm really pleased for you, Luce,' Jane said, tapping Lucie on the knee. 'Ooh, this stuff is delicious. I think we might need a few more of these, don't you? They are really slipping down nicely just as Shelly said they would.'

Lucie laughed and held her glass out. 'Show me the way!'

All around them as the light had faded, the chairs had begun to fill up and the fires threw out heat, Jane and Lucie had chatted mostly about the wedding and Lucie's ideas on a dress. As the drinks flowed, they were laughing and giggling as the lights from the pier twinkled against the inky blue sky and Lucie filled up their glasses again. As Mr Cooke shuffled over towards the empty chair to Lucie's left, Jane could just make out the silhouette of a couple with a child headed for the last two remaining chairs on the other side of Mr Cooke.

Mr Cooke smiled and looked over at Jane. 'How did you enjoy the market?' he asked kindly.

Jane held up her glass and then indicated to the cocktails. 'I really enjoyed it. These are making the evening even better than it was earlier. Who knew rhubarb worked in a cocktail?'

'Yes. I've been looking forward to one of those all night.' Mr Cooke chuckled.

Lucie rummaged around in the tea chest, pulled out a bottle, flipped off the top, and started to pour the cocktail into a glass for Mr Cooke. 'We've just been talking about the wedding and wondering whether or not this might be a good little welcome drink. What do you reckon?'

Mr Cooke widened his eyes. 'Yes, if you want the whole wedding party to be worse for wear!'

Lucie laughed. 'Haha, we were thinking of a somewhat watered-down version. It's so nice.'

'It is that.' Mr Cooke sat down and let his weight rest back on the chair. 'I'll sit here and think about your wedding as I have a little tipple.'

As Lucie and Mr Cooke chatted, Jane looked across to where the couple were headed for the two chairs to Mr Cooke's left. Getting a whiff of the woman's perfume as she passed, Jane leant forward to say hello to the woman as she sat down on the other side of the tea chest beside Mr Cooke. The woman smiled, as she zipped up the coat of a little boy of about five standing in front of her. Jane turned towards the other chair as the little boy asked for a drink, and as the light from the fire flickered an orange glow of shadows over their faces, at first she thought she was seeing things.

She did a double take and, gripping the edge of her plastic glass like a vice, she went cold. She was filled with horror as the man in the other chair inclined forward around the little boy, as if to go to say hello to Jane. His face reflected the same amount of horror as Jane's face registered on seeing him. Jane coughed and nearly spurted her drink out as he said hello to Mr Cooke. She couldn't believe it! Sitting right in front of her doused in the orange glow of the fire and clearly with his wife and son beside him was the man from the hotel. Jane felt herself freeze. What on earth? It wasn't quite how she was hoping her next meeting

149

with Oscar would go. She hadn't foreseen in the scenario she'd played out in her head that he'd have a companion with him the next time she saw him. That he'd be on a cosy little family night out. She had just come face-to-face with the man she'd met in a hotel in Edinburgh, and here he was a few seats away sitting with his significant other who had been sorely missing when Jane had flung her bra at him. Jane closed her eyes and took a deep breath in. This was not pleasant. Not good at all. As she wanted the ground to open and swallow her whole, all the doors that had opened as part of Operation Le Romancer slammed tightly closed in unison.

Jane didn't know what to do. She was totally and utterly flummoxed. How in the name of goodness was she going to play it? Before she had a chance to think about it, Oscar got in first. 'Hello. I'm Oscar.'

So he was going to bury it. Jane coughed. 'Hi.' There was no way she was adding her name, even though he already knew it. She wanted to bash him over the head with one of the cocktail bottles as a mixture of fury, disappointment, and shock rumbled around her veins.

The woman twisted around and inclined her hand across the sand. 'Adele.'

Jane could see Adele more clearly now as the light flickered on her face. Pretty, little diamonds sparkling at her ears, a kind face. Jane felt sick as she thought about what she'd done with Adele's husband. Bile swirled around her stomach. It was all she could do to speak, she tried to steady her breathing and replied, 'Hi.'

Jane felt a bolt of anxiety punch through her and everything started to go in slow motion as she tried to concentrate on what Adele was saying to her. Something about the little boy and school. All Jane could see was herself kneeling up on the bed without her bra. The ridiculous, what she'd thought at the time sexy, wriggling. The silly daydreams she'd had about seeing

Oscar again hurtled into her mind at a trillion miles an hour. As she heard Adele say something else about the plastic cups and whether or not they were sustainable, Jane simply didn't know what to do.

As Oscar's wife or partner or whatever she was, turned to look at her son, Jane thought more about what her options were as she stared into her glass. She could totally land Oscar in it and be done with it. She could simply turn to the woman, tell her exactly what had happened, and show her the phone with the evidence. How well would that go down?

Oh hello, lovely evening for it. Just a little heads up for you; a while ago I was having wild abandoned sex with your husband in a business hotel in Edinburgh. Nice to meet you by the way. Can I interest you in a feta cheese ball?

No, Jane didn't think that was really an option. There weren't many good ways to find out that your husband had been unfaithful, but there had to be a better way. It would be pretty mean to be the bearer of such news considering the situation they were sitting in. As Jane considered what to do, she shook her head; no, she simply didn't have the energy to be the bearer of such grim news to Oscar's wife. Not in that instance, anyway.

As she sat in the chair feeling as if her whole world had tunnelled down to her, the woman near her, and Oscar on the other side, Jane thought about her second option; to simply get up and leave. That would be the end of it. Finito. The problem with that was Lucie was deeply engrossed in conversation about flora and fauna with Mr Cooke, and she would probably be wanting an explanation as to why Jane suddenly wanted to get up and go. Neither of her options were particularly good. She gazed into the flickering flames from the fire in front of her and considered what else she could do. She tried to think about how someone with a bigger life than hers would react. As her mind raced along, she decided that she would have to go with option three and just ride it out. She would simply have to get on with it. She couldn't change the past and at the end of the day, she was a grown-up who had made the decision at the time to have a no strings attached, flash-in-the-pan, fun time with Oscar. No one had forced her to go to Oscar's room or cajoled her into anything. It was just a chance meeting in a hotel that had turned into a little bit of fun on the side. Something to spice up an otherwise crappy evening. Clearly, that's what he had thought, anyway. He hadn't gone home and imagined it going further. It hadn't opened up his small life. He'd probably been more than happy to see the back of her when she'd sloped back off to her room.

She took a sip of the rhubarb cocktail, and however much she told herself that she'd known the way the cookie crumbled, she felt a little bit of herself die inside. Because at the end of the day, it had been a huge deal for her, there was no getting around it, no matter what she told herself. The episode with Oscar had prompted all sorts of things in Jane and it had meant a whole lot; it had started the Operation Le Romancer plan, it had provoked her into doing things she wouldn't normally do, it had caused her to have a good hard look at her life. Bottom line, it had made Jane's small life feel less small and more hopeful. It had given her a new lease of life and now as she sat on the beach with her feet in the cold sand and the salty sea air whipped around her head, she knew one thing for sure, she felt smaller than she'd ever felt in her life. Together with a little layer of stupidity nicely sprinkled on top.

Jane shifted in her chair and steadfastly ignored Adele, avoiding her gaze just enough to not be rude but enough not to invite any kind of interaction. She made sounds and gestures to ingratiate herself into Mr Cooke's detailed description of a foraging trip to the mainland, swigged back a massive gulp of her drink, and counted down the minutes before she could go home. *Go home, Jane, just go home.*

Lost in her thoughts and steering well clear of eye contact with Adele or Oscar, an hour or so later, as the evening began to unfold, Jane was jolted back to the present with a question from Lucie who had been chatting animatedly to Mr Cooke. 'Are you okay?'

'I'm fine,' was about all Jane could muster up to say.

Lucie frowned. 'You don't seem it at all. What's up?'

'No, no, nothing. I'm good.'

'You've gone very quiet, Janey, are you sure you're okay? Do you need something else to eat?'

Jane nodded and forced herself to smile. It wasn't very convincing she could tell, and Lucie knew her well. 'I'm just a bit tired.' She nodded towards the sea. 'It must be the sea air or something,' she said, attempting to inject some cheeriness into her voice.

Lucie didn't appear to be satisfied with Jane's answer, and she tapped Jane on the hand and looked directly into her eyes. 'You're very quiet. Do you want to make a move?' Lucie asked and gestured over towards the pier.

Jane tried to stop herself from jumping down Lucie's throat at the suggestion to leave, she couldn't wait to get away from Oscar but not wanting to ruin the evening, she tried to sound as if she wasn't bothered. 'Whatever you want to do. I'm easy. I'm happy to stay if you are,' she lied with a big smile. The smile on the outside was definitely not how she was feeling on the inside. She wanted to jump up from her chair, throw something at Oscar, or maybe shove him in the direction of the fire, and run for her life.

Lucie shook her head. 'I don't mind either, but it looks to me as if you've had enough. It is getting chilly. I'll phone George and see if he can come and pick us up.'

'Oh, you don't need to do that!' Jane replied with a shake of her head. 'Honestly, I'm fine to walk back to the house.'

'Don't be ridiculous! I tell you what, how about I walk with you back to yours and we can have a little nightcap there? Then I'll see if George can come and pick me up in a bit. It'll be nice to end the evening with a stroll. I could do with stretching my legs.'

Jane nodded and started to gather her things together. 'Yep, that's fine with me.' It was more than fine. It was music to her ears. She couldn't wait to retreat.

As Lucie was folding up a blanket that had been on her knees, she held up another bottle of the rhubarb cocktail and brandished it in front of Jane and laughed. 'How about another one for the road just before we head off?'

Jane had consumed more than enough of the rhubarb cocktail and another glass of it whilst Oscar sat nearby was the last thing she wanted to do. But, as Jane always did, she agreed. It was delicious, and she had to admit that downing the cocktail as if it was orange squash had taken the edge off a very tense situation. Maybe one more would actually do her good, maybe not? She accepted the drink, waited for Lucie to pour it into her glass, and gulped back a huge swig. Stuff Oscar and Edinburgh. And his wife.

There was no doubt that fifteen minutes or so later, Jane was definitely feeling the rhubarb cocktail. It had gone down well and she wasn't quite as despondent as she had been before. As she tidied up her chair, making a conscious effort not to look further than Adele and only smile at her every now and then, Jane went to put her plastic glass in the bin, and was certainly on the wobbly side.

Wrapping up with Mr Cooke, waving cheerio to Shelly, and

nodding to a few people as they left, they made their way up the beach. The pier twinkled against the inky blue night sky, and Jane couldn't quite get her head around how everything looked so pretty around her when inside she felt as if someone had turned the lights out. It had left her fumbling around in the dark, trying desperately to work out quite what was going on. She tried to stop thinking about Oscar and instead concentrated on walking back to the mews. As they walked along, Lucie put her arm through Jane's and giggled. 'What a lovely funny night that ended up to be, eh Janey? Rhubarb cocktails, sitting by a fire on the beach and watching silly dances in the sand.'

Jane didn't feel the same at all. It had not been lovely or funny as far as she was concerned. In fact, it had been one of the worst nights she'd experienced in a long time, in a very, very long time. Possibly up there with one of the worst nights of her life. As she always did though, she pretended she'd had a nice time. She kept her voice resolutely upbeat. 'Yes, it was a lovely evening.' She looked up at the sky full of stars and attempted to change the subject. The less said about the evening on the beach, the better. 'The stars are so pretty, too. These must be Darling Island stars; they seem brighter and sparklier here.'

Lucie giggled and followed Jane's gaze upwards. 'Yes, maybe they are. Darling seems to do everything better. That was my kind of market. I could do that all over again. And what about that rhubarb thingy?'

Jane grimaced and shuddered inside. She'd have to be paid a lot of money to go through that again. The crushing feeling that had swept over her like a tidal wave when her eyes had adjusted to the light and registered that the man taking a seat was Oscar was not a good one. Her idea of a fun evening was not bumping into the man she'd slept with on a whim at the other end of the country when he was being accompanied on a family outing with his wife.

Lucie rattled on. 'It's nice to have a little get together like this. I love it when we get to just chat for ages and there's no screen or time zones or anything like that. We need to organise another one with the girls. Like when we went to Tunbridge Wells. That was such a fab weekend.'

Jane nodded in agreement, trying to take her mind off the image of Oscar currently front and foremost in her mind. 'Yes, that would be nice.'

'I know. How about we arrange a weekend while you're in the house here? We could get everyone together and just chill out. I'll cook and we'll have a cosy evening in, like we did before my engagement party. What do you think about that? Would that be okay with Catherine, do you think?'

If Jane had been honest, she couldn't really have cared less; at that particular moment, all she could think about was Oscar sitting next to his wife as brazen as the day was long. Trying to sound interested in Lucie's chattering, she injected a sing-song into her voice. 'Oh yes, I'm sure she would be fine with that,' she replied and squeezed Lucie's hand. 'I'll get on it. I'll sort it out, and we'll have a Hold Your Nerve girls group here.' Inside, she cringed, considering that it could quite possibly morph into a Hold Your Nerve group meeting about the situation that had just happened that had done a very good job of rocking her small little life.

19

It had taken ages for Jane and Lucie's slightly tipsy stroll to get them back to the mews house, but despite Jane's mood, as they walked over the cobbles, the sight of the house nestled down at the end at least made her smile. Automated lights at the front lit up the door in a pool of golden light, and in huge pots bay trees covered in tiny little white lights shimmered into the night. Arriving at the front door, Lucie chuckled at the sight of a basket tucked in beside a pot. 'Ooh!' she exclaimed. 'If I am correct, I know what that is!' She picked up the basket and brandished it in front of her. 'This my lovely friend is a Bottles on Darling basket. Talk about appropriate timing!' Lucie tucked the basket under her arm as Jane keyed the number into the pad. Lucie smiled. 'Yes, I was correct, it is from them! Look what we have here.' She laughed as she wiggled a tissue paper covered bottle in front of Jane's face.

'You're nuts, Luce, I think that last cocktail has gone to your head.' Jane chuckled as she unwound the scarf from her neck. Sensible Jane kicked in and she laughed as they almost fell in the door. 'I'm thinking maybe we should have a water break and a big one at that.'

Lucie flipped her hands this way and that in front of her face. 'Absolutely no way I'm having a water break. I'm not Tally, you know! You don't need to look after me. I've hardly even had much to drink.'

'You'll love me in the morning.' Jane smiled.

Lucie giggled. 'It feels good to be a bit tipsy, though, know what I mean? I hope the rhubarb cocktail doesn't come back to haunt me tomorrow,' Lucie replied and giggled as a little hiccup emerged, she nearly tripped over a basket full of logs, and she dumped her bag near the front door and headed into the kitchen. Jane laughed as they got to the kitchen, and she turned on the sconce lamps in the window over the sink.

'Oh, this is such a cute, lovely little house!' Lucie exclaimed as she sat down at the island, and Jane unwrapped the bottle of gin. She took two glasses down from the shelf and looked around. 'I'm not sure if there'll be any tonic anywhere, hang on, I'll have a look in the pantry.'

'I'll drink it straight, haha!' Lucie laughed.

'We are in luck,' Jane said as she emerged from the pantry wielding a bottle of tonic water. 'Look, there are even some fancy garnishes,' she said as she held out a little brown paper envelope with a clear plastic window displaying dried orange and lime.

Lucie giggled. 'Well done, superstar.'

'Nothing to do with me. There seems to be everything you could ever want here,' Jane said as she clicked the top from the bottle of gin and took two glasses from the shelf. 'Catherine has thought of everything.'

Lucie sighed as Jane poured the drinks. 'Oh, I've missed you, Janey, it's so nice having you here, wouldn't it be lovely if we all lived near each other again? It would be just like the old days.'

'We definitely need to make the most of it while I'm here,' Jane replied, as she thought inside that she wouldn't be hanging around too long if it was the type of place where a married man slept with any old person in hotels at the other end of the country.

Lucie took the gin, wriggled around to get comfortable on her stool and looked across the table at Jane. 'So, Jane, the guy from Edinburgh, Oscar. We didn't get a chance to talk about it before. When are you meeting up again? Sorry you did say when you came for supper, but I've forgotten what day you said.'

Jane shuddered inside. What did she do now? Did she lie or did she tell the truth? With a massive, whooshing exhale, she decided she would tell Lucie exactly what was going on. What was the point of keeping it a secret? She was a failure anyway - she would just go back to her small, little life in her London street where she couldn't get things wrong and leave it at that.

Lucie frowned at the obvious change in Jane's body language. She leant forward. 'Are you okay, Janey? What's happened?'

Jane didn't quite know how to tell Lucie that the man they had been sitting near at the beach was the same man as the guy she'd flung her bra at in Edinburgh. She shook her head. 'I don't really know how to say this, but I'll just blurt it out anyway. The bloke at the beach is the same Oscar.'

Lucie frowned and wrinkled her forehead in confusion. 'Sorry. Wait, what? Hang on, I'm not with you, Jane. What are you talking about? You mean the couple who were on the other side of the drinks next to Mr Cooke?'

Jane tried not to let her irritation show. She was going to have to spell it out for Lucie. It wasn't surprising - Oscar had been the last person she had been expecting to see at the market, so it was no surprise that Lucie was confused. 'I am telling you that the guy from the hotel, Oscar, is the same guy as the one this evening sitting just along from us.'

Lucie placed her glass down on the table. 'I think I *have* had too much to drink. My friend, are you telling me right now that the man you slept with on a one-night stand in a hotel in Scotland is the same man that turned up with his wife and child this evening?'

Jane bristled, flustered, closed her eyes and sighed. 'Yes, correct, that is exactly what I'm telling you. The man there was the same man as the one in Edinburgh! It was him, and he was there with his wife this evening!'

Lucie fell silent and didn't say anything for a minute or two, and then squeezed her eyes together really tightly. 'Wow!' Lucie swore and continued, 'I didn't really catch his name anyway. Blimey!'

'I know.' Jane shook her head resignedly.

'How the hell did you sit through it?' Lucie asked and swore again.

Jane squirmed and raised her eyebrows. 'I really don't know; I simply didn't know what to do, so I just remained where I was.'

Lucie agreed. 'I don't blame you one little bit for not knowing what to do. I don't think I would've known either. Far out, the bloke you slept with turns up with his wife! What's that all about? What are the chances? Why would someone behave like that? What an absolute loser.'

Jane was the one who felt like a loser, she shook her head. 'I think I'm the one who's the absolute loser. I don't know about *absolute* loser - I am an *absolute* idiot, more like. I feel like I fell for the oldest trick in the book. I slept with someone in a hotel and he must have been laughing all the way to the bank. It really is as cut and dried as that.'

Lucie fiddled with the stem on her glass, fished out a piece of dried orange garnish and wiggled it in the gin. 'When you put it like that...'

Jane nibbled on the inside of her thumbnail and then exclaimed. 'I can't believe what an idiot I am! He must have seen me coming at forty paces. Lonely single woman in a hotel and all that.'

'You are *not* the idiot,' Lucie replied sternly. 'He is the unequivocal scum of the earth to have done that, especially with a young family. It's bad enough that he's in a relationship, but a child too. Euhh, horrible.'

'I know, and I was part of it. How terrible is that? Maybe I even encouraged it somehow?' Jane stated weakly.

Lucie raised her eyebrows. 'No, just no. Sorry, Jane, most responsible adults you would hope wouldn't behave like that. I guess I must be wrong and living in cloud cuckoo land.'

'You would think that, yes.' Jane nodded in agreement. 'But maybe that's just us.'

'What are you going to do, then?'

'I don't know. I don't really have any options, do I? I mean, at the end of the day, what do I say? Not that he'll even respond anyway. I haven't got a leg to stand on about any of it. I barely even know his name!'

'True, yes, no, I guess there is that side to it. What about all the texts, though? Why would he have been texting you? It's not like he shelved you afterwards, you've clearly had a text thing going on. I don't get it.'

'I've no idea. Maybe he was keeping me at arm's length for a reason.'

Lucie screwed her face up in confusion. 'What would his motive have been for that, I wonder?'

'He might have been texting me to keep me warm as an option.' Jane looked horrified. 'Oh no! He's been keeping me as a sex option!'

Lucie shook her head, her lips turned into an upside down grimace. 'Surely not? No, you can't have that. You want to be at the top of someone's list, not an option on the end of a text thread.'

'I was an idiot, but I played the game. I took the gamble, as it were. What's that saying? Them's the breaks or something like that?'

'I suppose that's one way of looking at it, but it doesn't sound nice to me. Sorry, but I can't really believe that people actually behave in that way and I'm sorry it happened to you. He must have just assumed that he would never ever see you again anywhere other than in a secret hotel somewhere. How little did he know...' She trailed off letting her sentence hang unfinished between them. Lucie fiddled with the cuff on her jumper and then swirled another piece of dried orange around in her gin. 'You don't think it could be something else, do you? We're assuming all sorts here.'

'Like what?' Jane replied, looking doubtful.

'What I mean is, what if it wasn't what it looks like?'

'I'm not with you at all, you need to explain what you mean. It looked pretty damn obvious to me from where I was standing, or sitting, rather.'

Lucie's eyes were wide. 'Say, for instance, that's not his wife at all or his son? Say it's something else entirely. What if it's something completely different from what we are assuming?'

Jane shook her head. 'I cannot see any reasonable explanation for it. I've been over it in my head so many times and couldn't think of a single reason that if it was something different, why wouldn't he have just said so? Got it out in the open as it were. Why did he pretend he'd never set eyes on me before and introduce himself.'

'I don't know,' Lucie replied. 'But maybe it's something else. I'm just putting it out there. There could be an explanation for it. Stranger things have happened at sea and all that.'

Jane got up from the table, turned around and took the kettle from its base and ran it under the tap. A commiserative cup of tea was needed. She turned back around and leant on the worktop. Just as she was about to take the tea bags from their container, her phone buzzed. Lucie slid the phone across the table, and Jane flipped open the cover.

'Oh my goodness! It's him! He's actually got the cheek to send me a text!' She exclaimed.

'What?' Lucie squealed. 'He's got some front, you have to give him that. Give it to me here, show me!'

Jane kept hold of the phone, tapped the message, and started to read.

Yeah, hi, Jane. Look, it's not what you think. I need to explain. Where are you? Can we have a chat?

'According to this text, it's not what I think,' Jane stated with her eyebrows raised.

'See! I told you, Jane! There's more to this than we thought.'

'I just don't know what he could say to explain that situation,' Jane replied glumly.

'The plot thickens though, doesn't it?'

'Does it? How does it change anything? He's just panicking, I reckon,' Jane deducted.

'Why would he text you if he didn't want to explain?'

'He's scared I'll drop him in it somehow. This is a small island, and he's here with his wife and the woman he shagged in Edinburgh appears on the beach. Not looking good for him at all, is it?'

'Mmm when you put it like that, it does sound quite bad.'

'It *is* quite bad.'

'Thing is, what have you got to lose by letting him explain to you?' Lucie mused.

'I don't want to even give him the time of day, to be quite honest.'

'I say you should message him back and see what he says. You never know.'

'But then I give him an option. I could just delete his number and block him and put the whole thing in the past. It's not as if I want to ruin his life or anything.'

'No, true. What if it *is* something innocent, though?'

Jane frowned and poured hot water into the pot. 'Maybe you're right, maybe I will reply.'

'At least you'll know then.'

'I suppose so. I just feel like such an idiot. Part of me thinks I'll just leave it. Ahh, I don't know what to do for the best.'

'Maybe give him the benefit of the doubt? Read it out to me again, what exactly does he say?'

Jane held her phone up and read the text out. 'Yeah hi, Jane. Look, it's not what you think. I need to explain. Where are you? Can we have a chat?'

Lucie held her hand out. 'Show me,' she demanded.

Jane slid the phone over the table, and Lucie read the message. 'I don't know, it doesn't sound as if he is overly concerned about you keeping quiet or anything.'

Jane took the phone back and reread the text. 'No, he doesn't, so I guess there is that.'

'He's not mentioned the wife or the son or anything,' Lucie stated.

'True, however, if he's going to try and wheedle his way out of this, why would he mention her at all?'

'Yes, maybe he's going to pretend and try to deny it.'

'Yep. I reckon that's it.' Jane sighed. 'He's hedging his bets.'

'On the other hand,' Lucie paused for added drama, 'Maybe she isn't his wife at all.'

'I just cannot see why he wouldn't have said anything.'

'You just need to try and wait and see and hear what he has to say.'

'Are you telling me that I should go and meet him?'

Lucie dragged her mug closer to her and took a sip of her tea. 'I don't know, Jane. I think maybe you should meet up with him, yes.'

'What, so I just message him back?'

'Yep. Do it. You have nothing to lose here.'

Jane sucked air in through her teeth and Lucie raised her eyebrows. 'We could have a meeting about it with the other girls. We could call a Crisis Talk meeting tomorrow to decide what to do.'

Jane shook her head defiantly. 'No, no way I'm doing that. I'm not blooming well dissecting this whole thing and thinking about it to within an inch of its life. It's bad enough as it is.'

'Just text back then,' Lucie said simply.

Jane chuckled wryly. 'Which means we have another problem to figure out.'

Lucie laughed. 'We do indeed. What the heck does someone respond to a text like that?'

'What's that thing they say? KISS. Keep it simple, stupid. Or something like that.'

Lucie laughed. 'I think on this occasion that is a very good plan of action.'

Jane laughed. The tension in the air broken briefly. 'See, what is the world coming to? How did I get myself into this? I need to put this to bed and forget it.'

'You don't want to meet up with him for a chat in person?'

'Do I really want to meet up with a married man and discuss this situation?'

'No, I suppose you don't really. Just put something noncommittal then.'

Jane picked her phone up and tapped the screen. 'Okay, here we go. Let me just read what he wrote to you again and see what you think. "Yeah. Hi, Jane. Look, it's not what you think. I need to explain. Where are you? Can we have a chat?" So what I'm going to put is something like "What is it then?" What do you think about that? Simple and direct.'

'I guess it's straight to the point,' Lucie replied.

'Keep it simple, stupid.' Jane laughed. 'That's what we said about half an hour ago.'

'You're not wrong.' Lucie chuckled.

Jane started to type out the message with her thumbs.

Hi, Oscar. Thanks for your message. I'm staying on Darling at the moment and I don't really want to have a chat about it. And if it's not what I think, what is it?

Jane showed Lucie her phone screen 'I'm gonna go with that. What do you think?'

'Yeah, no more messing around talking about it for ages. Hit send and be done with it. It is what it is.'

Jane pressed the blue button and right away her screen told her that the message had been delivered. In a split second, the blue dots were flashing to show that Oscar was replying. Jane looked up at Lucie. 'He's typing right now.'

Lucie sipped her drink. 'This is going to get good, where's the popcorn?'

Jane laughed. 'I need more than popcorn to get me through this. I need a Valium. Where's Tally when you need her?'

'Oh well, Janey, at least it will give us something to talk about at the next Hold Your Nerve group meeting.'

Jane let out a whoosh of air and shrugged her shoulders. 'Do you know what? I don't know if I want to go through it all with everyone.'

'Up to you, Janey.'

Jane looked down at her phone as the reply arrived.

I can understand why you must be annoyed. It was quite awkward this evening but I really would rather meet up for a chat and talk about it.

Jane looked at Lucie with her eyebrows raised. Lucie mused, 'Well, if nothing else, he definitely wants to meet up with you by the sounds of it.'

'Yeah, it does sound that way. Why would I do that, though?'

'I don't really know what to say for the best.'

'I'm just going to say no.'

Jane started typing with her thumbs.

Thanks, Oscar but I'm really not interested in meeting up with you.

The little dots flashed again as Oscar replied.

That wasn't my wife. Well, she was my partner but not my wife. It's complicated.

Jane turned her phone screen around to show Lucie who read the text. 'It's complicated? I've heard that before,' Lucie replied cynically. 'Isn't that the name of a film or something? I'm wondering whether you should just meet up with him and find out. Why don't you arrange something now and call his bluff?'

'And put what?'

'Just say that you will meet up with him somewhere very busy.'

'Okay.'

'Hold on a minute. How come he was in Darling in the first place? Someone must know who he is or at least know something about him. Everybody knows everybody on this island.'

Jane nodded. 'We should have thought of that before. Mr Cooke might have known something about him.'

'Obviously I didn't know anything about it at that point, but he didn't seem to recognise him.'

'No, he didn't. However, you two were deep in conversation and he was a few chairs away and around the other side of the circle, so maybe Mr Cooke didn't see him properly. It was also very dark,' Jane noted.

'True. However, wouldn't someone have spoken to him? Like Shelly, for example?'

'I suppose so.'

Just as they were sitting there discussing what to do, they heard a noise outside. A car engine parked outside the window and was turned off. Lucie got up from her stool. 'That must be George,' she said.

Jane whispered, 'Don't say anything about this, please. I don't want anyone to know at the moment.'

Lucie pulled open the old pale blue door and George walked in. His face cracked into a huge smile, and he kissed Jane on either side of her cheeks. 'Hello, how are you? It's so nice to see you. How are you getting on?'

Jane hugged George. 'I'm good, thanks.'

George looked around at the house, the beautiful kitchen, and down towards the sitting room area where the white sofa was flagged by two huge lamps. 'I should think you *are* good, this place is really nice.'

'Yep, I've done well.' Jane laughed. 'Not a bad house swap.'

George turned to Lucie. 'Right, are you ready to leave?' Lucie looked at Jane. 'Yep, I am. Are you going to be okay?'

George frowned and turned back to Jane. 'Why would you not be okay? Has something happened?'

Jane batted her hands in front of her face. 'Oh, no, no, everything is fine.'

Lucie interjected, attempting to fluff over her asking Jane if she was okay. 'All good, it's just that Jane got a bit cold on the way back.'

Jane agreed, 'Yes, the wind coming off the sea was quite chilly as we walked home.'

George nodded. 'It's a funny old time of year around and about now, one minute it's warm the next minute it's not.'

Jane laughed. 'Yes, I think I've worked that out for myself.'

Lucie picked her bag up from the dresser at the entrance, and Jane opened the front door. 'I'll see you tomorrow,' Lucie said.

Jane kissed Lucie on the cheek. 'Yes, thanks for a lovely evening.'

As Lucie hugged Jane, she whispered in her ear. 'Text me and let me know what's going on. Whatever you do, do not arrange to meet him tonight.'

Jane whispered back, 'Don't worry, there's no chance of that.'

20

The next morning, Jane woke from a fitful night. She'd had all sorts of horrible dreams, including one where she'd walked into the courtyard and was surrounded by snakes slithering around by the chiminea and hiding in the flowerpots. Fumbling around on the bedside table, she sat up in bed, took a sip of water, and opened her phone. There was nothing further from Oscar, just a text from Lucie asking her if she was okay.

Pushing her arms into her dressing down and padding down the steep stairs, she grimaced at the bottle of gin still in the middle of the island, grabbed it, and put it away in the pantry. Ten minutes later, she was waiting for the toaster to pop and had almost decided that she wasn't going to bother with the Oscar thing at all. She wasn't going to bother with anything at all. Jane would return to her small life. Operation Le Romancer would be put on hold and she would continue as she always had. The whole thing had been a stupid idea and a useful reminder of the benefits of staying small.

After spreading copious amounts of Darling butter on to toast, she followed it with a generous slathering of Marmite, picked up her plate and cup of tea, and went to stand by the window. Looking out over the front where rain poured down from the sky in sheets, she watched as it pitter-pattered onto the road. It was as if the road was alive with a million flies landing on its surface. The gutters filled with rushing rain as Jane ate her toast and watched raindrops form into little black circles as they landed on the water. The pouring angry rain was as grim as her mood.

As she stood there watching nature do her thing and wondering what to do, she was mightily cheesed off about the Oscar situation and wished that she had never started a text conversation with him in the first place. She stood there for ages thinking about the dilemma, well aware that she was over-thinking it completely, went back to the toaster, popped two more slices of toast and waited. What did it really matter? As she finished the toast, she looked at her phone and reread the message thread from him. Before she had time to think about what she was doing, she'd sent a message that she'd changed her mind and would meet him for a quick drink that evening at the pub. She didn't know if she was doing the right thing but something inside was telling her to give Oscar a chance. It was a good ten minutes before a reply came back by which stage Jane had had another cup of tea and was wondering if it was far too early for a salad cream sandwich.

Great, he had replied. *What pub do you want to meet in?*

Jane didn't really have any clue about any of the pubs on Darling Island. She'd been with Jane and George to a few and so Googled pubs on Darling. Not allowing herself to fuss over it any more than she had done the night before with Lucie, she texted back.

I'll see you in the Darling Inn at seven if that suits you?

This time Oscar's reply was instant. He sent a thumbs-up emoticon and replied that yes, he would see her there, unless she wanted him to come and pick her up.

She shook her head and raised her eyebrows. Who was he

even kidding? There was no way she was going to tell him where she was staying. She replied that she was fine to see him there and left it at that.

Jane didn't have too much chance to deliberate further about Oscar or anything else as shortly after she'd sent the text, she'd had a message from work about an old case where she had been the lead. There had been a problem that needed fixing pronto, and she'd been elected by her boss to sort it out. She'd emerged from the study just after two o'clock and pottered around in the kitchen, making herself a salad cream sandwich, and as she started to consider the Oscar thing, she had second thoughts about the pub meeting altogether. It was all very well saying that she would meet him at the pub, but at the end of the day, what was he going to say?

Drumming her fingers on her lips as she thought about it, her mind swinging wildly from thinking that she would just go along and see what happened, to not turning up at all and not bothering to text him either. With her feet tucked up under her, she pulled a book from Catherine's bookshelf and tried not to think about it. At about three o'clock, there was a knock at the door. She got up from the sofa, pulled back the curtain, and peered towards the front door to see Lucie standing there with a bunch of flowers. Jane rushed to the door, opened it, and Lucie stepped in.

'You didn't need to do that!' Jane exclaimed.

'I know, I know. I just wanted to pop in and see how you are. It's nice to have someone here. I know you said you were working today, so don't let me stop you,' Lucie said as she handed over the flowers to Jane.

Jane let her in. 'No, no, you're fine. I was just about to make a cup of tea anyway. Would you like one?'

Lucie took her jacket off and hung it by the door. 'I'll have a quick one. I can't really stop. I'm on my way to pick up some fabric.'

'So,' Jane said with a funny look on her face, 'let me tell you the latest.'

'That's why I'm really here, to see what's going on and make sure you're okay. The more I thought about it the more concerned I became.'

Jane gathered her hair up behind her and smoothed it into a tight ponytail. She tried to sound nonplussed. 'I'm just going to go and meet him in the pub and see what it was all about,' she stated.

'Right,' Lucie replied.

'What do you think about that?'

'Yeah, yeah, all good. I just want to make sure you're safe.'

'I'll be fine.' *I'm always fine.*

'How about we let George in on this?' Lucie said with her eyebrows raised in expectation.

'No!' Jane stated emphatically. 'I don't want anyone to know about this yet.'

'Just a suggestion,' Lucie said as she took her tea and Jane slid the biscuit tin over the table.

'It will be fine in there, it's a pretty busy pub.'

'Yeah, yeah, you'll be okay in there. What do you think he's going to say?'

Jane rested both her hands on the kitchen island. 'Do you know what? I'm really not sure. Last night I was thinking that he was awful but now I'm wondering what's going on here - he's openly meeting me in a pub in the middle of Darling Island. If he was up to something, then surely he wouldn't want to do that?'

Lucie nodded in agreement. 'So, anyway, I did a little bit of digging.'

Jane's eyes widened. 'I thought I said for you not to say anything to anyone...' She didn't finish her sentence.

Lucie shook her right hand back and forth. 'Don't worry

about it. I was very, very careful. I asked Mr Cooke when we were on our walk this morning if he knew anything about him.'

'Right. And what did he say?'

Lucie put her mug down and grimaced. 'Highly unusual for him not to know anything and not to notice but because it was dark, he said he didn't really know who I meant and because of the way the chairs were arranged, he couldn't see that well. He reckoned he might be a newcomer.'

'Right, I see. What did you say was the reason you wanted to know?'

'I just said I thought I recognised him from somewhere and wondered if he lived on the island.'

'It's a pity Mr Cooke didn't really see him, maybe we would have more of an idea and I wouldn't have to bother going along,' Jane stated.

'I think you're going to be fine, Jane. I think there's an explanation for this.'

Jane smiled. 'I won't be holding my breath.'

Lucie raised her eyebrows. 'No. I suppose not.'

Jane pursed her lips together. 'We now have another dilemma. What in the name of goodness am I going to wear?'

'Now there's a question.'

'It's not really a dress occasion, is it? Anyway, who cares what I look like?'

Lucie tapped the side of her temple. 'I think this is a simple nice jeans occasion,' she said with a smile.

'Good. I thought the same. I mean it's not exactly as if I have to worry about what I look like. He's kind of seen it all before.' Jane guffawed and inside grimaced at the flinging of her bra.

'Good point, that.' Lucie chuckled.

Jane joined her in the chuckling. 'In any case, it's not about the outside package, it's about what's inside. Isn't that right?'

'Haha, so they say. To me though, it's always better when you feel comfortable and you believe that you look nice. Who wants to turn up to something looking like a bag of you know what?'

'Exactly my thoughts on the matter,' Jane said with a smile. 'So you think jeans?'

'I do. I like the Frenchie look.'

'What's that when it's at home?' Jane laughed.

'Nice jeans, stripy top, ballet flats, and my navy blue jacket with the gold buttons. Do you have a stripy top with you?'

Jane nodded. 'I do, yes. That will do, I won't have to think about it then. I'll chuck it on and be done with it.'

Lucie went to get up from her stool. 'I'll drop the jacket over just before you leave. Are you going to walk over there?'

'Definitely, there's no way I'm driving and being stone-cold sober even though I had my fair share last night.'

'This is the part where you tell me that you were right to make us drink that water last night and to only have a small nightcap.' Lucie smiled.

'You didn't say that at the time.' Jane chuckled.

'I know, but you're always the voice of reason, aren't you?'

Jane nodded, whilst inside she thought to herself that maybe that was the problem. Always good old, sensible, little Jane with the small life. Jane the Widow. Ever the voice of reason. Perhaps that was her problem all along?

Lucie picked her bag up and made her way to the door. 'Okay, so I might see you later. I may just drop the jacket by the door because I'm going to be in a bit of a rush to pick up Darce later.'

Jane held the door open. 'No worries, thank you. See you later.'

〜

Jane had gone down a rabbit hole on social media. She'd typed in the hashtag 'Frenchiestyle' as recommended to her by Lucie and had taken a head-first dive into all things French style. As she scrolled and tapped through her phone, she got lost in all sorts looking at images on Pinterest of sullen looking women in trench coats, Chanel ballet flats, and in some cases berets. She forgot about Oscar and the dilemma for a bit as sitting tucked up in the chair in the corner of the courtyard, she closed her eyes and imagined herself moseying down a Parisian street wearing a stripy top, jeans, and a market basket over her arm with not a care in the world. In the daydream, she sat outside at a café with an espresso coffee, a just baked croissant, lashings of butter and jam, and a pack of Gauloises beside her. She then went on another jaunt to a fabulous French bakery with white café chairs outside and window boxes full of red geraniums. In the daydream, she ordered a baguette, tucked it into her basket and made her way home for lunch. The whole day was rammed full of carbohydrates and yet came completely calorie-free. In the daydream she remained skinny, sulky, and mysterious looking.

Unfortunately, Jane Le Romancer's actual life wasn't quite as idyllic as the French scenario in her head. In reality, life involved a small London existence peppered with the odd trip to a business hotel and sometimes (actually once) a one-night stand. A one-night stand with someone who most probably was very much taken by his wife. The thought of it made a little shudder of shame take a trip around the inside of her stomach. Dropping her phone into her lap, she stared around at the little courtyard. A pool of sunshine gathered on the block paved terrace and the pots of rosemary rustled in a breeze, filling the air with scent. Hopefully, the explanation from Oscar later on that evening would put her remorse to bed.

As she pottered around the house tidying a few things up,

checking her emails, and running a wipe over the coffee table, she made a decision. She would stop dwelling on the situation and she would approach the matter head first. She didn't need to fuss about it. She didn't need to dissect it every two seconds. She didn't need to stress and worry and overthink. No, Jane was going to approach the matter just as Oscar clearly was. She would turn up at the pub, find out the facts, assess the situation, and go from there. It really was that simple.

An hour before she was meant to be at the pub, Jane was standing in the bedroom. She had soaked in the bath, applied a sheet mask to her face, followed it up with all sorts of fancy creams, and had carefully blow dried her hair. She looked in the mirror; her hair was good, nails were painted and the shapewear she'd yanked on was doing a marvellous job. Lucie's jacket was hanging on the outside of the wardrobe and her jeans were draped over a chair. After trying them on, with the stripy top she threw the whole outfit on the bed in disgust. French chic she most definitely was not. English turnip described how she felt rather more aptly.

She spoke aloud to herself in the mirror. 'What am I even thinking? French chic! I have nothing to wear!'

She rummaged in the wardrobe where the few clothes she'd picked for the three-month stay on Darling hung. Rifling through the hangers, she stopped at a red dress with a square neck. *Would that do?* she asked herself. She shook her head and continued the rifling. A silk ruffle blouse with a fancy cuff? Finally, she came to a little black dress. She'd popped it in her suitcase just in case she'd needed to go to a work meeting. Maybe this was the occasion for it? Pulling on the dress, she then stood in her bare feet in front of the mirror and taking one look, she knew it was an absolute no.

With the clock ticking, she tried on a green work blouse with jeans. That was also a no. Surveying the pile of discarded rumpled clothes on the bed and not feeling any good vibes about any of it at all, she picked up the original stripy top, pulled it on over the shapewear, tucked her remaining muffin top neatly into the waistband of the jeans, slipped on her ballet flats, and pulled on Lucie's jacket. Standing with her head cocked to the side, and her right leg out to the side, she gazed in the mirror at the image looking back at her. It would have to do.

Jane chuckled to herself as she looked in the mirror on the dresser adjacent to the front door, lifted her chin, and looked at the precise line of black eyeliner on her top lid. As the French make-up tutorial on YouTube had instructed, a thick, tight-lined dousing of black clung to her eyelashes - she wasn't quite sure about the authenticity of it being French or not, but it looked not bad. Less turnip-like than the outfit.

As she closed the door behind her and walked down the cobbled street, despite being tightly held in by a layer of flesh-coloured spandex, she felt a flutter of wobbles in her tummy. Part of her was wondering what was the point of even going, and another part of her was hoping that the situation would turn out much better than she hoped. She rolled her eyes to herself as she walked along. Who was she fooling? There was also a corresponding feeling in the pit of her stomach that this wasn't going to turn out that well. At all.

21

Jane made her way to the pub and as she approached, she smiled at its glinting pale blue subway tiled exterior. Getting a whiff of Lucie's perfume from the jacket, she felt another wave of butterflies inside as she got closer to the pub door. She took in the beautiful setting as she approached; all the way along the front hanging baskets swayed in the breeze, an anchor shape was cut out of the door, and little lamps glowed from the windows. Stepping onto a thick navy-blue doormat inscribed with 'Darling Inn,' Jane pushed open the door. At the sight of the busy pub, she stopped, suddenly overcome with emotion, turned on her heel, and went to walk back out.

There was no way she was going to open herself up to anything by giving this Oscar the time of day. What had she even been thinking by responding to his text in the first place? She should have just left it where it was. She must have been out of her tiny mind to have not only considered meeting him, but investing her energy in it and having an actual conversation with Lucie about what she was going to wear and all that old codswallop. She was supposed to be an independent professional with her own home, a well-adjusted son and good career.

She did not need to be faffing around worrying about what she looked like going to a pub with tight-lined eyelashes and shapewear to meet someone who was clearly up to no good.

Stepping back out onto the pavement and walking along to the other side of the outdoor tables, she paused in front of the window, pulled out her phone and messaged Lucie.

Changed my mind. I'm going to head back. Crazy! I shouldn't have even considered this. Xx

Ahh, OK. I don't blame you. Tricky one xxx

Yeah, I know. I just suddenly thought I'm nuts. He could be a blooming serial killer for all I know. Jane let out a wry laugh. She hadn't let that bother her in the hotel.

I get you. Message me when you get back so I know you're safe.

Just as Jane was texting back, there was a rapping on the window behind her. She turned around to see Oscar peering out the window, smiling and holding up his hand in greeting. Jane did a little wave back and stood motionless for a second. In No Man's Land, she didn't move towards the door or start walking away; she stood rooted to the spot. A few seconds later, Oscar was on the street.

'Hey. How are you?'

'Err, I'm well, yep, fine.'

'Lovely evening despite all that rain earlier,' he said, looking up at the clear night sky.

Jane stuttered, completely wrong-footed at his casual mentioning of the weather. 'Yes, yes, it is.'

Oscar went to lead the way into the pub and Jane lamely followed him to the main pub door, then trailed behind as he made his way towards a table in the middle near the fire. Jane looked around at the packed pub where a gaggle of young girls sat by the window gossiping over their phones, a group of men with pints were playing cards, and there was a queue at the bar in the food area. The pub was heaving. It was not the sort of place you took someone when you were trying to be inconspicuous or trying to hide. There were only a few spare tables, and a barman was scurrying around with his arms full of plates. Touching her gently on the elbow, Oscar pointed to the table. 'It's a bit noisy here, but it was one of the last few tables. Are you okay with that?'

Still not having said much, Jane sat down, propped her bag under her chair and put her phone in her pocket. Oscar smiled. 'You look nice.'

Jane nodded, barely able to string two words together as her mind galloped along, confused at how this man seemed to be totally oblivious to the fact that the night before he'd been with his wife and son and now he was here with her. He continued, glancing around the pub. 'It's busy in here. What can I get you?'

Jane pushed her chair out, shook her head, and picked up her bag. 'Sorry, I'm not staying. I shouldn't even have come here. Big mistake, huge. I was just leaving when you came out. I should go.'

Oscar frowned and jumped. 'What? No, no! Let me explain about last night.'

Jane suddenly felt angry and even stupider than she had the night before. 'You know what? I don't really want to know.' She repeated what she had already said, folded her arms tightly across her body, and crossed her legs. 'I shouldn't have come here. Last night was awful, hideous, and this is probably going to be worse. No, I'm going.'

'It wasn't what you think. It wasn't my wife or anything like that,' Oscar blurted out. 'I know what it looked like. I, err, I didn't know what to do for the best, considering the circumstances.'

Jane stared into his eyes. 'The circumstances? What is that supposed to mean?'

Oscar flicked his hand back and forth. 'How you and I met, I meant.'

'Okay...' The look on Jane's face did not appear convinced. Her arms remained crossed.

'She's not my wife,' Oscar reiterated.

'I don't get it, then. Why didn't you say that last night? Why completely ignore the whole, umm?' Jane paused, trying to think of the correct word to use as she referred to the Edinburgh thing. She flicked her hand towards the window. 'You know, what happened...'

'That's my point. I wasn't quite sure how to address that. Plus, I wasn't certain what you were happy to have said about it. It's hardly something you, you know, broadcast. At least, I don't,' Oscar replied.

'And what about Adele?' Jane replied, lifting her palms upwards in question.

'Just let me get you a drink and I'll explain. It's complicated.'

Jane was taken in by the eyes, the prettiness, the everything. She adjusted her bag strap on her shoulder, unsure whether she should give him the benefit of doubt or not. Oscar continued, his voice urgent. 'Stay there and I'll get you a drink.'

Jane continued to keep her arms crossed. Unexpectedly, a vision of herself without any clothes, kneeling on top of him catapulted into her mind. She felt embarrassment flood through her body, she shook her head, and he touched her lightly on the elbow. 'What would you like?'

A triple vodka, extra strength, is what she thought in her head. 'A glass of white wine, please, but I'm only staying for one,' she replied, as she lowered herself back down into the chair and watched Oscar's back head off towards the bar. Whipping out her phone, she fired out a text to Lucie with her thumbs.

I changed my mind again. I'm in the pub with him now.

Oh! OK! Keep me in the loop. Text me if there's a problem.

With a queue at the bar, it was a good five or so minutes before Oscar was back at the table, he placed a glass of wine on a beer mat and sat down. He smiled. 'Sorry, they're short staffed.' He pointed to the wine. 'Okay?'

Jane took a sip of the wine, trying not to down it in one. 'Yes. Thank you.'

Oscar shifted his chair closer to the table and then held his pint up. 'Cheers.'

Jane wasn't sure if she wanted to toast anything but clinked his glass anyway. He wriggled in his seat and fiddled with the top of his glass. 'So, last night. I can explain it.'

Jane wasn't going to give him anything - she just raised her eyebrows. 'Yes? You've said that more than once now.'

'I used to be with Adele. We had Arlo...' He trailed off and looked up to the ceiling for a second, working out what to say. 'Then, she sort of went off with someone else.' He screwed up his face. 'Let me rephrase that; she didn't *sort of* go off with someone else, she went to live with someone else when Arlo was little.'

Jane didn't really know what to say so she just nodded.

'And that was that,' he stated.

Jane put her wine down and leant her elbow on the table and chin on her hand. 'Why didn't you just say that last night if you're not together? How hard would that have been? I don't get it. I really don't.'

Oscar exhaled and made a wincing face. 'She's difficult about it. I just couldn't be doing with the drama, and I didn't know what you were going to say, and I didn't really know what to actually call what happened between us.' He looked embarrassed and flicked his hand in between them. 'I don't make a habit of doing things like that as a rule.'

Jane swallowed. 'Me either.'

'Yeah, so, Adele. When she left, it was a relief for me. Then it all went pear-shaped between her and him, and she wanted to come back. She said that she'd made a "terrible mistake" as she put it.'

'Right, I see. You didn't want that?'

There was another very elongated sigh. 'No, I certainly did *not*. I'm not going to lie, I did consider it for Arlo's sake. Yeah, but no. It was never going to happen.'

'So how does that lead to last night? You're bothered about what she thinks?'

'She didn't take it well when she realised it was over and got all uppity about me seeing Arlo. It wasn't easy, plus there were loads of things to sort out and all that.'

'I see.'

'Meaning that last night, if I had said anything about what had happened in Edinburgh between us and who you were, she might well have flown off the handle. I don't care about what she thinks, but I didn't want Arlo to have to see that.'

Jane nodded. 'Hmm. What, so you can't see anyone else? Doesn't sound good.'

'Well, no, I can and I have, quite a few actually, but it's more that I sort of have to ease her into it.' He rolled his eyes a touch.

'Sounds tricky.'

'It is, which is why that happened last night. Which, I might add, I totally regretted once I was at home. What a complete idiot. I should have handled it differently, hence why I sent the text. I realised I was more than rude, especially after, well, you know what.'

Jane thought about how she'd felt sitting in front of the fire. 'You should have, yes. That did not make me feel good.'

'I'm sorry. So, what about Edinburgh?'

'What about it?' Jane replied, not giving anything away by the look on her face.

Oscar coughed. 'Very good from my end.'

Jane's face cracked into the tiniest of smiles and she felt the blood rush up her neck landing in a flush on her cheeks. 'Uh-huh. I wouldn't argue with that.'

Oscar took a gulp of his beer. 'I have to say, it was a shock to see you last night. Not the err… next part of the scenario I had in mind.'

'Yes, ditto.' Jane uncrossed her legs and sat back in her chair, her body language a little bit more open. 'You don't, umm, do things like that usually?' she asked.

'Bloody hell, no!' Oscar exclaimed.

Jane felt relief rush through her veins. 'So, now what?'

'Good question. I'm hardly an expert on the protocol after, ahem, something like that.' He chuckled, breaking the tension in the air and held up his beer. 'Another one of these and a cheese, onion, and salad cream sandwich?'

Jane giggled and felt her eyelashes doing the same strange thing they had done in the hotel. 'Works for me.'

W ith the wine softening Jane's edges, she began to ever-so-slowly let go. Flashes of the Edinburgh evening and how easy Oscar was to get on with, kept coming into her mind as she sat opposite him and the conversation flowed.

'What are you doing on Darling?' Oscar asked with an inquisitive look on his face. 'And how come you were there last night?'

'I could say the same to you.' Jane chuckled.

'I've just bought a place here.'

'Oh right, I see. And what about Adele?'

'No, no, they live over the water. Her grandmother has a retirement property here way over the other side.'

'Right.' Jane didn't want to say too much about her situation. 'I'm just looking after someone's house for a bit.' She'd tell him the details if and when the relationship went any further.

With her third drink, a soft one, Jane almost purred in plea-sure as the conversation ebbed and flowed. Satisfied he was telling the truth, she found herself happily chatting. She may or may not have fibbed here and there about her life and had had to fish around to make herself sound a little bit more interesting at some points, but Oscar appeared to be enjoying her company as much as she was his.

Time had seemed to both stand still as if they were the only two people in the pub and gone by in a flash. If Oscar had ulterior motives about the evening, or the thing about Adele and his son was not quite the truth, he was a master at deception. As far as she could make out, he was *genuinely* interested in her and *genuinely* nice. The fact that he was also *genuinely* gorgeous helped enormously.

The evening proceeded with easy, continuous chatting. Oscar asked a tonne of questions and seemed to be actually interested in Jane's life. She'd fibbed a bit more about a few things as the night had gone on and made her little existence sound not quite as small and found herself unravelling as she'd chatted to him. She'd even touched, unbelievably, on what had really happened with her husband, and as Oscar had strolled back over to the bar to get another round of drinks, she'd thought about Operation Le Romancer. She couldn't deny it; it was actually working. It was opening doors she hadn't even known were there. Leading her through them to a place where she was rather enjoying herself. Leading her to somewhere where she sat in the aura of a man she couldn't quite get enough of. She nodded to herself as she watched Oscar chatting casually with someone at the bar. Yes, this was what had been missing in her life. Not altogether him, but being out, doing something, chatting, learning, listening, *being*.

If she never even saw him again, she'd be forever grateful. Oscar and Edinburgh had not just opened invisible doors she hadn't been aware of, it was as if something had opened inside her too. Something that had closed many, many years prior when Jane had been saddled with not only grief, but debt, single parenthood, and mind numbing anxiety that had suffocated her every single day. All of those leading, ultimately, to where she was now and a very small life. But now the same doors that had slammed shut had slowly begun to open an inch. And as she sat in the pub relaxed, smiling and happy, she basked in the glorious golden light that had started to peep its way through the crack in the doors.

22

The next day, Jane woke up after a deep and solid night's sleep and relished in the evening before. She'd ended up staying in the pub with Oscar, they'd ordered fish and chips at the bar, and finished off the evening with a Cosmopolitan and a stroll home. As she put her slippers and dressing gown on and pottered around making breakfast, she thought about what had happened as he'd walked her to the door. For two people who had spent an abandoned night of passion in a business hotel, it had been stilted and awkward as the night came to a close. She'd stood under the light above the door, thanked him for the company, reached up and given him a quick peck on the cheek and said goodbye and that was that.

In the light of the morning after, as she sat in the courtyard under a blanket with tea and toast, she thought about how he'd seemed a bit awkward too. As she'd closed the door behind her, full of a lovely evening and happy thoughts, she'd almost yanked the door back open, scooted over the cobbles, grabbed him and pulled him up the steep stairs to bed. But something, she knew not what, had stopped her from inviting him in. And with a cup of rosehip tea, she'd sat in bed and mused the opportunity presenting itself to her. She'd batted it around her head like a tennis ball and wondered what would happen next and as she'd sat there, she'd realised that, in actual fact, that was the best thing of all. The not knowing was completely different to everything in her life; it felt sublimely delicious that whatever was coming around the corner was a complete mystery.

In the courtyard thinking about it all and contemplating whether or not to message him, she was too late when he got in first.

Lovely night. Thanks. Are you free this week at all to go for dinner?

Boom. The opportunity was happening. Operation Le Romancer was doing its thing. Jane read through the message twice, then she jumped up from her chair, formed both her hands into fists, raised her arms into a star shape, held them there, and squeezed her eyes tightly shut. 'Yessssss! Yes! Yes!' she squealed.

Did she want to go for dinner? Oh hang on a minute, let me see, she thought to herself with a chuckle. *I'll just have to consult my non-existent diary in my NOT SO small life.*

She sent a message back saying that she would love to go to dinner and a few minutes later it was locked in. Operation Le Romancer was most certainly in the room.

A couple of hours or so later, Jane walked into the Sailing Club with a smile on her face and spring in her step. Lucie was sitting in one of the wingback chairs with her head bent to her phone. Hearing the door open, Lucie looked up and beamed. 'Hello!' she said, jumping up and kissing Jane on the cheek.

'Hi.'

'How was it? I've been thinking about it all morning. He

wasn't a serial killer after all, seeing as you're still alive,' Lucie joked. 'All good?'

Jane shook her head in tiny little movements, a huge smile on her face. 'It was lovely. It ended up being such a nice evening. I'm so pleased I changed my mind and stayed.'

Lucie squeezed Jane's hand. 'I thought you were going to text me!'

'Sorry. The night sort of got away with itself and then it was late, and I didn't know if your phone was going to be on silent and I didn't want to wake you up.'

'It got late, ooh, interesting. So you didn't leave after one drink like you said you were going to?' Lucie said, rubbing her palms together.

'I did not. Nothing like it.'

Lucie shrugged her shoulders up. 'I cannot wait to hear all about it. Let's go and get a drink and a menu and discuss it all.'

Jane nodded, waited for a guest pass from reception and then followed Lucie through the club, past the ballroom to the bar. 'It's so nice in here. Look at the view today!' Jane exclaimed as she peered around at the old clubhouse where navy-blue and white tables and chairs faced out over the deck and a polished antique bar ran from left to right. 'It really is a gorgeous place for a wedding. Such a good choice.'

Lucie smiled as she shrugged her jacket off, and they stood at the bar. 'It is, and even better with the help of the wedding planner of my dreams.'

'Haha, I'll do my best. I can't tell you how happy I am for you after what old McKintock did,' Jane replied, referring to Lucie's ex-partner who she'd been with for years who had left Lucie, via a note, that he was trotting off to have a baby with somebody else.

'Who?' Lucie winked and wrinkled her eyebrows in faux confusion. 'I'm not sure who you are referring to. What was his name again? I can't quite remember.'

'I like it. Look how far you've come,' Jane acknowledged with a chuckle and a tiny little bit of envy inside at how well Lucie's predicament had turned out. Not that Jane wanted to get married or anything, of course she didn't.

'No idea who you mean.' Lucie chuckled. 'What are you having?'

'Something soft,' Jane said, running her eyes along to the fridges behind the bar. 'Pepsi or something.'

'Rightio, I think I'll have the same.'

A few minutes later, each with a drink in their hand, they shimmied in and out of the tables making for the doors out to a wide deck area straddling the beach. They stood looking out, contemplating whether or not it was warm enough to sit on the deck. Yanking the door open, Jane poked her head out. 'I think we'll just about be okay if we sit around the corner there out of the wind.'

As they made for the corner, strolling past Adirondack chairs topped with nautical blue striped cushions, Jane turned and looked out towards the sea. 'Not a bad spot to discuss what happened in the latest instalment of Janey and the Man From the Hotel story,' she joked.

Lucie put her drink down on a small outdoor coffee table and chuckled. 'Ooh, there's a name for it now. This is beyond exciting. The girls are going to be so jealous that I'm getting to hear this first. We should have done a broadcast from here. That would have been hilarious.'

'They will be,' Jane agreed.

'Come on then, spill the beans. I'm taking it that there was a plausible explanation for all that went on the other night, or should I say what didn't go on.'

Jane nodded. 'Yes. Adele, the woman from the other night, *was* his partner.'

'Was?'

'Yes, she left him when their little one, Arlo, was small.'

'Ouch.'

Jane shook her head. 'Well, actually, not quite, because apparently, Oscar was relieved when it happened.'

Lucie frowned. 'Really? Thing is, Luce, why didn't he just explain all that at the time? It doesn't add up, does it?'

'Hmm, I know it appears that way.'

'Sounds a bit iffy to me. '

'I asked the same thing.'

Lucie leant forward in her chair. 'And he said what?'

'Adele is tricky, apparently,' Jane stated.

'What does that mean?' Lucie asked, wrinkling up one side of her nose.

'I don't know much more than that. She wanted to go back to him and realised that she had made a mistake when she left him. Long story short, he said no, and it didn't go well.'

'Right. I see. I'm not sure if I'm buying it. Are you?' Lucie questioned.

'I am,' Jane stated. 'Unless I am a terrible judge of character and he is an out and out con artist, he's telling the truth.'

'But why all the weirdness on the beach? Why didn't he just acknowledge that he knew you?'

Jane screwed her face up. 'We did have a one-night stand, remember? He said he didn't even know how I felt about that, etcetera, etcetera.'

'I suppose it does make sense,' Lucie admitted with a nod. 'But he could have said he'd met you in the bar or something. He didn't have to let on about that bit of the evening.'

Jane batted her hand in front of her face. 'Anyway, we barely mentioned it again for the whole evening. It flew past. It was the same in the hotel. I'm not quite sure how, but it was just nice.'

Lucie started laughing. 'Was the end bit the same? Was it that nice? Is this where the story gets juicy?'

Jane's face changed, and she shook her head. 'Actually, it's not.'

'Oh! What happened then?'

'Dunno, it was really strange. He walked me home and it sort of got very awkward, as if none of the stuff in the hotel had happened at all. It was kind of embarrassing, yes that's the word.'

Lucie screwed up her nose. 'That *is* strange. On the other hand, it is understandable.'

'I know,' Jane agreed.

'What, so you didn't invite him in for a supposed coffee which was really an invitation for something else? I assumed that's what you were going to say was what happened next.'

Lucie shook her head. 'Nup, I did not. It didn't feel right. I left him at the doorstep.'

'Interesting. Very interesting. I thought you were going to say the opposite. I presumed this was the bit in the story where you told me you rotated your bra around your head again.' Lucie hooted.

'Nowhere near it. In fact, I almost shut the door in his face, I was so desperate to get inside,' Jane clarified. 'It was a bit weird. I'm not sure how I could tell, but I think he felt the same.'

'Okay, so now what?'

'So, now I'm going on a proper date. Go me.'

'Lalala! Whoopee!' Lucie squealed. 'This gets better and better. Where?'

'I don't know yet. A restaurant for dinner.'

Lucie rubbed her hands together. 'This is so exciting and all because of a strike and a bit of bad weather.'

Jane couldn't even believe the words that were coming out of her mouth as she said them. 'You have to let doors open for you, don't you?'

Lucie nodded and clinked her glass against Jane's. 'Yes, oh my word, Janey, you most certainly do.'

23

I t had been a drawn-out week in the days leading up to the dinner with Oscar, with more than a few problems with a case Jane was working on. Despite being a long way from the office, technology had done its job in keeping her very much in the loop on something that had gone wrong, and there had been a plethora of problems that unfolded from one to the next. Subsequently, Jane had woken up on the day of the date with Oscar with a head full of numbers and emails and had not put much thought into the evening at all. She'd barely had time to think about anything and with her unwashed hair scraped up on top of her head in a messy knot, a comfy old sweatshirt, and jogging bottoms she'd not come out of the study much for air. There had been a conveyor belt of conference calls and she'd drunk so much coffee, it was almost as if she'd had an IV of caffeine running directly into a vein.

As she put her mobile down and closed the corresponding shared document on her laptop for a break, she leaned her elbows on the desk and pushed the tips of her fingers into her eyebrows over and over again. She mentally went through her checklist of things she had to do before she could end her day and ran through the mammoth amount of goals she'd achieved whilst locked in the study that week. One thing was for sure, Jane Le Romancer was a powerhouse at work and her company got more than their pound of flesh and then some.

Locked in the study for work, however nicely decorated and quiet it was, had meant that some of the tension that had picked itself up and left her shoulders when she had arrived on Darling Island had plonked itself back on top. It sat there weighing her down. She pushed her chin backwards and forwards, felt the corresponding bones in her neck crack and then dropped her left ear to her shoulder and then did the same thing with the right. She was so frazzled, tired and tight from sitting at her computer that part of Jane wanted to cancel the date. Over dinner she would have to be all buzzy and zippy and pepper little white fibs through her narrative to make herself sound an incy bit more interesting and after the frantic work pace of the week, she didn't know whether she had the gumption to follow through with being Interesting Jane.

As she straightened her desk, picking up two dirty coffee mugs, she realised that she'd not really appreciated it before, but there were a few good things about a small life; mostly that sometimes you just didn't have to bother. You could finish your day just as you wished; bra off, hair up, carbs in, and coexist with a soft, cosy sofa and not have to exchange a word with anyone at all. Sometimes it was quite nice being small.

She wondered how a text would go down.

Oh, hey, Oscar. Yeah, about tonight. Just wondering if you wouldn't mind popping over instead. Any chance you could bring a cheese, onion & salad cream sandwich, two rounds if poss, white bread from the bakery on Darling St??? Sweet. I'll be in my ratty old pyjamas & not sure if I'm up for any bra flinging tbh. Thx so much. Janey.

Jane chuckled to herself, strolled out into the courtyard, and held her head up to the sky for some fresh air. She'd have to get a move on, there was a requirement for some primping and fluffing to get herself over the hump of feeling small and grey. She had no clue what to wear and needed to do all sorts of prepping for what might come. It was all very well jumping into bed with someone in a hotel room, but what happened when you were meeting up for real?

As she stood in the courtyard doing shoulder rolls and clasping her hands behind her to stretch her back before she went back into the study, she vowed not to get bogged down in worry about what to wear that evening. He'd probably not even notice and the whole thing likely wouldn't go anywhere anyway. Just like her actual life.

As she rested her hands on her knees and stretched her shoulders down from left to right, and thought more about how the last time she'd got ready to go out she'd felt like a turnip, she tried to banish the thoughts from her head and talk herself up. She was a modern woman who was not going to value herself on how she looked. No, she would not go down that route. She would have a nice long shower, do her hair and make-up, put on something pretty and comfortable and be done with it. She would arrive at the pub in a flurry of modern self-confidence, in a swish of perfume, and a smiley face as if she regularly attended casual little dinners with men she'd randomly slept with in a different country. She would push away all images of a relationship and would concentrate on the fact that this was a friendly meeting, whereby Oscar may or may not become a casual friend she saw every now and then. Yes, this was just an informal little dinner between two friends, nothing more, nothing less.

Strolling back into the kitchen, she made a salad cream sandwich, poured a long glass of cordial, went into the sitting room, and sat there thinking about the date with Oscar. In her comfy old clothes, the sofa folded around her and all her bravado and ideas about a friendly, casual relationship, maybe with friendly, casual sex began to slowly dwindle away and she had asked herself quite what she thought she was doing. What was Jane the Widow as she often presumed people referred to her as even thinking? As she snuggled back into the cushions and the salad cream sandwich went down, more and more doubts crept in. It would be much easier to just stay on the sofa in her dressing gown. Just like she always did.

Later, as she plonked herself back at her laptop, the more the afternoon wore on, the more she began to feel jittery about the whole thing. All sorts of things were trudging through her brain and every time she stopped pouring over the numbers on her screen, she thought of another reason why she would be much better off to shelve the Oscar thing altogether. Not only that, indeed shelve trying to make her life less small. She could just settle, like she always did, and stay with the devil she knew. Just so much easier.

As a mixture of anticipation, nerves and questions ran through her veins, every time she felt the jitters, she made another half round of cheese, onion and salad cream sandwich in an attempt to numb things. Even at about two-thirds of the way through a loaf of bread, she had to admit to herself that the sandwiches were not working at all in comfort eating her way to the date and by early evening she'd talked herself down into a hole and didn't want to come out. Forcing herself to shut off her computer, she dragged herself up the steep narrow stairs and stood in the shower letting the hot water soak away her apprehension and the unremitting call of comfort coming from the cashmere throws on Catherine's sofa. As she stood there in the hot water, she contemplated Oscar and thoughts ran through her head at a hundred miles an hour.

What if he realises I'm not very exciting? Jane the Widow. A forensic accountant? Blah. Ahhh, will it be awkward at the end? Will he expect me to jump into bed with him and perform? What if I do that, and I'm such a letdown?

All the questions swilled around as she smoothed conditioner into the ends of her hair and then commanded herself not to mull it over. She made a pact with herself that she wasn't allowed to think about it until she was out of the bathroom with her hair dried and curled and her make-up on. Once she was in a fit state to go, then she'd think about it a bit more.

When her hair was done, make-up on and she was dressed, she stood in front of the mirror with a downward cast face. She'd decided on slim-leg trousers which could be dressed up or down and dressed them up with a cream pretty billow-sleeved cutwork blouse. She stood sideways onto the mirror, took a gigantic inhale, sucked her stomach in, and pushed her ribs out. Then, looking over her right shoulder, she peered behind her at her bum. Massive. Absolutely gigantic. What in the name of goodness? More pumpkin than turnip. She couldn't go out with that in tow.

Whipping the trousers off, she did precisely what she told herself she wasn't going to do and started to desperately rummage through not only the wardrobe, but the few remaining things she had left in her case. Three outfits in, she sat on the bed, her hands in her lap. Dumpy, cellulite-y, saggy in various places, and though small in her actual existence, not in the size of her posterior. Jane wanted to cry. Mostly because she felt *pathetic*. There was no doubt in her mind that Oscar wasn't standing in front of a mirror examining the size of his behind. First and foremost, he really didn't need to and second, he'd probably have a shower, throw on a shirt, possibly spritz a splash of aftershave and head out the door. He wouldn't be trying on or thinking about outfits and whether or not he should have run to the shop to buy a fresh mascara.

Not happy with anything, she put the black trousers back on and examined herself again, fluffed an extra layer of radiance-giving blusher on her cheeks and checked the time and let out a shriek. 'Ahhhhhhhh.'

She'd now lost so much time cavorting around in front of

the mirror trying to work out why her bottom seemed to have both grown *and* dropped at the same time she was close to being late. And Jane Le Romancer was never late.

Nearly tumbling head first as she tried to run down the steep stairs, she slipped her feet into wedge shoes, grabbed her jacket, yanked her bag from the dresser, slammed the door behind her and began to leg it for the tram. Finally arriving at the empty tram stop, her phone buzzed with a video call from Tally. Answering in light of Tally's divorce problems, her chest rising and falling, her breathing hard, she pressed the button and waited as Tally came onto the screen.

'Just calling to say hope it goes well. Oh wow, yes, super, you look really nice.'

'Do I? Crikey, Tals, honestly there's something wrong with me. I told myself I wasn't going to do it and then I spent ages looking in the mirror and my inner brat continued to chastise me on the size of my bum. I mean, really? I thought those days were over? I thought that was a teenage thing. Why, oh why, do I continue to do it to myself?'

Tally shook her head. 'If I had the answer to that, I would be very rich. We all do it. It's been brainwashed into us by years and years of media abuse.'

'It's pathetic, and there I was thinking I was hippity-hoppity body positive,' Jane stated.

Tally burst out laughing. 'Too funny.'

'I've been having second thoughts about this all day. What was I thinking? I'm all sorts of nervous.'

'I bet there have been a few salad cream sandwiches in the vicinity of that mews house.'

Jane waved her hand in front of her face. 'You don't even want to know.'

Tally burst out laughing. 'Many?'

'There may have been a few rounds, yes. And now I'm

roasting hot because I messed around trying on things to make my bum look smaller when it was never going to be.'

'How exciting is it though, Janey?'

Jane's face suddenly dropped and she looked down to her armpit. 'Ahh, I'm like really nervous; I think I might be sweating through my jacket. Oh my goodness, can you see it?' Jane said, angling her phone down towards her chest.

Tally squinted towards the screen. 'I don't think so, hmm, maybe...'

'You don't think so! Ahhhh! Sheesh, I'm going to turn up with big damp patches under my arms along with having my gigantic pumpkin bum in tow.'

'Stop the negative self-talk. You'll be fine. Where has this even come from? You've already been out with him twice!'

'I know, but the first one was, well, you know what that was, and the second one wasn't a date as such, it was more a clarification...'

'I see, not,' Tally joked.

'Why am I putting myself through this? Why? I should have just stayed small.'

Tally frowned. 'Stayed small? What? What does that mean? Small? I've never heard you say that before. You're not small.'

Jane looked flustered and batted her hand in front of the screen. 'Nothing, nothing, look, sorry, I'm going to have to go. I need to pull myself together a bit.'

'Yeah, yeah, take some big breaths. You'll be more than fine.' Tally chuckled. 'It's not as if he hasn't seen everything anyway.'

'Ahhh, oh dear, oh dear, that's what I'm worried about! Flipping heck Tals, you're not helping.'

'Put a message in the WhatsApp group while you're there. We'll all be with you virtually.' Tally laughed again. 'Most of all have fun, Janey. You deserve it. See ya. Oh, and remember to fling your bra.'

~

Jane took off her jacket, puffed air into her blouse as she stood at the tram stop, and slowed her breathing down. Five or so minutes later, as a blue and white tram slowly trundled to a stop, she got on, sat right at the front, and stared out the window as it made its way through Darling. Arriving at the correct stop, the bell rang as the tram slid away and Jane, with her jacket over her bag, walked along in the sea air telling herself to remain cool for her underarm's sake.

Operation Le Romancer opening doors, Operation Le Romancer opening doors, she repeated over and over to herself as she walked along the road past Doctors on Darling until she could make out where she was meeting Oscar. From a distance, she could see him in a navy-blue jacket and jeans standing peering into a shop window. *Operation Le Romancer,* she said again to herself as she arrived, plastering a huge smile on her face to hide her nerves. She couldn't quite fathom why, but this time meeting him for an actual date it felt all kinds of different.

'Hi, hello, lovely evening,' she said in a bright voice, sounding a whole lot more casual and relaxed than she was inside where she felt as if a freight train was running up and down her veins pumping her blood so fast she was going to explode at any second. She realised she was doing the thing with her hair again as she looked up at Oscar. He kissed her hello on the cheek, and surprising herself, instead of pulling away awkwardly as she had done after the pub, she stepped forward and put her arm onto his back and gave him a hug. As she breathed him in, he matched her enthusiastic greeting, put his hand on her hip and in one fell swoop, she relaxed. She looked up into his eyes and felt the same thing as she had in the hotel; an unknown thrill of what might arise.

'I walked from the other side, lovely evening but there's still a nip in the air.' Oscar asked, 'Have you got a jacket?'

Jane pulled her bag and jacket around to the front. 'Yep, it was warm on the tram.'

Oscar pointed along the pavement to where they were going, and Jane strolled along beside him as they walked away from Darling Street. As they ambled and fell into step, he chatted and asked a few questions; about her house in London, about her son and work. The conversation batted back and forth until they arrived at a small cluster of shops at a crossroads where a café, sweet shop and bistro stood on each side of the road. A gorgeous old corner shop turned restaurant with a white front door with brass plates, old entrance bell, and tessellated tiled floor stood in front of them.

'Ooh, it looks nice. Nearly as nice as the pub the other day,' Jane said as Oscar pushed open the door and gestured for Jane to go in.

Inside tiny tables were lined up all the way along the left-hand side. A shelved bar heaving with bottles was wedged in on the right and at the back a tiny narrow outdoor courtyard was lit up with white lights. Cosy, homey, lovely, not fancy. The sort of place you might get a really nice old-school lasagne, no streams of elaborate drizzled sauce on the edge of oversized plates. A vague feeling that you could well be in someone's home. It was just the sort of place Jane was at ease. She loved that he'd chosen it as a place to bring her. Her shoulders dropped for the first time that day.

They stood by the bar and waited until a young waiter with a beard tapped an iPad and looked up in question. 'Table for two?'

Oscar nodded. 'I've booked in the name of Oscar.'

The man ran his eyes down the screen. 'Great, follow me.'

As they sat down, Oscar smiled. 'Fancy a glass of bubbles?'

Jane felt more of her nerves slip away as she nodded. 'Yes. Thank you, that would be lovely.'

Oscar looked up at the waiter. 'A bottle of house sparkling for us, cheers. Champagne if you've got it.'

Jane sat back and made herself comfortable as the bubbles arrived super quickly and the waiter poured their glasses. Oscar picked up his flute and held it aloft. 'Champagne to apologise for the other night and to say thank you for the night before that.'

Jane felt herself blush, heat burning in her cheeks, but she answered boldly. 'I'll drink to that. Cheers, Oscar.'

'I wonder where the night will take us?' Oscar joked and laughed as he took a sip of his champagne, clinked Jane's glass, and picked up the menu. 'The food here is great. Is there anything you don't like?' Oscar asked. 'I'm not seeing many salad cream sandwiches on here, though.'

Jane laughed to herself, if only he knew, she'd had the best part of a loaf of bread that afternoon and had an emergency sandwich carefully wrapped in foil in her bag. She was so bloated she could barely think about food. Hungry she most definitely was not. There was no way she was going to tell him that though. 'I'm ravenous. I'll eat anything really, but I'm not a lover of lamb,' Jane said, as she scrolled down the menu. 'This all looks delicious.'

Jane drained her champagne much quicker than she should have done and revelled in the slow magic that started to wipe away the anxious feelings of the afternoon. Enjoying the beautiful restaurant, most of her ragged nerves from earlier had evaporated as Oscar regaled her with tales of all sorts. She sat lost in it all; forgetting for a moment Jane the Widow, forgetting having to fib to sound interesting, forgetting how small her own life actually was. With this man in front of her and the bubbles slipping down nicely, she didn't feel quite as small anymore. Perhaps there was more to Jane Le Romancer after all.

She sat there looking at him, getting lost in his eyes and thinking about all the little daydreams she'd had since he'd unknowingly opened a door for her. Before he'd plonked himself down in front of her in a bland hotel bar and mistaken her for someone else. Now she was having ludicrous daydreams about relationships, house swapping with strangers and examining how much her bum had slipped down to meet the tops of her thighs.

'I'm just going to pop to the loo,' Jane said and gathering her bag, she pushed out her chair, sucked in her stomach and made her way through the restaurant to the toilets. Once in the safety of the cubicle, she hooked her bag over the hook, leant on the back of the door, and furiously texted the Hold Your Nerve girls group.

I'm here. He's blimming gorgeous! She stood and waited, seeing that Anais was messaging back.

I've been wondering how it was going. We all have!!! How are you feeling?

Don't know! I can hardly fit any food in. I've been eating sandwiches all afternoon b/c I was so nervous.

Hah hah, course you were. How many rounds in your handbag?

Shut up!!! What do I do if he wants to come back??

Do it.

Jane cupped her right hand over her mouth and blew breath into her palm and quickly tried to sniff at the same time.

**** I reek of onion. It's been making its presence known out the other end too!!!

The screen flashed as Lucie started typing.

As if he'll care about that. Overthinking, Janey.

Rich to you, Luce!

Tally arrived online. *Go for your life is my advice. In fact, I'm commanding you to do it. You only live once. Ask me how I know that?*

Yes. Anais agreed.

Have a good old-fashioned night of bonking, just like you did on the first date, hahaha, Libby added.

Ahhh. I'll let you all know later. Xxx

Hold. Your. Nerve.

Once Jane was back at the table, after having tried to do something about her onion breath in the toilet, the evening moved swiftly on and she felt as if little zaps of electrical current were running between her and Oscar; when he caught eyes with her, when she said something that made him laugh, when he deftly caught her glass as she nearly knocked it over.

But most of all, as Operation Le Romancer powered into full swing, Jane felt as if, all of a sudden, she was starting to do something interesting with her life. And above everything else, that was the best thing of all.

24

A few weeks or so later, Jane had been sitting at the little desk in the study since her alarm had shrilly awoken her earlier that morning. With her head down and her laptop open, she'd been lost in a maze of work that had sent her around and around, not giving her time to think about anything other than where the numbers didn't add up. The time had flown by since the dinner date, and her text thread and time she'd spent with Oscar had continued to move on at an alarming rate. Jane Le Romancer was enjoying it very much.

Finishing off an email, she closed her laptop and walked into the kitchen. As she filled coffee into the top of the Baccarat coffee pot and put it on the Aga, she thought more about what was going on with the two of them. They'd been out more than a few times since the dinner, and she still couldn't quite believe how it had all seemed to magically appear in her life out of nowhere. She wondered where it was going to go, and more importantly, what she wanted to happen next. If indeed she wanted anything to materialize at all. The best thing about it in its own fabulous little way was the uncertainty of not knowing what was going to happen.

For someone who a few months earlier knew how every single second of every single day was going to pan out, she relished the uncertainty. For so long she'd been able to predict just how her whole week, her whole month, her whole year would go. With the Oscar thing, her future was not quite as mapped out; it pointed in all manner of different ways and even if it went nowhere, she was somehow, oddly, fine with that too.

While the coffee pot burbled away, she popped a cinnamon bun in to warm and stood looking through the French windows into the courtyard, thinking about everything that had happened since she'd met Oscar in Edinburgh. Meeting him had been the start of a whole new chapter in her life. It was as if part of her life had lain dormant for years and now was ready to pop up its head again and get ready to party, taking her along for the ride.

Once the coffee was ready and the bun warmed, she pushed open the courtyard doors and stood surveying the area. Whoever it was who had originally planned the courtyard had clearly studied its pros and cons; the little patch of sun that fell deftly onto the table and chairs, the trickling water feature on the right creating the perfect ambience, and the two large potted olive trees rustling in the breeze. An idyllic little spot, just right for an alfresco candlelit dinner for two and Oscar coming over that night.

With her coffee mug nestled into the crook of her arm, she stood with her head cocked to the side, squinting at the little table tucked into the corner. Five or so minutes later, her coffee was finished and she'd dragged a smaller table over and placed it to the side. Then she'd gone around the house finding lanterns and had gathered them into a grouping around the little spot. Next, she'd found fairy lights in a Christmas box in the cupboard under the stairs, plugged them in to check that they worked and wound them in and out of the olive trees. On the spot above the table, she'd added an oversized rattan heart also found under the stairs.

Following Catherine's instructions, she'd added paper and kindling to the chiminea and crossed her fingers it would light. As she pottered around setting everything up, she folded two throws onto the back of the chairs and added hurricane candles alongside the table whilst she thought about her little life. How when her husband had died and she'd found out the truth, it had been like, somehow, he'd drawn the life out of her too. As she smoothed a flax linen tablecloth onto the table, she realised with a jolt that her life had been in freefall pretty much ever since. Down and down it had gone, until there hadn't been much left at all. The first few years after he'd gone had been a scrambling of trying to keep herself together, the next few more of the same just about keeping her head above water, and then her career had turned a corner and it had all very slowly started to get better. But, despite how it looked on the outside and having everything nicely under control, Jane had simply fallen into the role of someone juggling all the balls, doing all the grown-up things all of the time. Actual Jane, the person, had fallen by the wayside. Actual Jane was lying in a muddy ditch waiting for someone to turn her life back on. And it was Oscar who had been that person. He'd popped into her life by way of a bit of fog and a cancelled plane and switched the switch, whereupon she'd emerged from the ditch and was slowly but surely flicking off the mud, becoming Jane again.

As she pottered around thinking about Oscar, with little butterflies inside, she realised that somehow in the last few years she'd been purposely keeping her life small. A small life meant no problems, a small life delivered itself without any hurt, and a small life meant simplicity. But now she was ready. Ready for new things, different experiences, and candlelit dinners in courtyards with lovely men. Bigger things were on the horizon.

As she finished off the table, setting plates and wine glasses, she smiled to herself. She wanted everything about the night to be dreamy and perfect, just like it had been a few nights before. Jane Le Romancer was ready. She no longer wanted to be small.

Jane put the phone down from her son. He was having a whale of a time and she'd known he was more than okay when he'd surreptitiously asked for money. She'd put her phone on speaker and transferred a healthy little lump sum as they'd been chatting. When she'd got off the phone, she wondered when she'd be mentioning to him that she was seeing someone, if that was indeed what she was doing.

Looking around at the courtyard, she was pleased with her efforts. It looked lovely in the corner with the chiminea lit as soft plumes of smoke drifted off and up into the early evening sky. Jane hoped the surroundings and the food would lead to a good night. More than a good night. Much more. As she made her way through the house and up the steep stairs, she surveyed the bedroom; the bed had been changed, everything was sparkling, the little lamps glowed and it was ready for anything that might come its way. Not that she was hoping for that. *Oh, maybe just a teensy bit.*

After a quick hot shower, she took the new black silky camisole she'd had expressed delivered and slipped it on over the matching bra. As she looked at the pretty delicate lace edging, she smiled to herself; it was a far cry from the underwear she'd been wearing in Edinburgh. There was one good thing about that; the only way was up.

After doing her hair, lavishing herself with one of Catherine's luxurious body lotions, and spritzing perfume not just behind her ears but anywhere else she thought it might be enjoyed, she gazed down from the window to the fire flickering in the chiminea in the courtyard. Everything was set up; delicious cooking smells wafted up from the Moroccan chicken in the tagine and in the corner of the bedroom chamomile essential oil pumped from a diffuser on the bedside table. Operation Le Romancer, the Dinner for Two episode, was in motion and Jane was ready to go.

Just as she was chastising herself for even a glancing thought at a salad cream sandwich to soothe her anticipation nerves, she heard a gentle knocking on the front door. Scooting down the stairs, she opened the door and felt herself stumble into the dreamy waft of Oscar. The evening had got off to a very good start. The eyes, him, the prettiness, all stood there in the doorway with a bunch of flowers and a bottle of wine. Lovely, glorious Oscar in all his fine form. Jane tried to remain casual, breezy, and nonchalant as she propped the door open wide for him to come in. What she really wanted to do was chuck a bucket of water over the chiminea, dump the tagine and the flowers in the bin, and drag him up the stairs to the freshly made chamomile-scented bed.

'Evening. Wow, you look amazing! Are you expecting someone special?' Oscar joked as he stepped in and kissed her on the cheek. He looked around and peered into the courtyard as Jane led him to the kitchen. 'This place is lovely and whatever you're cooking smells even better. I think half of Darling will be able to smell it. What are we having?'

Jane couldn't give two hoots about the food. She was much more interested in the end part of the evening. She played along and pointed to the tagine. 'Moroccan chicken. I should clarify, my version of Moroccan chicken.'

'Nice pot. What, umm, is that?' Oscar frowned at the tagine.

'It's a tagine. It's Catherine's tagine,' Jane clarified.

'Right, I'm none the wiser. What's in it is more what I'm interested in. Moroccan chicken will do me.' Oscar chuckled. 'I'm ravenous. What's in it?'

Ravishing more like, Jane thought to herself as she stared at him, images of the night in the hotel rushing into her brain. She wondered what it would be like running her fingers up and down his back. Would it feel different than it had in the hotel? Nicer? She didn't really care and imagined it anyway.

'Hello? Jane?' Oscar said, waving his hand in front of her face, breaking her daydream.

'Oh, yes, sorry. It's just chicken with saffron, garlic, ginger, paprika, preserved lemon, and olives, seeing as you asked. You pop it in there and, yeah, it quite simply ends up lovely.'

'Whatever it is, I'm good with it. There's not much I don't eat, as you know.'

Jane nodded. 'I hope it tastes as good as it smells.'

Oscar touched Jane on the arm as he sat down at the kitchen island, and Jane went to walk around to put the flowers in a vase. 'You really do look lovely this evening.'

Jane tried to appear breezy and confident at the compliment as she pulled the brown paper from the flowers. She had to laugh to herself; there had been no stressing about what she was wearing. Once the fabulous underwear was in place, she'd just pulled on a pretty top Lucie had made her with jeans, put her hair in a ponytail, did her usual makeup and left it at that. 'Thank you. So do you. What would you like to drink?' Jane opened the fridge. 'Beer, wine, gin, Baileys.' She reached into the fridge and pulled out a bottle of sparkling wine. 'Bubbles? They might be nice to start with. Hang on, actually, there's a bottle of Campari in the pantry I spied earlier. How about that?'

'I'll give it a go,' Oscar replied. 'I don't think I've ever had it before.'

Jane took the Campari from the pantry, poured two small glasses and handed one to Oscar. Her hand brushed his as he took the glass from her and she hid a gasp as the buzz between them felt as if fire was running from her fingers.

'Cheers,' he said, holding up his glass. 'We seem to be doing a lot of glass clinking, you and me.'

Jane's eyes widened, it had been so much more than a bit of glass clinking for her. 'Ha, yes we have indeed.'

'It's all, err, moving quite fast.'

Jane nodded, popping her drink down on the table and putting a bowl of olives between them. 'Yep.'

'Anyway, cheers. I'm good with that if you are?'

Was she good with that? Was the sky blue? Again she pretended to be casual, breezy, nonchalant. She waved her glass around. 'Yeah, yeah.'

'So, what's the go-to with this place?' Oscar asked.

'Like what?'

'How long are you here and everything? You said it was three months.'

'I'm here, yes, for three months. That was the initial plan, anyway. As I said before, I can work from home anyway so it doesn't make a huge amount of difference and when I went into the office last week, it was no drama to get the fast train once I was there.'

'Right. Yep, agree, that train makes a world of difference.'

'Are you missing your house?' Oscar asked as he took a sip of his drink.

Jane shook her head. 'Not really. I miss the routine of my life a little bit, but no.' She started to tell him more about her house in London. How she loved being able to get into the bustle of the city easily but still lived on a quiet little road. They chatted about some of the excellent London pubs and the Albert Hall. She kept it to herself that in reality, though she was a stone's throw from all the goings on of the capital, really she didn't do that much at all.

Oscar popped an olive into his mouth. 'I know what you mean about the routine of living somewhere. You get to know stuff.'

'Yep, you do, even though you don't realise it. Like I used to talk to the woman at the tube station every morning.'

'Yeah, yeah. I suppose it takes a while to get the ins and outs of a place.'

'It does.' Jane changed the subject, moving it onto Oscar's ex. She'd been wanting to ask him every time they'd met up but hadn't wanted to seem too bothered. 'How is it with you and Adele?'

Oscar waved his hand in front of his face. 'Fine.' He then indicated back and forth between the two of them. 'I told her about us so it's out in the open from the start.'

About us! What the! So there is an us. Excellent. Jane nodded and swallowed. 'Good. So she's not as tricky as you said she might be.'

Oscar chuckled. 'It's none of her business, but I know how she works now and for Arlo's sake it's always good to just keep her on side.' He cleared his throat. 'I, err, elaborated a bit on the initial thing. No, not elaborated, I should say that I told a white lie.'

Welcome to my world, Jane thought and looked back at him with a frown, confused. 'What did you say?'

'I just said we met when we were away on business and had a drink and left it at that. Which is technically what happened.'

Jane raised her eyebrows. That was putting it one way. 'Yes, thanks. I don't really, well, you know.'

'Want to broadcast the other thing?'

'Yep, precisely. Not that it's anyone's business. Okay. Glad that's sorted,' Jane replied and lifted the lid of the tagine, giving it a stir. 'Right, this looks ready, and I've set everything up in the courtyard. I hope it's warm enough out there. Let's go out there, shall we?'

~

An hour or so later, the Moroccan chicken was long gone. Sitting in the corner of the courtyard with the chiminea glowing and lights twinkling, the conversation had flowed and Jane was thoroughly enjoying herself. She had lit all the little tea lights in the lanterns, the water feature burbled and a chocolate cake with two wedges missing was perched on a white cake stand between them. Oscar nodded to the cake and gesticulated to the kitchen. 'Bit of a cook on the quiet. That was delicious.'

'Ahh, I dabble.' Jane laughed, she went to say that she loved to entertain but rarely had anyone over and stopped herself just in time. 'I don't like anything fancy.'

'That was plenty fancy enough for me,' Oscar replied good-naturedly and drained the last of his drink. 'Delicious.'

'Thank you. I try my best,' Jane joked.

'So, you're looking forward to the evening in Darlings?' Oscar asked, referring to the tickets to a special dinner they had booked in Darlings café.

'I am.' Jane pointed her index finger to the house next door. 'The neighbour here says it's a really good night.'

'Can't be worse than the Twilight Market,' Oscar replied, laughing.

Jane flushed, remembering how awful she'd felt sitting in the cool air coming in off the sea and the flames flickering onto Oscar and Adele's face. 'Not a night to remember, no.'

'No. Then again, it did lead to this,' Oscar stated, sweeping his right hand around the courtyard.

'True.'

Jane's phone pinged from her pocket. 'Sorry, that's my son. It's a funny time for him to message me. I'll just check.' She looked down and read through.

'Everything okay?'

'Yep, he's clearly had a few drinks, but everything is fine. I transferred some money earlier, he's just saying thanks.' Jane adjusted herself in her chair, picked up her drink again, and surveyed the courtyard. 'Well, that was very nice.'

Oscar agreed, glancing at his watch. 'Yeah, it's flown by. That always seems to happen with you.'

Jane nodded, it had. As she sat there gazing around, everything felt glowy inside. It was like she'd been bathed in some sort of Oscar Light and she felt more content than she had in years. Chatting in the courtyard of Catherine's mews house, having a nice meal, good conversation, and having all the feels about Oscar was lovely. They both stared up at the stars for a moment until she broke the companionable silence between them. 'Who would have thought when we met in that hotel that we would be here at the other end of the country sitting in this courtyard?' Jane mused. 'What a funny old turn up for the books.'

'I never would have picked it, no.'

'If it hadn't been for the striking baggage handlers, fog...' Jane trailed off.

'Yes, I thought that the other day. How much was I complaining though? I was not happy when I plonked myself down in front of you.' Oscar chuckled, putting his empty glass down on the table and stretching out his legs in front of him.

'Another one?' Jane offered, pointing to his glass.

'Think that might be me done for the night, actually.'

'Coffee. Cup of tea?'

Oscar chuckled. 'Thought you'd never ask.'

Jane pushed herself up from the chair and called out over her shoulder as she walked in. 'I'll bring out a pot.'

When Jane came back outside with a teapot and two mugs on a tray, Oscar was sitting on the other side of the courtyard on the outdoor sofa peering into the water feature. 'I was just investigating this.'

Jane put the tray down and sat down next to him on the sofa.

'It sounds lovely, doesn't it?' She passed over a mug of tea. 'There you go.'

'Thanks. No salad cream sandwich with it?' Oscar joked as he took the mug.

Jane giggled. 'I don't think even I could fit one in at the moment. Never say never though. I've been known to have one just before I go to bed. In actual fact, at all and any time of the day.'

'You are funny. Funny and lovely,' Oscar said and rested his hand gently on her leg.

Jane smiled and turned her head to him and looked into his eyes. 'Thank you. So are you.'

'I was determined to get that sandwich for you that night in the hotel. I haven't told you this bit though; I actually slipped the waiter a few notes to get it sorted.'

Jane giggled. 'What? You didn't let on at the time! You did that for me?'

'Yeah, I was wondering who this gorgeous woman was who was making my heart do all sorts of things, and I was saying to myself that if it was the last thing I did, I would get the sandwich sorted.'

Jane didn't know what to say. She gazed at him as more of the feelings she'd had every time she'd seen him raced around her body, whooshing through her veins. She put her hand on his and smiled, surprised at how all the confidence from the night in the hotel had vanished, and she wasn't quite sure what to do next. She'd been so small for so long, being with this man and wanting to do more than fling her bra at him had taken her by surprise.

Oscar put his mug down, pulled her close to him, put his arm around her waist and kissed her gently on the lips. Jane felt her whole body release and relax as she lost herself in the kiss as the gentle sound of the water fountain trickling went through her ears.

She inched herself closer so their legs were together and stroked her hand up and down his broad shoulders as Oscar pulled her even closer and caressed the back of her neck. He started to press her, more insistent, and she slid her hands to the top of his jeans.

Jane Le Romancer was lost in the glow, the rushing blood pounding through her veins, the excitement of it all searing around her body. It felt amazing as, in the flickering light, she realised that Oscar had come into her life and all of a sudden, just like that, she was no longer quite as small.

25

J ane strolled along Darling Street feeling nothing short of fabulous. After an early start with a Zoom breakfast meeting she'd been locked in the study working, had called it a day around one, and had indulged in a long walk taking in the back streets of Darling. Waiting at the tram stop not far from the busy bustling bakery, she stood in the warm sunshine observing Darling going about its business. Watching one of the old blue and white liveried trams slide along to the stop, she waited until it had come to a full halt and stepped on.

'Hello. How are you?' Shelly the conductor asked with a friendly smile and inquiring eyes.

'Good, thanks, you?'

'I'm well. I'm just back from a week off, actually.'

'Ooh, lovely. Did you get off to anywhere nice?'

Shelly helped a woman with a buggy as she chatted. 'A bit of a staycation and days out in the end. I was thinking of trotting off to France but with the lovely weather, I decided to stay at home. It was one of my better decisions. Can you really beat good old England when the sun is shining?'

'Ahh, right, good idea. Saves all the messing about travelling too. It's a nightmare at the moment at the airports and the ports. Have you seen what's going on in Dover? Queues for miles.'

Shelly stood with her hand on the back of one of the seats. 'I know, I decided I'd rather steer well clear. I booked a full deep house clean on my last day of work, got a seven-day pack of those dinner things, and sent my washing to the laundry so everything was done and dusted. Talk about a treat.'

'Goodness, that's pro-level staycationing,' Jane acknowledged. 'I like how you roll.'

Shelly nodded. 'The thing is, I knew if I didn't do that I'd just end up doing stuff at home the whole week. I'm not one for sitting around in mess. I like my place shipshape.'

'True. I've done that before when I'm meant to be taking a week off. What did you get up to?'

'All over the place! I found all sorts of things on Darling I'd never seen before and had a couple of days out on the other side of the water. Took a ride on the fast train and all sorts. Yes, it was a thoroughly nice week. I need to do it more often and get out and explore my own backyard.'

'Good to hear.'

'How about you? What have you been up to?'

Oh, you know, doing all sorts of things with Oscar, staying overnight in a hotel on a whim, buying fancy underwear, going on dates. You know, stuff like that. Jane thought in her head but smiled noncommittally. There was no way she was giving away her business on the tram. 'Oh, this and that. Mostly work. I've been keeping myself busy.'

Shelly nodded with a twinkle in her eye. 'I see. Sounds like you've not been up to much.'

Jane had a funny feeling Shelly knew exactly what she had been up to, but she didn't play along. She was not going to be telling anyone anything yet about the ins and outs of her love life. 'No, not really. I've got a lot on at work, so that has been keeping me occupied and on the computer a lot of the time.'

'Right you are,' Shelly said as she moved over towards the front of the tram. 'It's always good to be busy, I believe. You know, keeps you out of trouble.'

Jane nodded as Shelly walked to the front of the tram. 'You're not wrong there.'

Twenty or so minutes later, Jane made her way to Darlings café and smiled affectionately as she approached. There was something about the little place that made you feel comfy even before you'd ventured inside. The window boxes full of flowers seemed to smile, a sweet old dog was snoozing under one of the outdoor heaters lazily opening one eye as Jane got close, and an upside-down timber fruit crate displayed a huge basket of freshly picked rhubarb, besides it was a neat stack of trays of eggs.

A bell tinkled overhead as Jane walked in and she looked around with a smile on seeing Mr Cooke sitting in the far right corner with a group of old men playing cards. A couple of women sat with their laptops open, chatting and a table of swimmers sat with steaming bowls of coffee and little white baskets. The café was filled with a low hum of chatter, the scent of freshly ground coffee beans and cinnamon buns filled the air, and there was a hiss of steam from the coffee machine at the back.

Evie, the café owner, scooted up with a smile as Jane looked around for a seat. 'Hi, Jane, how are you?'

'Well, thanks. Busy, I should say.'

Evie gestured her hand around to the tables. 'We've just quietened down a bit, you picked a good time.'

'Perfect, thank you.'

'Lucie's just popped over to the bakery, she should be back any minute now. Can I get you a coffee?'

'Love one, thanks,' Jane replied despite having caffeinated herself since early morning, she was ready for a Darlings coffee which took the consumption of caffeine to a whole new level.

'Basket? We've only got a couple of lunch baskets left.'

Jane nodded. What she really would have liked to ask for was a cheese, onion, and salad cream sandwich but she wasn't sure how well that would have gone down. Her mugshot would probably have been posted around Darling and she would never be spoken to again as the news spread around that she'd turned down a Darlings basket.

Two minutes later, Evie was back and as Jane then sat with a little bowl of frothy milky coffee, she smiled as she thought more about Oscar. She couldn't quite believe the soppiness of herself, but she loved how he made her feel. She could still feel the imprint of him on her, the warmth of him, the smell. She sat with her hands cupped around the coffee, lost in a world of her own, the bustle of the café around her, gazing into space and thinking. She watched as Lucie squeezed in behind the counter at the back of the shop, a huge baker's flour bag in her arms and then smiled as Lucie made her way through the tables.

'Hello.' Lucie's voice was bright and cheery. 'How are you?' She dropped her voice to a whisper. 'How was the dinner the other day?'

'Lovely.' Jane beamed. 'No, it was much, much better than lovely. It was fabulous.'

Lucie perched herself on the side of the table, her ankles crossed, the long Darlings' apron draping against her legs. 'I hear you had a very nice time, and he stayed.'

Jane shook her head in exasperation. 'Blimey, Luce, news sure does travel fast around here. I'm still getting used to it. How come everyone knows what you're doing every two seconds? It's weird. Who told you?'

Lucie shrugged and chortled. 'Ahh, I can't divulge my sources. Small town life, I suppose. I've got used to it now. George reckons it's the only downside of living here. It drives him up the wall.'

'I guess it's better than getting mugged in broad daylight,' Jane suggested jokingly.

'Yes, works for me. Anyway, how was it? I'm thinking we can't call this dating any longer, Janey. You've seen him loads. You're sort of a thing now, aren't you?'

Jane inclined an eyebrow. 'Are we? I really don't think we would be calling it that at this stage. It's not like we've spoken about it or anything.'

Lucie looked unconvinced. 'You've seen him more than I've seen George and we live together! You have to admit that.'

'Yes, I guess I have when you add it up,' Jane replied, her cheeks flushing pink.

'And you've done the deed.' Lucie giggled. 'More than a few times.'

'Correct. There's that too.' Jane attempted to sound casual and breezy. 'We're just friends, Luce. I'm just thinking of it like that. I don't want to get too caught up in it.'

Lucie held her hand up in a stop sign. 'Yeah, right, you can stop with the nonchalant act right there. I'm not buying it. Not at all, so you can stop pretending. How long have I known you?'

Jane grimaced. 'Hmm, probably too long for me to get away with pretending, yes true.'

'Yes, you said it, too long. I know, and we all know that you don't see random blokes. We all know you never do things on a whim like what happened in Edinburgh, and we all know that you have very high standards. Meaning that we all also know that this is serious.'

Jane swallowed. 'Wow, sheesh, when you say it like that, you're right. You know me better than I know myself.'

'Maybe I do.' Lucie smiled, patting Jane on the hand and then glancing at the time on her phone. 'I'd better get back to work. We've got loads to sort out for the Darlings evening still.' Lucie motioned her head towards the back of the shop, rolled her eyes a little bit and lowered her voice. 'It's like a *huge* deal here. There was an argument earlier between a couple of women from the open water swimming group. I was chuckling to myself out the back there as I listened to it all going on.'

'Ooh, gossip. What happened?'

'One of them thought she'd bought eight tickets but turned out she'd only booked two. Evie said there was no way she could squeeze in another six people and there were words.'

'Gosh, so I should be honoured to have a couple of tickets for this highly sought after event, should I?'

Lucie's eyebrows shot up. 'Honoured? Crikey, Janey, you need to guard those things with your life.'

'Guard what with your life?' Evie asked as she arrived in a flurry at the table with a lunch basket in her arms.

Lucie chuckled. 'The tickets she has for the evening.'

Evie laughed. 'Yeah, be careful, you might get mugged for them after what's been occurring in here today.'

'I thought it was going to kick off earlier,' Lucie joked. 'I was going to run for the hills.'

'They know better than to mess with me.' Evie smiled, shooting Lucie a funny look. 'Anyway, I hear you were having all the fun and games the other night too.'

'Blimey, am I the talk of the town or something?' Jane asked.

'You are, Janey,' Lucie said as she slid off the table, winked and made her way to the back room.

Evie nodded in confirmation. 'That you are. It doesn't take much to get us talking, you know. A bit insular, haha.'

'Yes, I think I've clocked that now.'

'We like a bit of a love story on the island too, so there's always that,' Evie said with a wink and with a woosh, she was back behind the counter at the end of the shop and Jane was left with her basket. As she unknotted the fabric top, she reasoned with herself. Was what she had going on with Oscar a love story? She pressed her lips together and closed her eyes. From her end that pretty much summed it up in one fell swoop.

26

Jane was all about the doe eyes as she finished getting ready for the evening in Darlings, a special one off occasion she was attending with Oscar. She'd had a long, luxurious bath with indulgent bath oil, slapped a treatment on her hair and was dressed in a gorgeous handmade floaty boho top with a high neck and pretty long sleeves made for her by Lucie. And, though the weather was iffy, she'd decided to give the espadrilles an outing. Raising her eyebrows as she stood in front of the mirror, she smudged more deep midnight black into the outer edges of her eyes and nodded to herself at the result. She might have a small life, but she could knock out a smoky eye blindfolded.

Two minutes later, after spraying her hair, she was standing in the hallway peering out at the threatening rain clouds when her phone buzzed. She looked down to see a video call from Tally and took a second to decide whether or not to answer. She didn't really have time, but it was an odd time of the day for Tally to be calling and she wondered if she was okay.

'Hey Tals, how are you?' Jane asked, holding her phone in front of her. She could see in one quick second that Tally was far from okay. She looked as if she'd been knocked for six. The little lines at the corners of her eyes etched deeper than usual and underneath sat a grey off-colour tinge.

'I'm good,' Tally replied, then shook her head. 'I'm not, I don't know why I'm even saying that; I'm not okay.'

Realising Tally needed more than a quick hello, Jane walked through to the sitting room, propped her phone up against a candle and sat down. 'What's happened?'

'Nothing has happened as such, I'm just really stressed out and I'm having all sorts of second thoughts about being on my own. It's all very well saying how unhappy I was being married, but now... I don't know. I just don't know. I'm questioning everything. I'm going to be screwed, basically. I barely keep everything together as it is. I know you've done it so...'

Jane stopped herself from replying 'welcome to the club' and widened her eyes. 'Honestly, you'll be fine.'

'I'm not sure if I will! The girls and everything - it's all just so huge now, all the responsibility, the doing everything, the keeping all the balls in the air. Oh, god, what the heck am I going to do?' Tally moped.

'You already do all that anyway,' Jane stated firmly. 'Nothing much is going to change. In actual fact, from what I've seen, you'll be better off because he'll actually have to start pulling his weight. He might have to actually parent his own children for some of the time.'

'I know, but it seems different. Plus, there's something else. I feel really bad because I know you went through this years ago being on your own and all that and I look back and wonder if I was present enough for you, hence my call.'

Jane batted her hand in front of her face. 'Of course you were!'

'Was I, though? Was I really? Or are you just saying that?'

'You seem to have forgotten when you arrived on my

doorstep with a bucket of cleaning gear when I was struggling and spent a whole day cleaning my house,' Jane stated.

Tally's face brightened. 'Oh, yes, I *had* completely forgotten about that. I cleaned all day, and it was sparkling by the end of it!'

Jane continued. 'When my car broke down and I had to get to the nursery, you drove from the other side of town in rush hour to come to the rescue. Remember that?'

'Wow, I must be losing my memory because of my crazy life because I'd forgotten that too.'

'I wouldn't have got through it without you lot being there for me,' Jane noted. 'So, yes, you did loads.'

'Good, that makes me feel much better. Talking of our lot, you're going to this thing with Luce tonight?'

Jane shook her head. 'No, I'm not actually going with her, she's working. It's an event the café puts on.'

'Ahh, I see, I didn't realise that. You look gorgeous by the way. Rocking the smokey eye as usual. You need to do me lessons one day.'

Jane laughed and angled her phone down towards her top. 'Luce made this for me, what do you think? It's quite boho for me, but I like it.'

'Yes, I can tell. Very Lucie. It suits you, though.'

'I really like it.'

'You look well, Janey, Oscar is clearly working wonders for you.'

Jane felt embarrassed, but she felt the same. 'Thanks.' She didn't quite know what to say about her and Oscar, but she was loving it. 'I think he is doing me the world of good, or maybe it's just me.'

'What does that mean?'

What Jane really wanted to say was that she was no longer quite as small, but there was no way she was going down that rabbit hole, she'd need more than a video call for that. She batted her hand in front of her face. 'Oh, I don't know. I just feel different.'

'You seem it. Good for you. Have a lovely time. Have a drink or six for me,' Tally said with a sigh. 'Put a picture in the group if you get a chance. What time is he picking you up?' Tally asked, glancing at her watch.

'I'm seeing him there because he had something on with his son. He's shooting home, having a shower and going straight there, so I'm just going to walk.'

'I see. Enjoy yourself then.'

'Will do. Keep your chin up. Honestly, you'll be fine. Just mark my words.'

'Thank you. I feel better just having a chat. We need to catch-up soon.'

'We do. Just message me if you need someone to lean on. I'll be there like a shot.'

'Thanks, Janey. Have fun. Love you.'

Jane stood by the French doors at the back of the house and then looked dubiously at the clouds overhead. Was it threatening to rain? She opened the front door, peered down the road, and then opened the weather app and frowned as she scrolled along seeing there was no forecast of rain. Maybe the app was right, that there was no impending rain and the clouds were possibly going in the other direction. Stepping back inside, she decided to trust the app and chance it and noting that time was ticking on, she left the house in a rush.

About halfway into her walk to Darlings, the sky darkened threateningly, there was a clap of thunder from above, and a deep rumbling in the distance. Jane quickened her step, her espadrilles wobbling on the cobbles, and she peered up through a canopy of cherry trees to a now purple-grey sky. A huge plop of rain landed on her jacket, then another on the top of the espadrilles, then another on her head. Jane felt the top of her head, patting for the wet spot, cursing the cobbles and for trusting the app and ignoring the actual dark clouds. A few minutes later, she was just coming to the corner when a cobblestone wobbled, her foot slipped, and she winced in pain as her knee went sideways. Flinching, she rubbed the back of it as it throbbed in pain and began to slightly limp along the road.

The back roads of Darling were quiet as she hobbled along the pavement and other people had clearly heeded the approaching rain clouds and stayed at home. As she limped with the throbbing knee, the rain suddenly moved from big plops of water to a downpour. Jane attempted to drape her clutch bag over her head and cursed herself for not bringing an umbrella as puddles began to form along the pavement and rain sloshed in the gutter beside her. Dodging clumsily out of the way of a lone passing car, she swore as water swilled over her espadrilles. Cursing as she squelched along, she finally saw Darlings with its twinkling lights ready in the distance as she got progressively wetter.

By the time she was approaching Darlings itself, she had given up her attempt to stay dry with her clutch bag on her head, her jacket clung to her skin, and she could feel her hair clamped to the back of her neck as rain pummelled onto the pavement. With water running down her cheeks and blisters forming on her feet as the now wet espadrilles rubbed onto her skin, she put her head down and plundered on.

'Marvellous. Blooming marvellous,' she said to herself as Darlings came fully into view. She could see other sensible people hurrying along under umbrellas and rushing in the door. Standing just down the road attempting to shelter in a doorway, she stopped for a second and gasped at the time on her phone. Because of the call from Tally and the knee incident, she was already a good fifteen minutes late and she'd heard from Lucie that it was not good to be late for a Darlings event. Shoving her phone in her bag, she gathered her wet hair onto the top of her head, tied it in a bun, took off her sopping wet jacket, put it over her arm, and made a last hobbling dash to the other side of the road. Straddling a growing puddle forming outside Darlings, she burst into the café desperate to get out of the heavy rain. As she quickly closed the door to the weather, she looked around at the café and gasped. The whole place shimmered in flickering candlelight, soft jazz music played and bottles of red wine were lined up on a dumb waiter by the door. Looking around in a rush and hoping to get to her seat before anyone noticed how late she was, she spied Oscar sitting in the corner by the window, dashed up to the table, shoved her bag under and sat down.

'Hi,' Oscar said with a smile and a funny look on his face as Jane shook her head and adjusted the neck on her blouse.

'I cannot believe I got caught up in that and slipped on a cobblestone! Sorry I'm late!' Jane blurted out in a jumble of words. 'I jarred my knee too!'

Oscar looked around the table as she held out her foot and examined her knee. 'Are you okay?'

'Yeah, yeah, I just turned it somehow. Plus, these shoes are not designed for rain.' She batted her hand in front of her face. 'Ahh, sorry, I just plonked myself down. How are you? Did you make the ferry okay?'

Oscar started chuckling and raised his eyebrows, Jane frowned. 'What?'

'Your err, make-up.'

Jane frowned again. 'What do you mean?'

Oscar made a wiping motion under his eyes. 'I'm not sure what it's called, but it's run a bit. Quite a lot. Loads.'

Jane snatched her phone up, held it in front of her, flipped the camera button, and gasped as she saw the smokey eye she'd so expertly applied earlier had slid halfway down her face and was now residing in the middle of her cheeks. She burst out laughing. 'Oh my goodness! What a total idiot. I didn't even think...' She trailed off giggling. 'I need a drink after that, haha. What a sight I am!'

Oscar put his hand on hers and smiled with a twinkle in his eye. 'What a muppet.'

'I know, sorry,' Jane said as she dabbed under her eyes with a tissue and not having much luck, twisted the tissue into a point, dipped it into her water glass and started to scrub. 'Sorry, sorry. I turn up here looking like a drowned rat.'

'I don't really care about that,' Oscar said gently, his voice different to how it usually was.

Jane looked up from her phone screen. 'You don't care that I turn up wet and with half of Boots cosmetics department running down my face?'

'You can turn up painted green and hairy for all I care.'

Jane stopped the frantic wiping of her cheeks, put her phone down, and looked into Oscar's eyes. She was reminded for the umpteenth time how good looking he was and wondered also for the millionth time how he was interested in someone like her. Jane the Widow. 'I could?'

'Yep.' He squeezed her hand. 'You look beautiful, even with wet hair, black cheeks, and a dodgy knee.' Oscar laughed. 'More or less the same thoughts that I had the first time I saw you.'

Jane felt her heart somersaulting around behind her ribcage. She'd met this man in a hotel bar, installed Operation Le Romancer in her life, and before she'd realised what was happening, she was sitting with him holding his hand and staring into his eyes. What had even occurred in her life? As she sat there, she realised in a woosh exactly what had occurred. It was nothing about plans and opening doors, and living a life less small or house swapping by the sea. It wasn't anywhere near as dramatic as that, because as Jane Le Romancer sat in her damp top, with her wet hair piled on top of her head and mascara running down her face, she knew that in actual fact it was all so much less complicated.

There was nothing complex about any of it at all. Because what had indeed happened was that she had done something very simple. Jane Le Romancer had gone and fallen head over heels in love.

As she smiled and gripped Oscar's hand, his words swirled around her head and she felt the little knot of loneliness that had sat wedged behind her ribs for so long get nudged out of the way by a new feeling. A feeling where she wasn't on her own, or boring, or lonely, or beige. Because as Jane sat there she realised that whatever happened with Oscar and Darling and love stories and her life, there was one thing that she was certain about: Jane Le Romancer was very much no longer small.

Get the next part in Jane's story *Just About Darling Island* at Amazon.

JUST ABOUT DARLING ISLAND

The brand new book from the author of The Boat House Pretty Beach. Buy now at Amazon.

The funny, and uplifting new novel in Polly Babbington's Darling Island series where the local time is so very far from care.

From the queen of setting and author of The Boat House Pretty Beach comes the next instalment in the tale of Jane Le Romancer and her adventure with a house swap by the sea.

For Jane, everything is looking on the rather lovely side of rosy. Her new beau Oscar is proving to be fabulous and her once beige life is no longer quite as small – in fact, it's growing every which way she turns.

As Jane settles nicely into her relationship with Oscar and falls not only in love with him but with Darling Island too, she wonders what the next few months will bring. She starts to ponder where her life is going and whether she could, indeed, stay put on Darling for a while, but when someone close is not quite as they seem, Jane starts to question many things. As the conundrum engulfs her in a sea of concerns, she actually begins to wonder if being small wasn't such a bad thing after all.

We watch from the sidelines, looking onto the cosy little island with its floating bridge, vintage trams, and heritage buildings, and cheer Jane on, as perplexed she surveys all around and wonders quite what to do.

'Polly Babbington creates magical books.'

READ MORE BY POLLY BABBINGTON

Beautiful Little Things in Pretty Beach
Darling Little Things

The Old Sugar Wharf Pretty Beach
Love at the Old Sugar Wharf Pretty Beach
Snow Days at the Old Sugar Wharf Pretty Beach

Pretty Beach Posies
Pretty Beach Blooms
Pretty Beach Petals

AUTHOR

Polly Babbington

In a little white Summer House at the back of the garden, under the shade of a huge old tree, Polly Babbington creates romantic feel-good stories, including The PRETTY BEACH series.

Polly went to college in the Garden of England and her writing career began by creating articles for magazines and publishing books online.

Polly loves to read in the cool of lazing in a hammock under an old fruit tree on a summertime morning or cozying up in the Winter under a quilt by the fire.

She lives in delightful countryside near the sea, in a sweet little village complete with a gorgeous old cricket pitch, village green with a few lovely old pubs and writes cosy romance books about women whose life you sometimes wished was yours.

Follow Polly on Instagram, Facebook and TikTok
@PollyBabbingtonWrites

AUTHOR

PollyBabbington.com

Want more on Polly's world? Subscribe to Babbington Letters